To Mackenzie,
Here's to a little
more magic in the
world!

THROUGH THE DOOR

THROUGH THE DOOR

Jodi McIsaac

47N RTH

The characters and events portrayed in this book are fictitious. Any similarity to real persons, living or dead, is coincidental and not intended by the author.

Published by 47North
PO Box 400818
Las Vegas, NV 89140

ISBN-13: 9781612183077
ISBN-10: 1612183077
Library of Congress Control Number: 2012955737

For Levi

PRONUNCIATION GUIDE

Before you start stumbling over words like "sidhe" and "Toird-healbhach" (don't worry, that one appears only three times), here is a rough pronunciation guide to some of the old Irish or otherwise unfamiliar terms that pop up in this story. There's a fair amount of debate on the correct way to pronounce some of these words (is *Tuatha Dé Danann* pronounced *Too AH ha day DAN an* or *TOO ah ha DAY dan ah?*), so please feel free to say them any way you like, as long as they sound good in your own head.

Tuatha Dé Danann—*Too AH ha day DAN an*
Tír na nÓg—*TEER na NOHG*
Sidh—*SHEE*
Sidhe (plural of sidh)—*SHEE*
Ériu—*AY roo*
Cohulleen druith—*coo CALL en DRU ah*
Fionnbharr—*FYUN var*
Fionnuala—*fyun OO la*
Nuala—*NOO uh la*
Brighid—*BREE yit*
Deardra—*DEAR dra*
Ruadhan—*ROO awn*
Toirdhealbhach—*TUR a lakh*
Muireadhach—*MWIR akh*
Aine—*AWN ye*
Mallaidh—*MAUL y*
Osgar—*US gar*

PROLOGUE

Today was the day.

She was finally going to tell him.

Cedar ran her fingers through her long black hair, her stomach twisting with nerves. She was weaving her way through the crowd at the Halifax Busker Festival, her boyfriend, Finn, following in her wake. Anything could happen here, with its cacophony of street performers and artists and musicians, and that was why she never missed it. This year, she hoped, would be one to remember. It all depended on how he took the news.

"So? What do you think?" she asked, spinning around and fixing her mossy green eyes on him. He was looking over his shoulder at something behind them, but at her question he turned back to her and grinned, brushing a wave of brown hair off his forehead.

"The festival? I think it's beautiful chaos. Sort of like you," he said, his eyes crinkling. Cedar laughed and kissed him. He smelled like honey and lime and pepper, and it made her fair skin blush, even though the air around them was thick with salt air, hot pavement, street kebabs, and the sweat of performers. The crowd poured itself between stalls hawking everything from incense to kilts, and gathered in knots to watch the entertainment. There were bodies everywhere—some dancing, some singing, some drawing, some coaxing music out of unrecognizable instruments, everyone beckoning and beguiling the passersby. Cedar watched, amazed, as a contortionist twisted himself into impossible positions, and a fire dancer spun and leapt and tangoed with the flames. She lingered at every artist's stall, admiring the work and discussing technique and influences.

"Maybe next year you should bring some of your work," Finn said.

"Mmm, maybe," she said. They stopped and talked to a chalk artist creating what looked like 3-D images on the pavement, and Cedar's face lit up when the man told her he had seen her latest show at a local gallery. Cedar and Finn joined in an impromptu swing dance and then continued on to the next street corner where some old-timers were entertaining the crowd with a set of Cape Breton fiddle tunes. Finn winked at her and pulled his tin whistle out of his back pocket, joining in with a tune here and there as the men played and sang. Then one of the old men hauled him in from the crowd and sat him down on an upturned bucket, insisting he put his whistle to good use and join them for a song or two. Finn laughed and quickly complied, his brown waves bouncing as his body moved with the music. The crowd loved it: this young pup who could keep up with every song the wizened fiddlers threw at him. Finally, he bowed his way out and rejoined Cedar, who had been clapping and dancing along with the rest.

"Two years together, and you can still surprise me," she said, wrapping her arms around his neck and kissing him again.

"Surely not. I'm an open book," he said, his rich golden eyes widening in mock surprise.

Cedar swallowed. "So, listen, there's something—" she began, but stopped when she noticed he was no longer paying attention to her. He was looking away, his brow furrowed. She turned to follow his gaze, but didn't see anything out of the ordinary.

"What are you looking at?" she asked. He shook his head.

"Nothing. I just thought I saw someone I knew, that's all." He dropped her hand and continued down the street. She followed him, glancing back at where he had been looking. Maybe this wasn't the best time to tell him. But she didn't want to wait much longer.

Finn stopped in front of the theater and looked back at her, his eyes sparkling mischievously. "Want to go see the magic show?" he asked.

Cedar groaned. "Oh, no. You're not going to try to convince me again that magic is real, are you?" As an artist, Cedar thought magic was a lovely and romantic notion, but lately Finn had been taking it far more seriously, bringing home dusty old tomes from the university library and telling her stories of gods and heroes as if they had actually existed.

"Magic *is* real," he answered her. "If you want it to be. You just need to open your mind a wee bit more." He put his hands on her head and ran his thumbs along her eyebrows, which were arched in skepticism. She laughed and pulled away.

"You're all the magic I need," she said. "But, yes, I'll come see the show with you. Emphasis on the word *show*."

The sun had set when Finn and Cedar left the theater and joined the crowd spilling into the warm August air. The show had been highly entertaining, even mystifying, and Cedar had found herself daydreaming about what life would be like if magic *were* real, as Finn insisted.

The plaintive strains of Bob Marley accompanied them as they flowed through the throngs of people. "Come," she said to Finn, taking his hand and pulling him toward its source. A crowd was growing around three young musicians playing "No Woman, No Cry." Finn moved behind Cedar and wrapped his arms around her waist, bringing their bodies together. Cedar closed her eyes, and together they swayed to the music, wrapped in the night air and the knowledge that, at that moment, they were the only two people on earth. *Now,* she thought to herself. *Now is the time to tell him.*

Without warning, she felt a cold wave sweep over her, and Finn stepped away as if she had shocked him. She looked up at him and noticed with alarm that all the color had drained from his face.

"What's wrong?" she asked, putting her hand on his arm. He jerked away and continued staring off into the crowd, a look of horror marring his beautiful features.

"Finn?" she asked. "What's going on? Are you okay?"

He shook his head, but when he turned back to her, his face had relaxed and his eyes were clear and calm. "I just felt sick all of a sudden," he said. Then he smiled, though it seemed forced to Cedar. "Maybe too much street meat for one day. I think I should head home." She nodded, and they made their way through the crowd. She watched him carefully. His eyes kept darting around them, and his body was tense, as if ready to fight. She tried to follow his line of vision, and for one moment she thought she saw a bright flash of red quickly disappear around the corner. Then there was nothing. When they reached the door of her apartment, he didn't follow her inside or kiss her goodnight.

"I'm sorry our evening had to end early," he said, standing a foot away from her. "It was an amazing day. One I'll always remember." Then he turned and walked away.

The next day Cedar went straight to Finn's apartment after work, only stopping to pick up his favorite takeout curry for dinner. Her stomach was once again fluttering nervously. They would be alone together, with no distractions, and she would be able to share her news. She let herself in, and then stopped short.

It was empty. The furniture was gone; the walls were bare except for the holes where her paintings had once hung. A window was open, and the breeze made a few dust bunnies dance slowly around the floor toward her. In a daze, Cedar walked through the apartment, looking for a note or some indication of what had happened. There was nothing. She stood where the bed used to be and slowly pulled her phone out of her pocket. The automated voice on the other end told her his number had been disconnected. She sent him an e-mail, and felt a bone-deep cold creep over her as she read the immediate reply. *No such user here.*

When she spoke, her voice sounded hollow, as void as the apartment that loomed around her. "I'm pregnant," she said. But there was no one to hear.

CHAPTER 1

Seven years later

Cedar looked at the clock on her computer for the hundredth time, and then started shutting down files. She took one last glance at her e-mail and was about to shut that down too, when the message popped up on her screen: *Just got revisions from the client. Need you to make these changes before you go home.*

So close. Cedar was a graphic designer at Ellison Creative, one of the top marketing firms in the country. It was a demanding job, but a solid one, and she figured stability was worth a little overtime. She sighed and started opening files again. An hour later, she finally packed up and left the office. She picked up Eden's favorite pizza on the way home, thinking it might soften the blow of being late. Again.

"Hey, I'm home!" she called as she opened the door to her downtown condo.

"Mummy!" squealed Eden as she rushed to greet her. Cedar set the pizza on the counter, and lifted her daughter up into her arms. Eden was small for her age, all fine bones and olive skin and wavy brown hair that fell to her waist. She was the spitting image of her father, right down to the flecks of yellow in her golden eyes.

"Hello, my heart," Cedar said, kissing her daughter's cheeks and setting her back down. "Did you have a good day?"

"Yep! Gran took me to the art gallery!" Eden said.

"Oh!" Cedar said with a twinge of disappointment. She had been hoping to take Eden to the art gallery that summer, but hadn't found the time yet. "Hey, Mum," she called. "Sorry I'm late."

Maeve McLeod poked her head out of the kitchen. She was short and slightly plump, with a face that still held some vestiges of gentle beauty. Now it was marred by a disapproving scowl.

"No need to apologize to me," she said, though her tone indicated otherwise. "How was work?"

"Fine," Cedar answered distractedly, admiring the drawings Eden was showing her. "Had some last-minute revisions for a client, that's all."

Maeve pursed her lips.

"What?" Cedar asked, annoyed.

"You should be more firm with them. They know you have a daughter to get home to. They make you work late too much."

"Yes, but they also know I need this job."

Maeve sniffed. "Well, anyway, I made you dinner. I'll just take it out of the oven and be on my way."

"You didn't have to do that, Mum. I brought dinner home."

Maeve eyed the pizza box Cedar had set on the counter with an air of distrust. "Mmm" was all she said.

"Why don't you stay and eat with us? Are you going somewhere?" Cedar asked.

"No, not going somewhere," Maeve said, "but I'll go. I've been here all day, and you two need to spend some quality time together." She set a casserole and salad on the table, put on her coat, and left after kissing Cedar on the cheek and pulling Eden in for a hug.

Cedar took the casserole off the table and put it in the fridge, alongside the leftovers of the other meals her mother had made for them. She opened the pizza box and handed Eden a slice on a paper plate before serving herself. "So, how was the art gallery?" Cedar asked.

"Good," Eden answered, her mouth full. "Gran said you were a painter. Were you?"

Cedar's mouth tightened. Why was Maeve telling Eden how things used to be?

"I was," she said. "Sort of. It was just for fun, nothing serious. It was years ago. I had more time then." *And I was happier too*, she added to herself. Unbidden memories came back to her: drop cloths splattered with bright colors, the mixed smell of strong coffee and paint as sunlight bounced off her canvas on a Sunday morning, walls crammed with art she had either created or been inspired by, Finn's laughter as she tried to squeeze in just one more frame, his suggestion that she decorate the ceiling next.

Eden looked around at the apartment's walls, which were bare save for the bookshelves and a couple black-and-white photos of Eden. "Can I see your paintings? Where are they?"

"No," Cedar said, so forcefully that Eden swung back around to look at her. She tried to soften her voice. "They're not here. I put them away."

"Why?" came the inevitable question.

"I just did." Cedar didn't think she could explain the complexity of her decision to a six-year-old, and it wasn't something she wanted to discuss, or even think about, for that matter. How could she explain to Eden that those paintings had come out of the happiest time of her life, that her best, most creative work had been done in the years she'd shared with Eden's father, when she had been so full of inspiration and passion that the paint had seemed to flow from her veins straight onto the canvas? How could she explain to her daughter that the only time in her life she had felt truly alive, truly at home, truly, deeply happy, had been before Eden was born?

She changed the subject. "So what did you like best at the gallery?" she asked.

Eden shrugged. "Dunno." There was a pause while Cedar tried to think of a suitable follow-up question.

"How come I never see you painting?" Eden asked.

"Eden, forget about it, okay? I just don't."

There was another awkward pause, and Cedar found that she wasn't very hungry anymore.

"Was my dad a painter too?" Eden asked.

Cedar stood up abruptly and started clearing the table. *He was more than a painter*, she thought, feeling tiny shoots of pain blossom inside her and wrap around her heart and lungs. *A true artist. He was happiness and beauty and excruciating pain.* She reached for Eden's plate, but Eden grabbed it back, saying, "Hey! I'm not done!"

"Sorry," Cedar said. "No, he wasn't a painter. I'm going to the bathroom." She dumped her own plate in the trash and headed through her bedroom into the en suite. She closed the door and leaned against it, pinching the bridge of her nose. She didn't feel ready to have this conversation, although she knew the questions would only keep coming. The problem was that she didn't have any answers, at least not the kind Eden would be looking for. *I don't know why he left me. I don't know where he is. I don't know if he's ever coming back. I don't know if he ever truly loved me.*

"I'm done my dinner. Can I be excused?" Eden called through the bathroom door. Cedar opened it.

"Yes, of course," she said. "Do you want to watch a movie before bedtime? I've got some work to do tonight."

Normally this would have induced a squeal of glee and a race for the sofa, but instead Eden just stood there, chewing on her lip.

"Hannah says she doesn't believe I have a dad because I don't know anything about him," she said. "She says I'm a test-tube baby, and they're going to put me in the zoo. Am I?"

Cedar stared at her, shocked. Were six-year-olds really that cruel? "Are you a test-tube baby? No, my heart, of course not. There are lots of kids who don't really know their fathers. I didn't know mine, remember?" Cedar's father had died when she was just a baby. Maeve had never remarried, so it had always been just the two of them. She knelt down and wrapped Eden in her arms. As a child, Cedar, too, had been full of questions about her father, but it had never been a topic of conversation her mother had encouraged. There weren't even any pictures of him in the house. After a while, she had stopped asking about him. She wondered when Eden would reach that same point. "Hannah's just being mean, and you don't need to listen to her. Of course you have a father. He's just not part of our family. You and I are a family, and that's all we need."

Cedar could feel her daughter's little body start to shake in her arms, and she tightened her hold. "But I want a dad," Eden wailed. "Everyone else has a dad!"

"Shh, it's okay," Cedar said, rubbing Eden's back. Tears were pricking at her own eyes, but she tried to hold them back. "Your father was a really good person. He loved music and books, and his favorite pizza was ham and pineapple, just like yours. And you look a lot like him."

"But why isn't he here?" Eden sniffed.

Cedar took a deep breath to steady her voice. "I don't know, to be honest. I wish I did. He went away before he knew I was pregnant. He didn't leave because of you, Eden. That's really important for you to understand. I know it's hard, but he probably doesn't even know about you. He left before I could tell him. When you came along, I tried to find him. But I couldn't. I'm sorry."

Eden pulled away, her face twisted. "It's not fair!" Cedar tried to hug her again, but Eden yanked herself free and stormed down the hall. Cedar stood and watched her disappear around the corner. She'd give her a few minutes of alone time, and then go talk to her again. She listened for the inevitable slamming of Eden's door. It didn't come. Instead, Eden's screams died off as suddenly as if she had run out of air. The apartment fell silent, a sharp contrast to the storm of six-year-old anger that had been raging only moments before.

"Eden?" Cedar called out. Nothing. "Eden?" she tried again, starting to walk down the hall.

"Mummy? *Mummy!*" came Eden's voice.

Cedar quickly rounded the corner and saw Eden standing in the hallway outside her bedroom, staring open-mouthed through the gaping doorway. There was some sort of light reflecting on her face. It glimmered and shifted and created strange shapes and lines on her skin, casting her in an otherworldly glow. A slight breeze was lifting the edges of her sundress, brushing it against her legs. A small trail of fine sand crept through the doorway and was starting to collect around her feet.

"What is it, Eden?" Cedar asked as she moved to stand beside her daughter. Then her jaw dropped. "What the...?"

The two of them stood in shocked silence, looking into the room. The air in the open doorway was sparkling with a thousand points of light, like the surface of a pond catching the mid-afternoon sun. Strangely, the sight reminded Cedar of looking through the windows in her old apartment. She and Finn had covered them with clear plastic to help keep the cold out. They could still see what was on the other side, but through a film. In this case, the film glittered and moved. Even more remarkable than the way the air had changed in the doorway was what was on the other side.

"Pyramids?" Cedar whispered. No longer could she see Eden's room, with its pink walls and bright, flowered bedspread. Instead, she was looking at the unmistakable form of two giant pyramids. The sky around them was black, but they were lit by huge spotlights and were glowing like fallen stars embedded in the desert. Cedar glanced at her bare feet, where she could feel the breeze swirling around her ankles. She slowly bent, picked up a few grains of white sand and rolled them between her fingers. Eden reached over and took hold of her hand.

Cedar tore her eyes away from the spectacle in front of them and asked the first question that came to mind. "Can you see them too?"

Eden nodded.

"What did you do?" Cedar asked.

"I didn't do anything! It was just like this when I opened the door!" Eden said, still holding onto Cedar's hand. "It's like magic! Is our house magic?"

"No," answered Cedar automatically, thinking of what Finn had said about magic. *You just need to open your mind a wee bit more.* "I mean, of course not. That's impossible. There's got to be some logical explanation." But even as she said it, she felt something shift deep inside her, like the tectonic plates of reality were being realigned.

Still, she considered the options. She was pretty sure she was awake, but she grabbed a fold of skin on her arm and gave it a hard pinch. Ouch. Maybe they were sharing some sort of collective hallucination. Maybe they both had a brain tumor. Or maybe there was some sort of toxic gas in the air that was causing them to see this. But the sand felt real, and a few grains were still stuck to her fingers.

"I'm going to close the door," Cedar said.

"What if it goes away?" Eden protested. She let go of Cedar's hand and stretched her arms across the door as if to guard it.

"Yes, well, let's just see what happens," Cedar said.

She reached out a hand toward the doorknob, but in order to take hold of it she would have to move her arm through that glittering… whatever it was. She pulled her hand back. "Did you touch this?"

"I went through it. Just, like, one step," Eden said. "But I came right back out."

"I think we should test it," Cedar said. "I want to see what happens."

Looking around, she spotted Eden's favorite stuffed animal lying on the floor of the hallway and picked it up.

"Is Baby Bunny very brave?" she asked. Eden nodded, eyes wide. Cedar gently lobbed Baby Bunny through the shimmering doorway. The pink-and-brown rabbit landed in the sand on the other side, raising a small poof of dust in the air. Cedar leaned forward as far as she dared and peered at the rabbit. "She looks all right, just the same as usual," she said. She took a deep breath and slowly stretched her hand through the air and toward the doorknob. She expected to feel something, a tingling sensation maybe, but there was nothing. It was like passing through ordinary empty air, except that the air on the other side felt slightly warmer. She grabbed hold of the doorknob and quickly swung the door toward her.

The click of the latch echoed in the hallway as she and Eden stared at the closed door. There was still a small mound of sand on the carpet, and Eden bent down and poked her fingers into it. Then she stretched out on her stomach to look under the door.

"I think it's still there," she said.

Cedar opened the door a crack before pushing it more forcefully. The same eerie scene met their eyes: Egyptian pyramids surrounded by an inky black sky. It was undeniably there.

"Why Egypt?" Cedar whispered.

"I like Egypt. I watched a show about the pyramids with Gran. Can I go in?" Eden asked.

"No!" Cedar said. "It's not safe! It's not…normal. We have to get your bedroom back. Maybe if I go through, I can figure out a way to fix this from the inside." She gave Eden a stern look. "You stay here; I'm going to get a rope or something to hang on to, okay?" Eden nodded. Cedar ran down the hall and started rummaging through her closet. After a minute she came back, armed with a bike lock, two of Eden's toy dog leashes, and a skipping rope.

Eden was nowhere to be seen.

"Eden?" Cedar dropped her makeshift ropes, her heart pounding. "Eden!" she screamed. Through the shimmering veil she could see Eden standing ankle-deep in the sand, looking around with wonder. "Eden! Get back here right now!" Cedar yelled. Eden was smiling and waving at her, but she didn't seem to hear her. Cedar swore and stepped through the doorway after her daughter.

CHAPTER 2

It was incredible. The air was only slightly warmer than it had been in the apartment, but the way it smelled, the way it felt on her skin and tasted in her mouth, these were all different. The sand was cool beneath her feet. She was standing about half a mile from the base of one of the pyramids. The other loomed even farther in the distance, and a massive pile of rubble lay a few hundred yards to her left. There was a fringe of trees, or maybe buildings, in the distance, silhouetted by yellow streetlights. Cedar had never been to Egypt, but she had seen her share of *National Geographic* magazines, and this looked like the real thing. Other than the two of them, there was no one nearby. It was so quiet Cedar felt as if they had walked in on something private, some secret vigil the pyramids were having with the night sky.

"What are you doing?" she said in a hushed voice to Eden, who had picked up Baby Bunny and was brushing the sand off her. "I told you to stay put! We have no idea what's going on!"

Eden looked slightly abashed. "I just wanted to get Baby Bunny. It seemed okay when I stepped in the first time, so I thought it would be safe."

"You thought *this* would be safe?" Cedar waved her hands around them, feeling slightly hysterical. She exhaled slowly. "It's okay," she told Eden, who was looking at her with worried eyes. "I'm just a little freaked out." She took her daughter's hand, holding it more tightly than necessary, then turned and looked behind them.

The bedroom door stood open in the sand. The same shimmering, luminescent air danced in the doorframe. Cedar walked around to the other side of the door. Behind it was more sand. It was as if someone had put up a freestanding door, complete with a frame, in the middle of the desert. Cedar went back around to the front side. She was tempted to close the door from this side to see what would happen, but stopped herself. What if it disappeared? What if they became trapped in Egypt or wherever this place was? She panicked slightly at that thought. "We're going to go back now," she told Eden.

"Nooo!" Eden moaned. "I want to stay here!"

Cedar stepped through the doorway and into the hallway, pulling Eden with her. The familiar air of the apartment hit her in the face, and she shivered.

"This is the coolest thing I've ever seen in my whole life," Eden whispered, turning around and staring back through the door of what used to be her bedroom at their footprints in the sand.

Cedar blinked a few times, and then said, "I have no idea what to do." She closed and opened the door again, but Eden's bedroom did not reappear. The pyramids were still there.

"Let me try!" Eden said, and before Cedar could stop her, she reached through the shimmering air and pulled the door closed. When she opened it again, the pyramids were gone, and they were greeted with the familiar sight of pink walls and a fluffy speckled carpet.

Cedar stared at her daughter. Something inside her shifted again.

Eden scowled at the interior of her room as she entered it. She sat down on the edge of her frilly bed, then got up and crossed the room back out into the hallway, closing the door behind her. "What are you doing?" asked Cedar, who was still standing in the hallway. Eden stood staring at the door, her eyes narrowed in concentration. Then she opened it. Cedar gaped.

"Eden!" she said. She looked at her daughter as if she had sprouted wings or turned into a frog, both possibilities as likely as what she was now seeing through the doorway. Instead of white sand or girlish decor, she was looking at a small rustic cottage and the vast expanse of the Atlantic Ocean behind it. Cedar recognized it immediately as the cabin on Cape Breton Island that Maeve had rented for two weeks last summer. Eden had spent the whole time there, but Cedar had only been able to join them for less than a week because of work. The sky around the cabin was the deepening blue of early evening, just as it was outside the windows of their apartment.

The look on Eden's face was one of sheer delight. "This is so cool! Mum, look!" she said.

"Yeah, I can see," Cedar said, dumbfounded. "How are you doing this?"

Eden shrugged. "I dunno." She held up her hands and wiggled her fingers. "My hands feel kind of tingly."

Cedar's mind was still whirling and churning, searching for an explanation. Eden, however, wasn't nearly as concerned with finding an explanation as she was with discovering more about this newfound ability of hers. She gave her mother a grin and said, "Wheee!" before bounding through the open door onto the lawn of the cottage.

"Eden!" Cedar shouted, and then ran through after her. Immediately her senses were assailed—the cool ocean breeze on her face, the intoxicating smell of the salt air, the sight of the ocean stretching out in front of her and, when she turned and looked behind her, the gentle mountains of the Cape Breton coast. Eden was doing cartwheels on the lawn, squealing with joy.

"Shh!" Cedar said, looking around frantically. "There are probably people living here right now! Come here!"

Eden finished a cartwheel and ran over to Cedar, who was standing just in front of the disembodied doorway.

"What if someone sees us? How are we going to explain this?" Cedar asked, gesturing at the door. "We need to get out of here."

Eden reluctantly followed her back through the door. Again, Cedar tried closing it, but when she opened it, the cottage was still there. Then Eden closed and reopened it, and her bedroom reappeared. They sat down on the bed together. Cedar put her arm around Eden. "Eden, this isn't normal. How do you feel?"

Eden sprung off the bed. "Great!" Her eyes grew wide and sparkled almost as much as the air through which they had traveled. "I'm magic!"

"There's no such thing as magic," Cedar said weakly.

Eden ignored her. "Let's try your room!" she said as she dashed down the hall. Cedar felt as if she should stop her, but in all honesty, she, too, wanted to see what would happen. So she followed her daughter, who had closed Cedar's bedroom door and was standing outside it, face screwed up tight.

"You're sure you feel okay?" Cedar asked, her voice anxious. "You don't feel sick or anything?"

"Nope!" Eden answered.

"Okay," Cedar said slowly. "Where to this time?"

"Gran's house!" Eden replied.

"No!" Cedar said quickly. "We don't want Gran to know about this. I mean, we don't want to freak her out, okay? Let's pick a place where there probably won't be a lot of people." She searched her brain for a suitable location. "How about the library? It should be closed by now."

Eden rolled her eyes at her mother, but then closed them in concentration and reached for the doorknob. A second later, the stacks of the local library were dimly visible through the open door. They stepped inside and Eden started to move toward one of the shelves, when the ear-piercing wail of an alarm went off, causing both of them to jump and scream.

"Dammit! The alarm!" Cedar said as she grabbed Eden by the arm and they hurled themselves both back through the doorway. Eden slammed the door shut. They stood there for a moment, hearts racing, and then Eden burst into giggles. Cedar pressed her hand against her heart, but then a grin cracked her face and soon both of them had collapsed on the floor, laughing.

"Note to self," Cedar said. "Don't go to places that have alarms." Eden giggled again.

Cedar shook her head at her daughter. "This is insane."

They spent the next hour opening doors all over the house to see where Eden could take them. They took the scenic calendar of Atlantic Canada off the wall in the kitchen and flipped through the pages for inspiration. They went to Green Gables on Prince Edward Island, the Bay of Fundy in New Brunswick, and a remote lighthouse in Newfoundland. They never stayed for longer than a moment, but with each new foray, the reality of what was happening sank in a little deeper.

The only hiccup occurred when Eden wanted to try creating a doorway to a place she'd never seen before, not even in pictures. Cedar suggested Stanley Park in Vancouver, where she had spent many glorious afternoons during university. She tried to describe it to Eden, but when Eden swung open the bathroom door, nothing happened. Cedar grabbed a pencil and paper and made a quick sketch of her favorite beach in the park. She drew the huge drift-wood logs spread across the sand, the sailboats and freighters dotting the distant horizon, and even a few tiny sea stars clinging to the rocks. She couldn't help but smile as she drew—it had been a long time since she had created something other than a client's new logo. She showed the sketch to Eden, who examined it closely. But when she tried to take them there, it still didn't work.

"Huh. Well, it's just a sketch, and not a very good one. Maybe it doesn't work if you haven't been there?" Cedar said, squinting at the door. "But you haven't been to Egypt or Newfoundland either…"

Eden wasn't listening. She was looking at her fingers and pulling on each one as if she could activate the magic that way. Then she said in a voice so low Cedar could hardly hear her, "Was my dad magic too?"

Cedar felt as if the room had grown several times larger. She felt very, very small. She sat on the floor and pulled Eden onto her lap. "I don't know, Eden. I don't know why you can do this. Your father used to talk about magic sometimes, but I thought it was only talk. Now, I just don't know. Maybe. We'll find out what's going on, okay? You and me, together. We'll figure it out." Cedar wrapped her arms tightly around her daughter and buried her hands in the wavy brown hair that reminded her so much of the man she had loved.

I wish you were here, she thought. *I wish you could see her, and know her, and help me take care of her.*

As if Eden could read her thoughts, she suddenly lifted her head from Cedar's shoulder and said, "I know! We can find him! We can go anywhere! We can start right now!"

Cedar's eyes widened in alarm. "No, Eden! You can't go opening these portals or whatever they are all over the place to look for him, especially when I'm not with you. You could get lost or hurt or trapped somewhere. Remember when we were at the mall and you couldn't find me? Do you remember how scared you were? This would be a thousand times worse. I wouldn't know where you were, where to go looking for you."

Eden started to pout. Cedar put her hands on either side of Eden's face and looked directly into the mutinous golden eyes. "I know you are very excited right now, but you have to listen to me. This is very important. If people find out what you can do, I can't even imagine what will happen to you. They might take you away; they might do experiments on you, like Hannah said—not because you don't have a dad, but because you can do this. I don't know what would happen, but it would be bad. You can't tell anyone what you can do until we figure out what's going on. Not even Gran, not your friends, no one." Cedar's mind was reeling with all the things that could go wrong. She didn't want to scare her daughter, but she didn't know how else to protect her. She couldn't be with Eden all the time. In fact, she was hardly with Eden at all. "We'll figure this out, I promise. But don't go anywhere unless I'm with you."

◦✸◦

Several hours later, Cedar sat on the sofa nursing a Manhattan and staring at the screen of her laptop in frustration. The Internet was, for once, failing her. She had tried a number of searches, but subtle search terms such as "children with special abilities" led her to teachers' resources or websites about autism. More direct attempts like "warp zone" or "opening a portal" led her to sites about *Super Mario*, *World of Warcraft*, or lists of sci-fi/fantasy tropes. She found some unhelpful information about spiritual portals on a few astrology sites, and came to the conclusion that far too many charities used the phrase "opening doors" as their slogan.

The only remotely helpful thing she managed to dig up was an article on "Real-Life People with Mutant Superpowers." The article described the superhuman abilities of several people: a baby boy with bulging muscles, a woman who could not feel pain, a blind man who used echolocation, and a man who could eat and digest almost anything, including an entire airplane. As fascinating as all this was, the only thing Cedar took away from it was the possibility that Eden's "superpower" had something to do with genetics, a thought that had already occurred to her. Her best friend, Jane, had dragged her to the *X-Men* movies, after all. But if genetics were the cause, Cedar was pretty sure Eden's ability didn't come from her side of the family.

She leaned her head against the back of the sofa and closed her eyes. This was getting her nowhere. She needed help; she had to talk to someone. She picked up the phone and called her mother.

"Did I wake you?" Cedar asked when Maeve picked up.

"Of course not. What's wrong?" Maeve asked.

Maybe I'm just calling to chat, Cedar thought, but didn't say. She never called just to chat.

"Nothing's wrong," Cedar lied. "It's just that Eden has been asking me a lot of questions lately…about Finn."

There was silence at the end of the phone, and Cedar's stomach squirmed. Maeve's voice was terse when she answered, "I see. And what have you been telling her?"

"Nothing," Cedar said. "Only that she looks like him, and that I don't know where he is."

"She doesn't need to know that she looks like him. She doesn't need to know anything about him at all. You'll only make it worse for her if you feed her little tidbits. She'll start to imagine him in her mind; she'll be looking for a grown man who looks like her. You're only setting her up for more pain."

"I'm not trying to make it worse for her. I just thought it would be better if I answered some of her questions, that's all."

"Well, it's not better. What would be better is if the two of you forgot that he ever existed. Don't you remember what he put you through? You couldn't function for months. I had to practically peel you off the floor with a spatula. Don't go raising her hopes that she'll find him someday. I told you from the very beginning he was nothing but trouble. You chose not to listen, but for pity's sake, tell me you learned from your mistake and aren't going to subject your daughter to the same lesson."

There was another pause, this time on Cedar's end. Then she said, "You hated Finn before he even left me. I really don't think you're the most objective person—"

"Of course I'm not objective!" Maeve interrupted. "This is my only grandchild we're talking about! Maybe you need to be a little *less* objective. Try spending more time with her."

"Mum, how many times do we have to have this conversation? I *want* to spend more time with her, but I'm only human. I can't earn enough to pay the bills *and* be a stay-at-home mom. I think your expectations are a little too high sometimes."

"Or maybe yours are too low," Maeve sniffed. "Anyway, let's not quarrel, dear. I need to get to bed, and I'll see you in the morning."

Cedar wasn't sure what made her say it, but she blurted out, "Actually, that's why I was calling. Eden's running a fever, so I'm taking the day off tomorrow to stay home with her. You don't need to come."

There was a beat of silence, then a surprised "Oh" from Maeve. Cedar felt a bizarre sense of satisfaction. "Well, that's good of you, dear," Maeve said. "But are you sure? I really don't mind taking care of Eden when she's sick."

"You just said you thought I should spend more time with her. Don't worry, I've got it," Cedar said. "I'll let you know how she's doing tomorrow and whether I'll take the next day off too."

Cedar hung up the phone and went back to staring at her computer screen. Why had she said that? She couldn't take tomorrow off; she had three meetings lined up, and it was too late to reschedule them. She would have to take Eden to work with her, because there was no way she was letting her out of her sight.

CHAPTER 3

Cedar sat at the end of the long table in the Ellison boardroom, feeling the color rise in her cheeks as several pairs of eyes bore into her. She looked down at the table, which was made out of refurbished planks from a turn-of-the-century barn. Her thoughts were spiraling as much as the grain in the wood. It was the third time someone had asked her a question and she'd had to ask for it to be repeated. She mumbled an apology and tried to focus on the mock-ups on the screen. She had studied them yesterday in preparation for this meeting, but it felt like a lifetime ago. A wave of relief passed over her when one of the junior designers spoke up with an answer and the raised eyebrows around the table were directed away from her.

An hour later, Cedar escaped the boardroom and dashed back to her workstation, where Eden sat curled up in her chair, watching a movie on Cedar's tablet. She lifted one side of the headphones her daughter was wearing and said, "I'll be right back," before heading to the ladies' room and locking herself in a stall.

She leaned against the stall door and closed her eyes, fighting the hot tears that threatened to escape. She tried to take deep, calming breaths, telling herself that everything would work out. It didn't help.

Eden had wanted to do more exploring as soon as she'd woken up, but instead Cedar had bundled her into the car and stuck her in front of a movie while she slipped in late to her first meeting. Part of her thought that what had happened yesterday must have been a dream. But she knew it was real. She felt as if stepping through that first door had taken her to another plane of existence, and she couldn't go back.

She just wasn't sure how to go forward.

Cedar grabbed a wad of toilet paper and started blotting her cheeks. *Freaking out is not going to solve anything,* she told herself. She needed help. Which meant she needed Jane.

❧

With Eden trailing behind her, Cedar headed downstairs to Jane's office. Jane was director of IT and Cedar's best friend. She had arrived at Ellison four years ago, and the two women had immediately struck up a friendship. Cedar deposited Eden on a chair outside Jane's office, where she could still see her through the glass door, then walked in to find Jane scowling at her phone.

"Hey, Jane. How was the date?" Cedar asked her, trying to sound casual as she closed the door behind her.

Jane looked up through her long bangs, which were a surprisingly mellow shade of purple this week. Usually she went more for the shock value produced by neon greens and blues and fire-engine reds. The rest of her hair was ink black and curled under in a sleek bob. She had a lip ring, a nose ring, seven earrings in her left ear, and three in her right. The insides of both forearms were tattooed with quotes: one from the Buddha, and the other from *Star Wars*. They'd gone for tattoos together last year, and Cedar had gotten a small Celtic knot on the nape of her neck, hidden most of the time by her hair.

Jane's scowl disappeared. "Disastrous but fun," she answered.

Cedar shook her head. "Do I even want to know?"

"He took me to a *Lord of the Rings Online* tournament at the gaming store."

Cedar burst out laughing. Jane's love life was an endless source of entertainment for them both. "Oh, no! Did you remember to wear your trench coat?"

Jane shook her head. "It was frickin' hilarious, actually. I was the only chick in the whole place. I think the fishnets did them in."

"I'm sure they loved you," Cedar grinned.

"Hey, weren't you supposed to go on a date last weekend? How did that go?" Jane asked.

Cedar rolled her eyes. "It didn't. My mum was busy, and I couldn't find another sitter."

"Uh-huh," Jane said. "You could have asked me, you know."

"Yeah, because you love kids so much."

Jane shrugged. "If it gets you a date, I'll do anything."

"Gee, thanks," Cedar said, her eyebrows raised.

Jane stuck out her tongue. "You know what I mean. You're gorgeous, and you're lonely. I think some male companionship would do you good."

"In all my spare time," Cedar added. "Besides, there's some other stuff going on right now that's kind of…distracting. I was hoping I could talk to you about it."

"Really? What's going on?"

"Eden is, well, she's kind of sick or something. She's just been acting strangely."

"The same Eden who is camping outside my office?"

"Yeah, I had to bring her. It's a long story."

Jane sat down behind her desk and folded her hands. "Go on," she said.

Cedar wondered where to begin, and how to keep from saying too much while still getting Jane's opinion on what she should do. She settled into the chair in the corner. "I have a strange question," she began.

"Excellent. I love strange questions," Jane said.

"Do you believe in magic?" Cedar asked.

"That, my friend, *is* a strange question, and totally not what I was expecting. But since you asked, yeah, I do believe in magic."

"Really?"

"Sure, why not? I mean, think about it. The idea of magic has been around forever. There are tons of legends and stories and entire religions that deal with magic as a fact of life. I just don't think it can *all* be made up."

"Okay, but what about science? Isn't there a saying like 'Magic is just science we don't understand yet'?"

"Mmm, yes. That may be true in a sense, but I think there are some things science will never be able to explain. I dunno. Maybe it's just wishful thinking, or because I'm a fantasy junkie. But I like the idea of magic. And it's never been proven that it *doesn't* exist, so why not believe that it does?"

There was a pause while Cedar digested this. "You gonna tell me what's going on, or do I have to consult my crystal ball?" Jane asked.

"It's just that when I was with Finn, he, well, he thought the way you do. He talked sometimes like magic was real. I always just laughed it off. But I think he was serious."

"Yes, and he was also a first-class dickhead, leaving you the way he did. I thought you were over him. Why are you thinking about him now?"

Cedar chose her words carefully. "I *am* over him. It has nothing to do with that. It's just that Eden's been acting strangely. And it's making me question some of the things Finn used to say."

"Acting strangely how? Has she been riding a broomstick or moving things with her mind or something? Or is this unrelated to the magic thing?"

Cedar winced. She knew what she must sound like, and was starting to wish she had never said anything. "No, of course not, nothing like that. It's unrelated. I'm just worried about her, and I wish I had more answers. That's all."

Jane exhaled. Then she asked, "Do you want me to find him?"

"What?"

"Finn. Do you want me find him? If there's something wrong with Eden, and you think it might have something to do with him, then maybe you need to talk to him."

"Jane, I looked everywhere for him. I practically went out of my mind trying to find him. But he's gone. And it's pretty obvious he doesn't want to be found. Why would that have changed?"

Jane snorted. "Because now you know me, of course. I *am* a computer genius, after all. Plus..." Jane paused for effect. "I know people," she stage-whispered, her eyes wide.

"You know people?" Cedar repeated.

"Look, anyone can be found as long as you know where to look. And between me and some of my, er, friends, we know where to look. Like I said, I think the guy is a giant dick. He doesn't deserve you, and you're better off without him. But since you've obviously decided to never get a life *and* his kid is sick or messed up or something, I think it's time you found him. Maybe he can help. It's the least he can do."

Cedar sat there quietly silently for so long that Jane stood up and walked over to her. "You okay?" she asked.

"I know it would probably help. To talk to him, that is. I'm just..."

"Afraid he's going to reject you again," Jane supplied.

Cedar scowled at her, but then nodded. "It's been so long, and I really thought I had forgotten him. Honest, Jane, I thought I was done with all that. But now Eden looks more like him every day, and she's been asking questions about him, and it's all been coming back. And even if I could find him, there's no guarantee he won't just turn and walk away from me. Run, maybe. I don't think I would handle that very well."

"I understand," Jane said, giving her a hug. "But remember, you're not asking him to take you back. You don't *want* him to take you back because he's an insensitive, cruel jerk, and you are much, much better off without him. You just want to talk to him about Eden, right? At least think about it. I'll see what I can dig up and then you can decide what to do about it."

❧

Later that night Cedar lay in bed, unable to sleep. She had made it through the rest of the workday without any major embarrassments, fielded a phone call from Maeve, and caught Eden standing in a doorway staring with longing at the towering spires of Cinderella Castle. Cedar had threatened to put locks on all the doors if she caught Eden creating a portal again. She knew she needed to find answers, and find them fast. And unless she was willing to take Eden to a doctor or a psychiatrist, and God only knew what they would do with her, the best place to start looking for answers was with Eden's father. But she hadn't heard anything from Jane, and there was no guarantee she would be able to find him. There was no guarantee he was even still alive.

She felt a sharp stab in her gut at that thought and sat up, swinging her legs over the edge of the bed. She turned on the light and went into her closet.

She stretched up on her tiptoes and shoved a pile of wool sweaters over on the top shelf. Behind them was a tin coffee can from the era when she had made cheap coffee that came pre-ground in bucket-sized cans. Finn had introduced her to the glories of freshly ground beans and had insisted she own a proper grinder. But Cedar had kept this one can, and it had become her keepsake jar. The top was covered in a thick layer of dust. She hadn't touched it in years.

Cedar pried off the plastic lid and peered inside. She pulled out two ticket stubs. They had taken the train to Toronto to see U2. They had planned to take it all the way across Canada one summer. There was a picture of them at the busker festival, beaming into the camera and holding up giant gyros. A faded birthday card was curled against the inside of the can. In it, Finn had sketched a picture of Cedar's profile, her long black hair flowing out behind her as she lifted her face toward the sun, eyes closed. At the bottom he had written, "You are the sun that lights my world." Cedar set the card down, her teeth clenched.

Well, this is hardly helping, she said to herself, dumping her memories back into the coffee can and snapping the lid on. If she *was* going to face Finn again, she needed to do so from a position of strength, as a mother concerned about her child, not as an emotional sap stuck in the past. She pulled her robe on and stuck her feet into her slippers. She grabbed the can and carried it out of the apartment. Closing the door softly behind her, she headed down the stairs. *I don't need this anymore,* she thought, clutching the can tighter all the same. She let herself out into the night and walked around to the side of the building, where the big green dumpster was tucked behind a tall wooden fence. She felt a stirring of panic and tried to stifle it. She didn't want to have any expectations of him coming back into her life. She had a successful career, her own condo, her own child. She didn't need him, and she didn't need this old can of memories of a life that had died the moment he turned his back on her. She swung her arm back and threw the can as far as she could over the dumpster fence. She heard it crash and bounce off the top of the dumpster. No matter; it was as good as gone to her. A breeze swept through her and she shivered, pulling her robe closer. She breathed hard and gritted her teeth together, steeling herself against the tendrils of despair that licked at her like hungry flames.

She hurried back upstairs into the warmth of her apartment and poured a glass of wine. She just needed to take the edge off, to get some sleep. She glanced at her closed laptop on the counter, and then opened it. No new messages.

"Told you so," Cedar whispered. "He doesn't want to be found."

Just then her phone buzzed, and she picked it up. There was a text from Jane: *I found his parents. Did you know they live here in Halifax?*

Cedar stared at the phone in her hands, then texted back: *That's impossible. Finn told me they were dead.*

CHAPTER 4

The next morning, Cedar sat staring at the yellow sticky note in her hands. On it she had written the address and phone number for Finn's parents, Rohan and Riona Donnelly. She took a fortifying gulp of coffee and turned the note over, as if instructions on what she should do next would be written on the other side.

She heard Eden's bedroom door open and quickly stuffed the note into the pocket of her robe. "Morning!" she said a little too brightly. Eden gave her a strange look. Cedar got up and poured a bowl of Raisin Bran for them both.

"You hate Raisin Bran," Eden said.

"Yes," Cedar said, trying to keep the quiver out of her voice. "Yes, I do. Okay, I'm going to shower now."

Eden stared after her as she darted into the bedroom and closed the door behind her. Cedar pulled out the note again.

Finn's parents are here? In Halifax? They're alive? Finn had told her that both his parents had died in a car accident when he was younger. According to him, he'd lived with relatives for a few years before striking out on his own at age seventeen. He had never seemed particularly bothered by his past, but neither had he offered up any more information, so Cedar hadn't pushed it. But why would he have made up something like that? Maybe Jane was wrong. She supposed there was only one way to find out. She pictured the conversation. "Hello, I'm your son's ex-girlfriend. He told me you were dead. Do you happen to know where he is?"

She groaned and headed into the shower.

◦◦

The problem with open-concept office spaces was that personal phone calls were almost impossible to make. Cedar dumped her bag on her chair and headed for the stairwell. She leaned against the brick wall and stared at her phone. *This is ridiculous,* she thought. *Just call them.* She had called every Donnelly in the phone book after Finn's disappearance, just on the off chance that one of them was a distant relative who might know where he was. No one had ever heard of him. What if Jane was wrong, and this wasn't them, and she was back to square one? Or worse, what if Jane was right? What if she was only one step away from finding Finn? That thought was almost as daunting.

Cedar had thought about calling in sick so she could stay home with Eden. But she knew she was on thin ice after bringing Eden into the office yesterday and acting like a complete space cadet. So she had taken every single door in their apartment off the hinges except for the front door, telling Maeve some story about having them repainted. She had also given Eden a firm talking-to, threatening her with everything from no TV for a month to spending her life as a lab rat if she opened any portals. She'd even stooped so low as to warn Eden that the shock of seeing a portal might give her grandmother a heart attack. Eden had agreed to wait until it was just the two of them to do more exploring, seeming to take delight in the fact that this was a special secret they shared. Cedar had squeezed her tight and told her she'd be back as soon as she could.

But Cedar had to admit she was more than a little curious about this new mystery of Finn's parents. Maybe they were horrible

THROUGH THE DOOR

people; maybe they had been abusive. She supposed that that would have been reason enough for him to pretend they were dead.

She gripped her phone tightly and entered the number Jane had given her. She tried to control her breathing while listening to it ring. Once…twice…

"Hello?" A man's voice answered.

"Hello. Is this Rohan Donnelly?" Cedar asked.

"Yes. Who's calling?" The man's voice was not harsh, but there was no warmth in it either.

"Um, I'm an old friend of your son's."

"Which son?"

Finn has brothers?

"Er, Finn," she said. "I was just wondering if you might know how I can get in touch with him."

"Finn doesn't live here anymore," Rohan said, this time with a hint of gruffness.

"Okay. Do you know where he's living now? I just need a phone number, maybe an e-mail address?" Cedar said.

"I'm sorry. I can't help you," Rohan said. "Good day." And he hung up.

Cedar stared down at the phone. *What was that?*

Just then, the door to the stairwell opened and her boss stuck his head in. "There you are. We were going to meet first thing, remember?"

Cedar whipped her head around, and she immediately felt a piercing pain shoot through her neck. "Ahh, yes," she said, wincing.

As they walked down the hall, Cedar tried to drag her mind away from the mystifying phone call and back to her job. But the brusqueness of Rohan's reply to her simple question lingered in her mind. Why was he so loath to share any information about his son?

⤺

36

She was still puzzling over it at lunchtime. She considered calling Rohan back, but it had been far too easy for him to hang up on her the first time. He couldn't hang up on her if she was standing in his doorway.

She grabbed her keys and purse and ran down the stairs. The address Jane had given her was only ten minutes away, and hopefully she could make it there and back before anyone noticed she was gone.

A few minutes later, she was driving down Ashfield Drive, slowing to look at the house numbers. Finally, she spotted the right one and pulled over to park on the other side of the road. She sat and watched the house for a minute. It seemed friendly enough to her. It was an older building, as were all the homes in this part of town. But it was well kept, with butter-yellow siding and red window boxes filled with a cheerful mix of pansies. A small walkway led up to the front door. Cedar stepped tentatively out of her car and started up the walk. When she was halfway there, the door opened and a woman walked out, slamming the door behind her. When she saw Cedar, she stopped cold and stared at her. Cedar blinked in confusion. The woman was tall, willowy, and breathtakingly beautiful, with fiery red hair that cascaded in thick curls over her shoulders. Her skin was so pale it seemed to emit a soft light. She had powerful features: a long, straight nose, full lips, and strikingly high cheekbones. Her eyes were large, and a brilliant shade of green. And right now they were trained on Cedar with such hatred that it made her take an involuntary step back.

"What are *you* doing here?" the redhead asked, her voice filled with venom. Cedar tried to say that she didn't know what the woman was talking about, that she must be mistaking her for someone else, but her head suddenly felt like it was filled with fog. Her thoughts were sluggish, and she couldn't seem to articulate the words she wanted to say. The redhead turned to shoot another look at the yellow house, then seemed to make a decision. She snapped her head up and walked past Cedar without saying another word. Cedar turned and watched her walk away. Gradually, her head started to feel normal again, though she noticed her hands were shaking.

She forced herself the final few steps up the walkway and knocked firmly on the door.

A woman opened the door and looked at Cedar. Cedar thought the woman's eyes grew slightly wider at the sight of her, but then the moment passed and she was only gazing expectantly. She appeared to be the same age as Cedar's own mother. But whereas Maeve was short, plump, and graying, this woman was tall and slim, like a dancer. She had olive skin that looked so soft Cedar wanted to reach out and touch it. Her dark hair was swept up into a casual bun. She smiled at Cedar, who didn't quite know how to start. "Can I help you?" the woman asked.

Cedar cleared her throat. "Yes," she said. "I called earlier this morning. I think I spoke with your husband, Rohan. I'm an old friend of Finn's, and I'm trying to get in touch with him. My name is Cedar. Your husband told me Finn doesn't live here, but, well, I was hoping maybe if I came here in person you might be willing to help me. I just want to get back in touch with Finn, that's all. Do you know how I could get ahold of him?" Cedar took a breath and realized she had been rambling. The woman gave Cedar a hard look, but not an unkind one. "May I ask why you want to contact Finn?" she asked.

"Oh…well…" Cedar said, and then fell silent for a moment, kicking herself for not thinking this through, for not making up some plausible story. She still felt rattled from her encounter with the strange woman on the walkway. "Er, Mrs. Donnelly?" she began again.

The woman smiled, and then said, "I'm so sorry. I haven't even introduced myself, and here I am keeping you out on the doorstep. Yes, I am Riona Donnelly. Riona will do just fine. Please, why don't you come in for a minute?" She stepped back from the door and waved an elegant arm, indicating Cedar should follow her inside.

Cedar walked into the house and stood in the small entryway, not sure what to do next. Riona closed the door and gave her an appraising glance.

"In fact," she said, "why don't we have some tea?"

"Oh, I don't really..." Cedar was about to say that she didn't have time, but it didn't seem like Riona was going to just jot Finn's phone number down on a sticky note for her anytime soon. Maybe a cup of tea would be a good way to break the ice. "Sure," Cedar corrected herself. "Tea would be lovely, thank you."

Riona led her into the living room and told her to make herself comfortable, then disappeared into the kitchen. Cedar looked around. It was quite possibly one of the most beautiful rooms she had ever been in. Compared to Cedar's minimalist, black-and-white apartment, this room was a riot of color. Green potted plants sat on the sill of the large picture window and hung in woven baskets from hooks in the ceiling. The walls were adorned with richly colored paintings and intricate wooden carvings. A harp stood in the corner of the room, the sunlight glittering off its polished wood. Across from the chocolate-brown sofa was a tightly woven wicker papasan with a large bright-red cushion. Under Cedar's feet was a thick rug in many colors. The effect of so much going on in this one room should have been cacophonous at best, but Cedar felt that it worked perfectly. It was a room filled with life. It made her heart ache a little.

Riona came back from the kitchen carrying a tray laden with the tea service and a plate of small sandwiches and set it on the coffee table. "When I was in the kitchen I realized that it's lunchtime, so I brought out a few sandwiches in case you're hungry," she said.

"Oh. Thank you."

Riona sat on the other end of the sofa and poured the tea. As she handed a delicate china cup to Cedar, she said, "That's better. Now, you were about to tell me why it is you're looking for my son."

"I haven't heard from him in a few years and wanted to get back in touch. See how he's doing," Cedar said with an attempt at a casual shrug.

"Mmm," said Riona. "Yes, Finn has been abroad for the past several years. I'm afraid my husband told you the truth if he said we don't know exactly where he is."

Actually, he just said he couldn't help and hung up on me, Cedar thought. "But surely you must have a way of getting in touch with him for emergencies or something," she said.

Riona stirred her tea. "Well, as I'm sure you know if you were friends with him, Finn is a bit of an independent spirit. We haven't heard from him in quite some time, but the next time we do, I'll be sure to tell him you stopped by. It's Cedar, right?"

Cedar stared into her cup. That was it? That was all she was going to get—a polite dismissal? She decided to try another tack. "Yes. You know, it's odd. When Finn and I were friends, he seemed to indicate that his parents were…well, dead." She immediately regretted saying this. What mother would want to know her child was going around saying she was dead? But Riona didn't seem upset by this information. She just raised her eyebrows and smiled.

"Did he?" she asked. "Yes, well, Finn has always been very private. And creative," she added. She patted Cedar's knee. "Don't worry, dear, there's nothing so very dreadful about us that compelled Finn to say we were dead. I'm sure he had his reasons at the time."

40

Cedar set down her cup and stood up, disappointment and frustration burning in the pit of her stomach. She started to turn to leave, but stopped herself. She had to take the risk. "This might seem intrusive," she said, "but could you tell me if there's any history of medical conditions in your family?"

There was a long pause. Riona stood up as well and was looking at her with renewed interest. "Any medical conditions?" she asked slowly.

Cedar nodded, watching the older woman closely.

"No, there is nothing like that to worry about in our family," Riona said.

Cedar's stomach sank. This wasn't going to work. "Okay, well, thanks then. And thanks for the tea. It was nice meeting you," she said. She reached into her purse and pulled out a business card, handing it to Riona. "If he ever gets in touch, this is where he can find me."

Riona took the card and read it. "McLeod," she said. "Your last name is McLeod."

Cedar was alarmed. Riona's olive skin had gone pale, and she was swaying on her feet. Cedar put a hand under the older woman's elbow. "Are you okay?" she asked.

"Yes, yes, I'm fine," Riona said, but her voice shook. "McLeod... and you were asking about..." She stared intently at Cedar. "Impossible," she breathed.

"What's wrong?" Cedar asked.

"Forgive my boldness, but did Finn father a child with you?" Riona's eyes bored into Cedar's, and Cedar quickly looked away. Then, almost imperceptibly, she nodded.

The house was so quiet Cedar could almost hear the dust in the air as she watched it swirl in a sunbeam shining though the window. "Does he know?" Riona asked.

Cedar shook her head. She wasn't sure how much to say. But it was out there now, the truth. She felt unsettled, as if she had just arrived in a strange city and hadn't quite gotten her bearings yet. "No. He left me before I could tell him I was pregnant. I tried to find him. I just thought he should know. But he didn't exactly leave a forwarding address. I guess he wanted to make a clean break of it."

Riona was still staring at her, and her gaze was filled with pity… and disbelief.

"I didn't come here to get anything," Cedar said quickly. "And I'm not looking for Finn because I want money or child support or anything like that. I just want to talk to him, to ask him some questions, and that's it. He doesn't even need to see me."

Riona ignored this. "How old is the child?" she asked.

"She's six," Cedar said, and then added, "Her name is Eden."

"Eden," Riona repeated. "That's a beautiful name." She walked over to the picture window and stood there for a while, staring out at the marigolds. "But how?" she said, her face strained. "Tell me, Cedar, why were you asking about medical conditions? Is she unwell?"

Cedar was about to sidestep the question when she heard a door slam at the back of the house. Riona turned in the direction of the sound and called out, "Rohan, is that you? We have a guest. Come meet her."

A few seconds later, a man emerged from the kitchen and filled the doorway to the living room. Cedar was surprised. Although Finn was fine-boned and slim, his father was an imposing ox of a man. He stood at least six foot five and must have weighed 270 pounds. His full beard was dark red and peppered with gray. He had small but sharp eyes and a slightly hooked nose. Cedar thought of the stories Maeve had told her about Paul Bunyan, the lumberjack giant.

"Hello," she said, nodding to him, as he did not seem inclined to cross the room to shake her hand.

"What is she doing here?" he asked, looking at his wife.

"Rohan, this is an old friend of Finn's. Her name is Cedar. Cedar *McLeod*," Riona stressed Cedar's last name and gave her husband a significant look.

He held his wife's gaze for a long moment, and then looked at Cedar again, his eyes narrowed.

"McLeod? Any relation to Maeve McLeod?" he asked.

"She's my mother," Cedar said, not sure where this was going. "You know her? She never mentioned knowing Finn's parents."

"Yes," he answered.

"Actually, dear, there's more you should know," Riona said to her husband. "Cedar tells me she has a child by our son."

Rohan's expression grew dark, and there was a long silence. "That's impossible," he finally growled.

"Why is that impossible?" Cedar asked.

"Finn can't have children," Rohan said, a challenge in his eyes.

Cedar raised her eyebrows. "Well, he did. I'm raising one."

"No. Impossible," Rohan repeated. "It can't be his."

Cedar was indignant. "Excuse me? She *is* his! I am one hundred percent sure of it, not that it's any of your business! Look, I'm sorry that Finn didn't tell you about me, but he told me you were dead! We were together for over two years! And as I told your wife, I'm not here to get anything out of him, or out of you. I didn't even know you existed before yesterday. I just want to talk to him."

"Cedar," Riona said in a soothing tone, "please forgive my husband. We're just surprised at the news, after all. And you were about to tell me more about Eden, about your medical concerns."

Cedar felt her fingernails digging into her palms and unclenched her fists. "Look, it's really just Finn I need to talk to. Don't trouble yourselves," she said.

She turned to leave, but Riona put a hand on her arm. "We want to help you. If Eden is ill, maybe there's something we can do."

"She's not ill!" Cedar snapped. "At least, I don't think so." She tried to regain her composure. "She's just…special. She's different, in ways that I'm not, so I thought it might have something to do with Finn. But if you won't help me find him—and it's obvious he doesn't want to ever see me again—then there's nothing that can be done."

"*How* is she special?" Riona asked.

Cedar shook her head. "Honestly, Mrs. Donnelly, you wouldn't believe me if I told you, and it really doesn't matter if you can't help me."

"But you said she's special—different in ways that you're not," Riona persisted. "These special traits she has, you don't have them?"

Cedar frowned at the strangely worded question. "No. I'm extremely ordinary, believe me. Eden is, apparently, extraordinary."

Rohan was staring at Cedar as if he were trying to determine what particular species of plant she was. Then Riona spoke up again. "Cedar, could you give us a minute? I know you probably have to go, but this is a lot of information for us to digest, and I'd like to have a minute to talk with my husband before you leave. We won't keep you waiting long, I promise."

Cedar sighed and nodded as the couple retreated into the kitchen. She sat back on the sofa and picked up her cup. The tea was cold, but she needed something to do with her hands. She could hear their whispered voices but couldn't make out what they were saying.

After a few minutes, they reappeared.

"Thank you for waiting," said Riona. She looked at her husband, who cleared his throat.

"I apologize for the way I may have received you earlier," he said stiffly.

"Don't worry about it," Cedar mumbled.

"We've been telling you the truth," Riona said. "We really don't have a way of getting in touch with Finn. But he does call every so often, and you have our word that we'll pass on your message at the first opportunity." Cedar nodded.

"I don't mean to keep you," Riona continued, "but would you mind just telling us a little bit about Eden? What is she like?"

"She's beautiful," Cedar said, smiling despite her agitation. Thinking about Eden always made her smile. "She looks a lot like Finn. She's smart, very smart. She taught herself how to read when she was four. She likes to draw, and she's very good. She loves animals, and she likes watching shows like *National Geographic*. She says she wants to be a world explorer when she grows up." Under her breath, she added, "Ironically enough."

She had meant the comment to go unheard, but Riona immediately asked, "Why is that ironic?"

"It's not," Cedar said quickly. "I was just thinking of something else. You know what, I really have to get back to work. Thank you again for your time, and please pass on my message to Finn the next time he calls."

Cedar stood and walked purposefully toward the door. She swung it open and walked out, but before it closed behind her she thought she heard Rohan's gruff voice say to his wife, "Call the druid."

CHAPTER 5

I must be insane, Cedar told herself as she drove around the streets of Halifax later that evening. Nothing about her day had been normal. As soon as she had arrived back at the office from the Donnellys' house, she had called her mother to ask her why she hadn't said anything about knowing Finn's parents. There had been no answer. After a distracted meeting at work, Cedar checked the messages on her cell phone. There was one from Maeve, who sounded tense, but she didn't say anything except that Cedar should make sure not to come home late. The moment Cedar walked in the door, Maeve had rushed out, without the customary small talk and recap of the day's activities.

After dinner, Riona had called, saying they had more information for her about Finn, but they wanted to discuss it in person, so she wondered if she and Rohan could come over to Cedar's place. Cedar hadn't been too keen on the idea, but she wanted to hear what they had to say, so she suggested they meet somewhere else. Riona had given her the address of a pub called the Fox and Fey, and Cedar had agreed to meet them there as soon as she could.

Now she was questioning her judgment on a number of levels. First, she had left Eden with Jane. Cedar had tried to call Maeve, but there was no answer, which was strange. She wondered if her mother was unwell. So she had begged a favor of Jane and told her, without giving too many details, it had something to do with Finn, which had sealed the deal. Children were not Jane's forte, to put it mildly, but she and Eden got along well enough, and Cedar was sure they'd be fine as long as Eden didn't convince Jane to give her a nose piercing or something.

Then there was the small matter of where she was going. When she punched the address into her GPS, it came up in a little back lane in the Hydrostone, a newly trendy area in the heart of the city's traditionally sketchy North End. Cedar was surprised. Her hair salon was in the Hydrostone, and she had never come across a pub called the Fox and Fey. Halifax had no shortage of pubs, but it wasn't such a large city that a new watering hole could pop up without generating some buzz at the office. Cedar wondered how long it had been open.

She parked on the side of the road and double-checked the address. The sign on the building in front of her said, ANGUS MCKENNA & ASSOCIATES, ATTORNEYS-AT-LAW. Most of the buildings in the immediate area were made of brick and stone, but this one had cream clapboard siding with dark brown crossbeams on the upper floor. According to Riona, the entrance to the pub was in the back of this building. Cedar shifted in her seat. Maybe she should have insisted on meeting at Starbucks.

She got out of the car and walked around the building toward the back lane. She looked at the exterior, expecting a doorway or entrance of some sort. But the back of the building was featureless save for two small windows on the second floor. A black iron railing wrapped around the building about three feet away from the outer walls, but the only doorway in sight was the one out front labeled LAW OFFICE. Cedar pulled out her phone and was about to recheck the directions when she stopped. A man was leaning against a large green dumpster in the lane just in front of her. Cedar's muscles tensed, ready to run. But then her mind engaged and she realized that this wasn't a man so much as it was a boy, or maybe a teenager. He was slightly shorter than she was, and thinner. Still, she didn't go any farther. He looked up and his eyes widened, as if he was as surprised to see her as she was to see him. "Cedar?" he said, and his voice broke on the last syllable.

Cedar's eyes narrowed. "How do you know my name?" she asked.

"Rohan sent me. He said you were coming. He asked me to keep an eye out for you," he said, standing up a little straighter and lifting his chin.

"I see. And you're what, his bodyguard?" Cedar said, raising an eyebrow.

The boy let out a burst of laughter. "I wish!" he said. "Nah, he just thought you might need some help finding the place. My name is Oscar." He walked over to her and held out his hand. Cedar hesitated, and then shook it.

"So, where are Rohan and Riona?" Cedar asked. "I'm supposed to meet them at a pub, but it's sounding kind of sketchy, to be honest." She looked at him closer. "And are you even old enough to go in?"

She could see the color rise in the boy's cheeks even in the dimming light. "It's just a pub," he answered. "It's not sketchy, it's nice. And it's kind of a family place, so, yeah, I can go in even though I'm not, er, technically nineteen yet."

Cedar started to ask another question, but Oscar interrupted her. "Oh, and I'm not really supposed to talk to you. Rohan said I should keep my mouth shut if it was at all possible. But I don't want to be rude, y'know?"

"Why aren't you supposed to talk to me?" Cedar asked.

The boy shrugged. "Dunno. We just don't usually...well, anyway, it's fine. It's not like I'm saying anything important. Do you want to go in?"

Cedar paused. *Did* she want to go in? Then she looked around. "Go in where?"

Oscar grinned, and Cedar felt a smile tug at the corners of her own lips at the way his face lit up and how he almost bounced on the balls of his feet. He reminded her of a dog she and her mother had owned before they moved into the city. She half expected to hear his tail beating against the pavement. "It's the coolest thing, really. Unless you're with me, you can't see it."

"Uh-huh," Cedar said, cocking one eyebrow again and waiting for him to point her in the right direction.

"Serious!" Oscar exclaimed. "Here, I'll show you." He held out his arm as if he expected Cedar to take it. She stared at the proffered arm for a moment. Then she sighed and placed her hand in the crook of his elbow.

Despite herself, she tightened her grip, as a staircase suddenly appeared in front of them where before there had been only concrete. The staircase led down into the ground, and at the bottom was a large wooden door. Cedar swore, and Oscar's grin grew wider. "It's always there, y'know. You just can't see it unless you're with me, or someone like me. Crazy, eh? I mean, I imagine it would be. I've always been able to see it, but it would be cool to see it appear out of nowhere."

Cedar stared alternately at the newly visible staircase and at the boy whose arm she still gripped. Then she let go and took a half step away from him. The staircase was still there in front of her. "How come I can still see it?" she asked.

"'Cause now you know where it is," he said with a small shrug. "If someone walks by who's never seen it before, they'll just see the railing on top, like you did at first. It's there so no one falls in by accident. But now that you know what to look for, you should be able to find it without any trouble."

"Wait, how is this possible?" Cedar demanded. "Who are you?" Her mind was reeling. So Eden wasn't the only one who could do magic, or whatever this was.

"I'm just Oscar," he said, and his smile began to droop. "Hey, do me a favor, would you, and don't tell Rohan that I talked so much. I don't think I was supposed to make such a big deal out of the whole seeing/not-seeing thing. And he's going to kick my ass if he knows that I kept you standing out in this alley for half the night. C'mon, I'll lead the way."

With that, he headed down the stairs. Halfway down, he looked back and noticed that Cedar was still standing where he had left her. "C'mon!" he beckoned. "Don't be scared! It's totally safe. You're with me!"

Don't freak out, Cedar willed herself. After all, this was a good sign. If Oscar could make staircases materialize out of thin air *and* knew Riona and Rohan, it was becoming increasingly likely that they might be able to explain Eden's condition. A new thought occurred to Cedar.

"Are you one of Rohan's sons?" Cedar asked as she followed him down the staircase, clutching tightly to the side railing.

"Me? Nah. His sons are Finn and Dermot, and he's got a daughter, Molly," Oscar answered as they arrived at the bottom. They were standing in front of an intricately carved wooden door. Every square inch of the door was carved, not into one picture, but in seemingly random designs that nevertheless presented an incredibly pleasing overall impression. Cedar felt something inside her stir as she looked at the artwork. Then Oscar pushed open the door.

They stepped into a small, dimly lit room with round tables on one side and booths lining the other. The ceiling was low and made of a shiny, dark wood that was as intricately carved as the door. At the back was a long, polished bar, and set into one wall was a large fireplace that threw dancing lights on the brass rail. Behind the bar was a door that Cedar presumed led to the kitchen. As the bell above the front door signaled their presence, a few of the pub's patrons glanced toward them. Their gazes lingered on her for a moment, and then they returned their attention to their drinking companions. Most of the patrons, fewer than a dozen in total, sat in pairs or small groups.

Oscar was standing next to her, watching her sweep the room with her eyes. "See?" he whispered. "Nothing to worry about. C'mon, they're over here."

He led her to a booth near the back of the room, the closest to the bar. Rohan and Riona were sitting on the same side of the booth, and Riona waved to Cedar as she approached.

"Cedar! You made it! I'm so glad," she said. She looked as though she wanted to give her a hug, but she was trapped on the inside of the booth and Rohan sat solidly in place, his eyes focused on something behind Cedar.

Cedar turned to Oscar. "Thanks for your help," she told him.

He grinned. "No problem."

Cedar slid into the other side of the booth. Rohan gave her a nod of greeting. "Did you bring Eden?" he asked.

"No. I don't usually bring my six-year-old daughter to a strange pub at night," Cedar said. "She's home with a sitter." Rohan and Riona shared a disappointed glance.

"Forgive us, Cedar. I admit we were hoping you would bring Eden, but I see now how that wouldn't have worked from your perspective," Riona said.

"No worries," Cedar said. "So about that whole staircase thing outside. How did he do that? Is it an illusion of some sort?" she asked, although she had a strong feeling the answer would not be so simple.

51

Rohan squeezed himself out of the booth and stood up, ignoring the question. "Getting another drink," he said. "Can I get you something?"

"Sure. A Keith's," Cedar said. She watched as he walked up to the bar and spoke to the bartender, an older man with a thick white beard. Cedar thought the bartender would look more at home wearing a sou'wester on the docks than standing behind a bar. She turned her attention back to Riona, who had been watching her carefully. "It *is* an illusion, of sorts," the older woman said. "But it's more than that. You seem to be taking it quite well that some things are not as they seem."

Cedar picked up a leather coaster and turned it over in her hands. Was this some sort of test? "Maybe I'm finally getting an open mind," she said. "Finn used to talk about things being not quite as they seemed…about magic being real. Is that what this is? Magic?" She felt foolish once the question left her lips, but what other explanation was there?

Rohan returned and placed Cedar's drink in front of her. She mumbled her thanks but kept her attention fixed on Riona.

"In a sense, yes, it's magic," Riona said. "We can help you. We can help Eden. You said she's special, but she's not alone. Finn is special too."

Cedar grimaced. She was tired of all this beating around the bush. It was getting her nowhere. If she was honest, maybe they would be too. She took a deep breath, and a chance. "Eden can create portals to other places by opening a door. Is that what you mean by special? Can Finn do that? Can you?"

The silence in the booth was deafening. After a long moment, Riona spoke slowly, her measured words a contrast to Cedar's hurried frankness. "Finn has a similar gift, though not exactly the same. It is quite rare. The rest of us—everyone here in this pub and some others who are not here—are special too, but in different ways."

"What kind of people are you?" Cedar asked in a whisper, thinking of Finn. She had thought she'd known him better than anyone. Apparently, she hadn't known him at all.

"We're just different," Riona said. "Right now, the important thing is that your daughter is one of us. We think she is very special indeed. But I'm curious about you, Cedar. Are you from this area? Where did you grow up?"

Cedar frowned at the shift in conversation, but she answered the question because she didn't want to be rude. Riona followed it up with several more, seemingly fascinated by Cedar's mundane background. She asked questions about Cedar's childhood in small-town Chester, just outside of Halifax, her experience in art school, her return to Halifax, and her work at Ellison. Rohan remained silent but appeared to be listening closely. After twenty minutes or so had passed, Cedar managed to turn the conversation away from her and back to Eden.

"I've told you a lot about me," she said. "It's all pretty ordinary. You still haven't told me much about who you are, and why Eden can create these portals. But you know, don't you?"

"We have a very good idea, yes," Riona answered. "I paid a brief visit to your mother this afternoon to confirm what I suspected about Eden. And my suspicions were correct."

"Wait, you went to my apartment?" Cedar asked.

Riona looked uncomfortable. "You don't have to worry, I was very unobtrusive. Eden didn't even know I was there. Maeve was quite insistent that I couldn't meet her. She didn't even let me in, actually. Of course, I could have gone in anyway, but I want to be respectful of your family. I hope you know that. As it turns out, I didn't need to go in, or to see Eden in person. I could hear her. It told me everything I needed to know."

"Hear her?" Cedar asked.

Riona nodded. "You can't hear it, but each of us, everyone who is like Finn, sounds different than others do. It's like a musical signature, of sorts, called the Lýra. I could hear it coming from inside your apartment. We know Maeve isn't one of us, so it must have been coming from Eden. It's that simple."

"*Nothing* about this is simple," Cedar said. Just then she heard the door to the pub crash open, and she twisted in her seat to see who had burst in so violently. It was the last person she would have expected. Her mother stood in the entrance, her eyes wild and her gray hair askew.

Rohan stood up at once. He looked at Maeve and hissed through clenched teeth, "I told you not to come here!"

Cedar stared at him, then back at her mother. "Mum? What are you doing here?" she asked, also getting to her feet.

Maeve glanced at her daughter but then focused on Rohan. "What did you do?" she asked him, her voice shaking. "Where is she?"

"Who, Maeve? Who are you talking about?" asked Riona, stepping forward.

"The child, of course! You think I don't know? You think I don't have the Sight, just because I don't use it for your every whim?" Maeve's voice dripped with venom. "I have had a vision, a terrible vision, the clearest I have ever seen. I saw her with *him*. I saw her with Lorcan; I'm sure of it. Now tell me, *what did you do?*"

Cedar stared at her mother in shock. "What are you talking about, Mum? Why are you here?"

Maeve stumbled over to where Cedar was standing and grabbed her arm. "I have been trying to call you. Where is she? Where did you leave her?"

"Mum, you're freaking me out. Leave who? Eden?"

"Yes, yes, of course Eden! Where is she?"

"She's at home. Jane is with her. What are you talking about? You're not making sense. Here, sit down." She pulled forward a chair from a nearby table, but Maeve pushed it away.

"Damn it, Cedar, you don't understand what's at stake here!" Maeve said, raising her voice. Rohan cleared his throat and gave her a silencing look. She ignored him and looked pleadingly at Cedar. "Call her. Call Jane. Make sure Eden is safe. Then go home, and for pity's sake, don't leave her again."

Cedar pulled her phone out of her pocket. She had turned it on silent mode earlier in the evening, and sure enough, there were three missed calls from Maeve. Cedar hit "Jane's cell" on the display.

The pub was silent, and every ear seemed attuned to the ringing of the phone. It rang once…twice…then there was a click and Jane's voice, "Hello?"

Cedar tried to sound casual. "Hey, Jane, how's it going over there?"

"Cedar?"

"Of course," Cedar said, confused.

"Oh, Cedar…I think…I'm not sure…" Jane's voice trailed off.

"Hello? Jane, is everything okay?"

"No. No, I don't think so, but I don't know how…oh, shit."

"Jane!" Cedar shouted into the phone. "Tell me what's going on."

"This is impossible. I don't know how this happened."

"How what happened? Where is Eden, Jane? Is she okay?"

"I don't know how I got here. But Cedar, I think I'm in New York."

"New York? What? Is Eden with you?"

"Eden? No, of course not. Why would she be?"

CHAPTER 6

Cedar didn't remember much about the drive from the Fox and Fey back to her apartment. But she would never forget the cold feeling of utter dread that had engulfed her, the sensation that the whole world had dropped out from beneath her as she was sucked into a spinning vortex of sheer panic. Rohan and Riona had stuffed her into a car and had driven through the streets of Halifax at twice the speed limit, Maeve following in her own car.

When they arrived at the apartment complex, Cedar took the stairs two at a time and flung open the door, screaming Eden's name. Jane was still on the line, and Cedar yelled into the phone, "Jane, she's not here! Where is she?"

"I don't know," Jane wailed. "Honest to God, Cedar, I'm not making this up. I don't know how I got here. I remember you asking me to look after her; I remember driving over to your place, but that's it. After that, I woke up feeling like I had been drugged or something, and I was in Times Square of all the bloody places. I wasn't robbed or anything; I still have my wallet on me, thank God. But she's not here with me, not as far as I can tell. Ceeds, I'm freaking out here. What's happening?"

Cedar was so panicked she could hardly speak. "Just come home as soon as you can. And call me if you remember anything." Jane promised to be on the first flight home, and Cedar could hear her trying to hail a cab. Then Cedar hung up.

"Why did you leave her?"

Maeve was standing in the empty doorway to Eden's room. The doors were still off their hinges—all except for one. Jane had insisted Cedar put the bathroom door back on when she had arrived to watch Eden.

"Why did you leave her alone, knowing what she could do?" Maeve repeated.

"I was looking for answers," Cedar said in a strangled voice. "And I didn't leave her alone. I left her with Jane."

"Jane isn't…" Maeve shook her head as if to clear it. "Never mind. It doesn't matter; what's done is done. I'll tell the others to leave. Then we'll talk about what we should do to find her."

"We need to call the police!" Cedar said frantically, her voice still shaking. "Can you call them? I can't think straight."

Maeve spoke slowly. "I don't think calling the police is the best idea. First, we need to get rid of the people in your living room. Then we'll decide what to do."

Cedar followed her mother into the living room, where Riona and Rohan were standing. Riona immediately came to her side. "It's going to be okay, Cedar," she said, putting an arm around her. "We're going to do whatever we can to help you. I'm sure it was all just an accident. Eden will be home safe before you know it."

Maeve cleared her throat loudly. "Actually, if you don't mind, Cedar and I would prefer to be alone right now. I'm sure you understand."

Riona glanced at Rohan, who stepped forward. "This matter concerns us too, Maeve. The girl is one of us."

Riona, who was still standing with her arm around Cedar, said, "We can help. Cedar, look at me. All we want is to help you. We'll find her much faster if we work together. And I'm sure she'll be back at any moment."

"Why do you keep saying that?" Cedar asked, her mind still clouded by panic and fear. "How do you know?"

"Think about what she can do! Jane was here, now she's in New York. Eden must have used her ability."

"But Jane says she's not with her!" Cedar said, shaking off Riona's arm. "We have to call the police in New York so they can look for her there!"

"And how will you explain how she got there?" Rohan asked.

"Rohan's right; we don't want to involve the police," Riona said. "They would never believe you. And we don't even need them, Cedar. Don't you see? Eden can get back whenever she wants."

Cedar nodded slowly, and the incredible pressure under her rib cage lessened slightly. Riona was right. Wherever Eden was, she could get back on her own as long as she could find a door. But then why wasn't she back yet?

"That's enough," Maeve snapped suddenly. "Thank you for your willingness to help, but this is a family matter now. Cedar and I will handle things from here." She went to the door and held it open, looking expectantly at the others.

Rohan ignored her completely and addressed Cedar. "I know we haven't known you for long. We've only known about our grand-daughter for a few hours. But she *is* part of our family, and she needs our help. We are the best hope you have."

Cedar looked between the pillar of a man in front of her and her small gray mother at the door. Maeve's face was ugly with anger as she glared at Rohan. Cedar nodded.

Maeve let the door swing shut and looked at Cedar. "May I talk to you alone, please?"

Rohan cleared his throat and said, "Maeve…" She ignored him and took Cedar by the arm, steering her into her bedroom.

"Mum, what's going on?" Cedar said as soon as they were alone, though the lack of doors in the apartment meant that every word they spoke could be easily overheard. "Why don't you want them to help? Eden is missing! We need to do everything we can to find her! And I still think we should call the police."

"Believe me, there is nothing I want more than to find Eden right now," Maeve said. "But why didn't you tell me about Eden's ability? Why did you go to them first? If I had known, I could have kept all of this from happening in the first place."

Cedar felt a wave of anger—and guilt. "I thought about telling you. But you hate Finn so much. *Still.* And I thought this might have something to do with him."

Maeve pursed her lips. "Yes. I did tell you to stay away from him, and for good reason. They are nothing but *poison.* You need to stay away from them."

"Are you insane?" Cedar lashed out. "This isn't about you, or Finn's family and whatever quarrel you have with them. We have to find Eden!" She pulled out her phone. "You're all crazy. I'm calling the police."

"Think about it for half a second," Maeve said. "What are you going to tell them? That your child disappeared through a magic portal? They'll think *you're* the one who's crazy, or that you're trying to cover something up. And if you weren't their primary suspect, Jane would be. No. As much as it pains me to say it, Riona was right. This was probably just an accident, and Eden will come back at any time. But *we* need to be the ones who are here when she does, not these people who are strangers to her. Think how frightened she must be, and how she would feel if she's found by someone like Rohan."

Cedar narrowed her eyes and asked, "How do you even know what she can do? I haven't told you anything."

"I had an unexpected visitor today," Maeve said. "Your new friend Riona called me the minute you left their house, and showed up not long after. She told me you came looking for Finn, asking about their medical history. She insisted on meeting Eden, but I refused. I knew what it meant." She shook her head. "I've always worried that Eden would be like her father. You should have told me when she manifested. Instead, you went to *them.*"

"Mum, you act like you know them so well and yet you haven't said anything about them other than 'stay away.' Why didn't you tell me you knew Finn's parents? You knew I thought they were dead. Who are these people? How are they different from us? Why can Eden open these doors? Give me some answers here!"

Maeve's jaw stiffened. "Answers will come soon enough. But you need to send them away, tell them this isn't their concern. You and I will find Eden ourselves."

Cedar let out a roar of frustration. "That's not good enough!" She pushed past her mother and back out into the living room.

Rohan and Riona were standing close together, talking quickly in hushed voices.

Cedar looked at them fiercely. "Well?" she said. "You said you could help. How?" Maeve followed her into the room and stood glowering in the corner.

"We'll know more when Jane gets back and we can question her more thoroughly," Riona answered.

"Except Jane says she doesn't remember anything," Cedar pointed out.

"Well, it may have been the shock. She may remember more during the flight," Riona said. "Why don't you tell us more about what Eden can do? It may help us anticipate what she'll do next and how she'll come back. How does she open the sidhe?"

"The 'she'?" Cedar asked.

"Not s-h-e. S-i-d-h-e, or s-i-d-h for just one. It's the name of the portals, the gateways Eden can create," Riona answered.

Cedar started pacing. "It happened a couple of days ago. She was emotional. She ran to her room, and when she opened the door, her room turned into, well, Egypt. I know it sounds insane, but we could see the pyramids. Inside the doorframe, the air was all shimmery. We went in, and it seemed real. It was warm and there was sand and we could walk around. The door stayed there, and we came back through it just fine. I tried closing the door but the portal, the sidh or whatever you call it, was still there when I opened it again. I didn't have any effect on it. But when Eden closed the door and then opened it, it became her room again."

Rohan's eyes were narrowed in concentration as he nodded slowly. "So she can both open and close. Could she close the sidh from the other side? From Egypt?"

"We didn't try," Cedar admitted. "I was afraid we'd get stuck, that the door would disappear. So we always left it open until we were home."

"Always?" Riona asked.

"We tried a few other places," Cedar admitted. "The library, the cottage. We tried to go to Vancouver, where I went to university, but it didn't work, not even when I drew a sketch of it. It seemed like we could only go somewhere Eden could picture perfectly in her mind, places she'd either visited or seen on TV or in a picture. But wherever we went, she could always just close the door once we were back home again, and things would return to normal."

Riona looked thoughtful. "So Eden uses an actual physical door to open the sidhe?" she asked. Cedar nodded.

"Interesting. And when you go through it, the physical door can still be seen on the other side?"

Cedar nodded again. "I worried that it might go away if we closed it. And that we'd be stuck." Cedar felt the panic rising up again and tasted bile in her throat. "She's probably stuck right now, and we have no idea where she is." She paced faster.

"Shh, don't think like that, dear," Riona said. "If, as you say, she uses a door to open the sidhe, she just needs to find another door she can open. She's probably looking for one as we speak."

"But what if she's hurt? Or in the middle of a desert or New York City? What if she can't get back?" Tears started to run down Cedar's face, and her whole body trembled. "There has to be a way to find her!" Cedar looked through tear-blurred eyelashes at her mother, who was still standing a few feet away, arms crossed. "Mum, tell me, what can we do?"

"I told you what I thought we should do, Cedar. But it seems that you've decided to throw your lot in with these people instead of with your own mother. That's fine. It's your decision. But I have my own way of doing things, so I will go and do them."

"What? You're leaving? Now? Aren't you going to help me?" Cedar asked.

"I *am* going to help you, Cedar; I just can't do it here. I'm going to do everything in my power to find Eden and keep her safe. And believe me, I have considerable power." With that, she turned and left the apartment, leaving Cedar to stare at the closed door, mouth open. *What did she mean by that?*

Rohan cleared his throat. "We should go as well, and brief the others so they can help. We'll spend the night searching, and reconvene in the morning to question Jane." He looked expectantly at Riona.

Riona put her hand on Cedar's arm. "We'll call you as soon as we know anything."

"No, I should go with you," Cedar protested. She walked over to her desk and grabbed a notepad and pen. "We should make a list of all the places she could have gone. If Jane is in New York, shouldn't we start there? Or, she really wanted to go to Disney World..." Cedar sat down and put her head in her hands. "She could be anywhere."

"We're going to look everywhere we can, Cedar," Riona said in a soft voice. "We have considerable resources, and we can cover a lot of ground very quickly. But someone needs to be here for Eden when she comes back. Wherever she is, she's going to get tired and hungry, and then she's going to come home. And I'm pretty sure the person she'll want to see most is her mother. That's how you can best help, by making sure Eden has someone to come home to."

Cedar closed her eyes. Her rising panic was beating away at the remnants of her resolve. She took a deep, slow breath, trying to quell it before it reached the surface.

"Okay," she said to Riona without looking up.

Riona gazed at her worriedly, and then followed her husband out the door. Cedar breathed deeply, attempting to loosen the knot in her stomach. She tried to tell herself that Riona was right, that it would be okay, that Eden had just gone exploring somewhere and would be back soon. She repeated it to herself over and over again, a mantra that would hopefully help her hang on to her sanity.

A strange sound broke her concentration. It was muffled and seemed to come from the direction of the front door. She jumped up, her heart racing. "Eden?" she cried, rushing toward the door and flinging it open. There was nothing there. Then she looked down. Of course. It was the neighbor's cat, who spent as much time in Cedar's apartment as he did in his own.

"Oh, hey, Watson," Cedar said. "Did you get locked out again?" The cat walked past her into the apartment, and Cedar shut the door. She dug around in the cupboard for the small bag of food she kept for the cat's visits. Watson ignored the proffered food and jumped up onto the sofa. Cedar went and sat beside him, and the cat curled up in her lap and started to purr.

"Eden's not here, Watson," Cedar whispered as she stroked his fur. "She's missing. And it's my fault. Of course she wanted to show Jane. Mum was right—what was I thinking? And now something has gone wrong, and she could be anywhere in the world." She looked at her phone, wondering if she were making a huge error by not calling the police. She pressed her hands to her forehead and repeated her new mantra. *It was just a mistake. She'll come back. She can come back.* Everything she had learned in the past few hours pressed in on her—Finn's parents, their claims that Eden was "one of them," her mother's bizarre behavior. Cedar had the feeling she had just stepped into the middle of something much bigger than herself, and she felt completely out of her depth.

She moved to stand, and Watson jumped off her lap. She started pacing again. She made a pot of coffee. She made a list of everything she knew about the situation, and then stared at it incredulously. She paced some more, every nerve in her body tensed, waiting for a door to suddenly appear in front of her, waiting for Eden to walk through it. She forced herself to keep moving, as though that could distract her from feeling completely helpless. She wiped down all the counters in the kitchen, swept the floors, and dusted every surface in the living room. All the while, Watson sat and watched her or circled around her legs or jumped up into her lap if she happened to sit down.

It was 3:00 a.m. when Watson wrapped himself around Cedar's legs, purring loudly, then walked into her room and jumped up on the bed. Cedar felt ridiculous, following this cat around her own house, but the warmth of his presence was no small comfort to her. So she made sure all the lights were on, and then curled up beside the small, warm body on her bed. She stared at the ceiling for a while, not moving, letting silent tears run down the sides of her face and into her hair.

As her body yielded to sleep, she dreamed of a man walking through a field of the dead. It was a dream she'd had before, a recurring nightmare she'd experienced since childhood. It was always the same. A tall figure, hooded and cloaked, walking with arms open wide through a barren field piled high with bodies. The bodies were torn apart, limbs missing and entrails spilling onto the ground, and Cedar's dream gaze tried to avoid them. A thick mist rose from the ground, and the air was filled with a high-pitched keening coming from somewhere far away. The hooded figure walked on, and it seemed as though the field of bodies would never end. Tonight, however, something was different. Usually she just watched from a distance, but tonight she followed him, stepping around dismembered limbs and trying to look at anything except the staring faces of the bodies around her. Then, out of the corner of her eye, she saw a scrap of pink lace. She tried to look away, but her head turned as if forced by unseen hands. She tried to close her eyes, but they stayed as open as the unseeing eyes around her. The lace was torn, hanging by a thread from a little girl's nightgown. Cedar felt her feet move until she stood so close she could have reached down and touched it. Eden's lifeless body lay limp at her feet, her nightgown shredded and her face caked with blood. Her eyes and mouth were open. Then, as Cedar watched with horror, Eden's head turned, and she looked directly into Cedar's eyes without blinking. Her mouth moved and emitted a ghostly whisper, "Where were you, Mummy?"

CHAPTER 7

Cedar woke only a couple of hours later to the sound of her phone ringing. She picked it up and was immediately awake.

"It's Jane; I'm downstairs, let me up."

Jane. *Eden.* Everything flooded back in one agonizing blow to the pit of her stomach. She jumped off the bed, dislodging Watson from where he had settled for the night, and ran down the hall to Eden's room, buzzing Jane in on the way. It was empty. She stared wildly around the apartment, looking for any sign that Eden might have come home. Then Jane knocked on the door. Cedar flung it open and dragged her inside.

"Tell me what happened," she demanded.

Jane looked terrified, and close to tears. She backed away from Cedar with a pleading look, her hands in the air. Her purple bangs hung limp on her forehead, and she had gray circles under her eyes. "I swear to God, it's just like I said on the phone. I don't know. I told you everything I can remember."

Cedar breathed deeply, trying to fight the impulse to rage at her. How could she not remember? From the look on her face, Jane could tell what Cedar was thinking. "Damn it, Ceeds, I am so sorry. I would never let anything happen to Eden. I'll do whatever I can; I'll tell the police everything I told you, and maybe something will help."

Cedar sat down at the table and put her face into her hands. "The police aren't involved—yet," she mumbled through her fingers.

"*What?*" Jane said. "You haven't called the police? Why the hell not?"

"It sounds insane, I know. I can't even explain it to myself without sounding like a lunatic," Cedar said.

Jane crossed her arms and raised her eyebrows at Cedar. "Ceeds. I just found myself in New-bloody-York with no memory of the last several hours. And you're worried that *you're* the one who sounds like a lunatic?"

Cedar took a deep breath and then exhaled slowly. She watched Jane closely as she said, "Remember how I was asking you about magic, if it was real?" Jane nodded. "Well, Eden seems to have this, um, magical ability. If she thinks of a place, and then opens a door, any door, that place appears on the other side. And you can walk right into it, no matter how far away it is."

Jane's mouth was slightly open, and her eyes were wide. "For real?"

"Yeah, I know how it sounds. But it's true; I've gone through those doors myself. And I'm assuming that's how you got to New York."

Jane's eyes were still wide, but she had closed her mouth and was nodding slowly. "Okay. So, let's pretend for a moment that you and I are both still sane. Why can't I remember what happened? Do these doorways or whatever make you lose your memory?"

"No. At least, that never happened to me when I went through them."

Jane sat down beside Cedar. There was a long silence. Finally, she asked in a small voice, "How is this possible?"

Cedar glanced over at her best friend. "You're the one who believes in magic."

Jane's response was cut off by the buzz of the door downstairs. Cedar ran to the speaker and shouted into it, "Hello!"

"It's Rohan," came the deep voice against the backdrop of morning traffic. Cedar hit the buzzer to let him in. She opened the door, and Watson ran out and around the corner. Soon she heard the elevator door open. Rohan stomped into the apartment, followed by several others. Some she vaguely recognized from the pub, others she had never seen before. Riona brought up the rear of the group.

"Well?" Cedar asked Rohan.

Rohan looked frustrated. "Nothing yet. I want to talk to your friend. You've told her about Eden." It wasn't a question.

"How do you know that? And who are all these people?" Cedar asked.

It was Riona who spoke. "I'm so sorry, here we are bringing strangers into your home and we haven't even introduced them to you. These are some friends of ours who have been helping us look for Eden." She waved her hand at a pixie-like platinum blonde. "This is Nevan Blakney. Over there is Anya Kelly." She pointed at a tall middle-aged woman by the door. "And you met her son Oscar yesterday." Oscar grinned and waved. "Then there's Felix Dockendorff in the back." Cedar recognized him as the barkeeper from the night before. "And beside him is Oscar's father, Murdoch, and Murdoch and Anya's other son, Sam. He's with Nevan. And this here is our other son, Dermot, and our daughter, Molly."

Cedar sort of wished she hadn't asked. Her gaze lingered on Dermot. He had the same mouth as Finn, the same gentle curls. She forced herself to look somewhere else. "Thanks," she told Riona. "This is my friend Jane."

Rohan had crossed the room and was now glowering at Jane, who glowered back in return. "Cedar?" she asked. "What the hell is going on?"

Cedar rushed over. "This is Rohan Donnelly, Finn's father. And this is Riona, his mother."

"Hey," Jane said, skepticism written large across her face.

"Let's sit down," Cedar said. "This isn't an inquisition, Jane, but why don't you tell them what you told me. Maybe they can make some sense of it."

"*This* is what you're doing instead of calling the police?" Jane asked.

"The police will never believe us," Cedar said. "And these people are like Eden. They want to help. I think we should let them. They're our best chance of finding her." Cedar led Riona and Rohan to the table where Jane was sitting. Everyone else remained standing or found seats on the sofa or floor.

"Tell us again what you remember," Cedar said.

When Jane had finished, Rohan was staring hard at her. She bristled under his steady gaze. "Listen, I know what you're thinking, but I'm telling the truth. I don't know what happened. I'm not making this up. And who are you, anyway, to come barging in here? You didn't even know Eden existed before yesterday. And why are all these other people here?" She made an angry gesture at the crowded room.

Rohan looked at his wife. "You may be right," he said to her, ignoring Jane.

"It's the only thing that makes sense," Riona said, her face earnest. "I just can't believe I didn't see it before."

"*What* makes sense?" Cedar interjected, her gaze swiveling between them. Rohan's face darkened.

"There is only one way to know for sure," he said. "Jane, I believe I can help you remember what happened last night. But you must be completely honest with me."

Jane glanced at Cedar and then said, "Um, okay."

"Do you like children, Jane?" Rohan asked.

Jane looked confused. "What?"

"Do you like children? In general. Do you enjoy spending time with them; do you want to have children of your own?"

"Sorry, but what the hell does that have to do with anything?" Rohan glared at her, and then turned to Cedar. "Tell her to answer the question."

Cedar was indignant. "How about you tell us what you're getting at? What do you mean, you can help her remember? How?"

"If it works, you'll understand. But if she doesn't answer my questions, we'll never know what happened," he said with more than a hint of impatience.

"Fine, jeez," Jane said, with a sideways look at Cedar that clearly said she thought Rohan was crazy. "No, I don't want to have kids. There, does that answer your question? 'Cause I still don't remember anything more."

"Do you like them?" he asked.

"What are you trying to get at? That I hate kids and I kidnapped Eden or something? This is bullshit." Jane stood up, and so did Rohan, towering over her. Jane shot a look at Cedar. "I'm sorry I helped you find this guy. I didn't do *anything* to Eden, I swear."

"Jane, I believe you! Please, sit down. I don't think he's accusing you of anything. Are you?" Cedar asked, looking up at Rohan.

Jane sat down again and crossed her arms in front of her chest. Rohan sat down as well, but it was Riona who spoke. "I'm sorry, Jane," she said. "We, well, *I* have a theory about what happened, but we need to be sure. If you could just give us the benefit of the doubt. Even if his questions don't make sense right now, they will soon, I assure you."

Jane looked mutinous, but nodded. "Fine," she said. "I don't really like kids, no."

"Did you want to come over and look after Eden last night?" Rohan asked.

"I wanted to help my friend, yes. But if you're asking me if babysitting on a Friday night is my idea of a good time, then the answer is no."

Murdoch called out from the sofa, "Rohan, where is this going?" He was a short, burly man with red cheeks and gray hair that looked like bristles. His sons, on the other hand, were tall and lean, and they were both watching the proceedings with keen interest.

Rohan didn't look at him, but Cedar could see the muscles in his face tighten. "Wait," he said to Murdoch. Then he spoke to Jane. "I'm going to touch your head," he said.

Jane recoiled in her chair. "Like hell you are."

"Do you want your memories back or not?" he snarled. Then his tone softened slightly. "Please. If you would. It won't hurt."

Jane gave Cedar a panicked look. "What kind of a crazy cult did you get yourself into?"

Cedar took her friend's hand. "I don't understand it either, but please, just try. I'm right here."

Jane glared at Rohan, but then stiffly nodded her assent. His hands could cover almost her entire head, and Cedar had a fleeting, horrible thought that he might crush her skull. In the background she could hear someone mutter, "This is bullshit," but it wasn't Jane this time.

"Look into my eyes, Jane," Rohan said, "and tell me if you start to remember anything." Jane nodded as much as she could with her head in his grasp. "When Cedar called you, did you want to come watch Eden?"

"No," Jane whispered. "No. I did come, of course, because she said she was in a real bind. But I had, um, other plans for the night."

"What plans?" Rohan asked.

Jane's cheeks turned crimson. "Not that it's any of your business, but I had a date. Sort of. Online. I was supposed to chat with this guy." She frowned. "Wait. I did talk to him. I remember being here, and texting him on my phone."

"You were sexting while you were looking after Eden?" Cedar asked, incredulous.

"This is good, Jane. You're starting to remember!" Riona said, patting her knee.

"How did you feel when you were talking to this person?" Rohan asked.

"Well, um, I felt kind of guilty because, obviously, I'm the world's worst babysitter. Oh, my God, I think I'm starting to remember. Eden wanted me to play with her. I hate playing with kids, and I was, you know, busy. So I told her to leave me alone. But then I felt bad because she looked so sad, and I was worried she would tell Cedar how much I sucked. But that's all I can remember."

The room was so quiet Cedar almost forgot it was full of strangers. Riona interrupted the silence. "There's your hook," she said to Rohan.

Rohan looked at Cedar. "I need you to do something." Cedar nodded.

"Forgive her."

"What?"

"It should release her memories," Rohan said.

"Okay," Cedar began. "Jane, I forgive you." Then she looked at Rohan. "Like that? Did it work?"

"No," Rohan said. "It only works if you mean it."

"I did mean it!" Cedar protested.

"Just…try again," Rohan said.

Cedar looked at Jane, hunched miserably at the table with her head still sandwiched between Rohan's massive hands. She felt tears spring to her eyes again, and she squeezed Jane's hand tightly. "Oh, Jane, of course I forgive you. I should never have asked you to watch Eden; I know it's the last thing you would want to do. It would be like you asking me to go to one of your meditation classes or something. You know I'd hate it. You're an amazing friend, and you were so sweet to say yes to something you hate because you knew it would help me out. Please don't feel bad about it." She tried to give Jane an awkward hug, ducking under Rohan's arms.

Jane sniffed. "Thanks. Oh, shit. I think…I can remember… OH!" She wrenched her head out of Rohan's grasp and turned to stare at Cedar, wide-eyed. "Bloody hell, Cedar! You weren't kidding about those doors!"

Cedar leaned forward. "What? What do you remember? What happened?"

"It was like I said. I was kind of ignoring her, and she kept bugging me. So I told her to go away, and she did. A few minutes later she came back and said she had something really cool to show me. I thought if I looked at this one thing it would make her shut up. Sorry," she said, wincing as she looked at Cedar. "Anyway—can I be remembering this right?—she had the door to the bathroom open, and inside was…it sounds impossible, but it was Times Square. In New York. You know, just like in all the movies. I couldn't believe it. She told me she could open a door to anywhere in the world and wasn't it the coolest thing ever. It *was*."

"It's called a sidh, apparently," Cedar said. "So, did she go through it?" Her whole body pulsed with anticipation. Finally, some answers.

"No," Jane answered slowly. "She said she felt bad because she wasn't supposed to show anyone. Then this woman just walked into the apartment. I have no idea how she got in, Ceeds. Anyway, she goes, 'That's a pretty impressive talent you've got there!' and Eden kind of freaked out and went to shut the door, but then the woman said she had been sent by Eden's father. Eden just stood there, staring at her. I asked her who she was and how she had gotten in, but she just ignored me. She was totally focused on Eden. She told her that her father was just like her and had been looking for her, but they had to leave right away." Jane looked at Cedar, who had gone so pale Riona had wrapped a blanket around her shoulders and was holding her hands.

"I tried to stop her," she continued. "I told her to get out or I would call the police. But then she said something to me. It was the first time she had even acknowledged I was there. I'm trying to remember… She told me to go to New York, that I really wanted to go, and I wanted Eden to stay behind. And she told me to forget I had even been at your apartment." Jane looked horrified. "That must be what I did. I must have gone through that door. And then I forgot all about her." Jane took a moment to swear profusely, then continued, "Who was that bitch?"

Before anyone could answer, Rohan spoke. "Tell us what she looked like."

"She was gorgeous—stunning, actually. I just couldn't take my eyes off her. She was tall and thin, like a supermodel, and she had the most amazing wavy long red hair."

Cedar thought of the woman she had encountered outside Rohan and Riona's house, and the way she had looked at her with such hatred. Could she be the woman who had taken her child?

Rohan stood up. "Thank you, Jane," he said. Then he turned to the others. "And now we know."

There was a stunned silence in the room. Then Anya said, "Are you saying you think Nuala took the child?"

"That's a hell of an accusation! How do we know she's telling the truth?" Murdoch said, jumping to his feet and pointing at Jane.

"Why would she lie?" asked Riona.

"Because maybe she's the one who took off with Eden or lost her or got her killed, and now she's trying to cover it up!" Murdoch yelled, pointing a finger at Jane, who sat frozen.

"Jane has never met Nuala!" Riona said. "And she described her perfectly. She must be telling the truth."

"Nuala is hardly the only woman in this world with red hair. How do we know you didn't tell this woman what to say?" Murdoch demanded of Riona, coming closer, thrusting his chin out. "He said this was your idea. How do we know you're not just trying to pin the blame on her?"

Rohan turned on Murdoch, burning with suppressed rage. The other man seemed to grow smaller as Rohan stared him down. "We have the proof of it right here! You think we would lie to all of you about something like this? *Think!* Riona has it right. Nuala has every reason to want that child. But the longer we spend arguing about it, the more dire the situation becomes."

Cedar finally managed to find her voice. "Who is Nuala? Is she the woman I saw at your house? She looked like she hated me. But why? Who is she? What would she want with Eden?"

Several glances were exchanged around the room.

"I'm sorry, Cedar," Riona said. "I didn't realize the two of you had crossed paths. Yes, Nuala was at our house yesterday, before you came. She came back after you left, and demanded to know why you were there. I'm afraid I told her about my suspicions regarding Eden. She wanted to come with me to your apartment to find out for sure, but I said no. Nuala is unpredictable, and I didn't know how she would react. But I guess we know now. I think...I believe Nuala wanted Eden to use her ability to open a sidh for her."

"Where to? And why did she need to take her?"

"To a place that isn't safe for any of us," Rohan answered.

"I think you're right," said Nevan from her seat on the floor, cutting off Cedar's next question. "I don't want to believe it any more than the rest of you do, but look at the facts: there's a witness, there's a motive, and I think she's actively blocking me. Everything I send just bounces back. It all looks pretty guilty."

Jane frowned at the petite blonde. "What do you mean, she's blocking you?" she said.

Nevan raised an eyebrow, and then Cedar jumped as she heard a voice in her head.

Hey, Cedar. Hey, Jane.

"Whoa! Did you hear that?" Jane asked Cedar.

It takes a little getting used to.

Cedar didn't take her eyes off Nevan's lips, which had not moved.

"Are you reading our minds?" Jane asked.

Nevan smiled, and Cedar heard, *No. I can speak directly to you, but I can't read your mind. And if you concentrate hard enough, you can shut me out. It takes some practice, though.*

"Whoa," Jane said again. "Who the hell *are* you people?"

Rohan looked as if he had forgotten Jane was there and had just been uncomfortably reminded. "I think you should head home, Jane. Let me walk you to the door."

"Are you kidding me? No way," Jane protested, looking at Cedar for backup.

"We are grateful for the assistance you've provided," Rohan said. "However, from this point on, this needs to remain a family matter. Having one outsider is going to prove difficult enough." He looked at Cedar when he said this, and she bristled at the insinuation.

"Cedar, I am not leaving you alone with these people. Tell him I'm staying," Jane demanded.

"Of course you can stay," Cedar said. "She's staying," she snapped at Rohan. "Now tell me more about Nuala. She told Eden that Finn sent her. Did he?"

"No, Cedar," Riona said, her face anxious. "I can assure you, Finn had nothing to do with this. Nuala must have just been using him as a way to get Eden to go with her."

"Then why does she want Eden? If she just wanted her to open a sidh, she didn't have to take her."

As she had half expected, the faces in the room all turned toward Rohan. "We've told you all we can right now" was all he said in response.

"You haven't told me anything at all!" Cedar shrieked, her fear and frustration boiling over. "You're all just sitting here! You say I shouldn't involve the police, yet you spent the whole night searching and came up with nothing! Now we know it wasn't an accident. Eden was kidnapped by one of your people, and I want to know why! How else am I supposed to find her? Tell me, damn it! This is all your fault!" She punctuated her last few words with a series of hard punches against Rohan's chest. Then she stepped back, breathing hard.

When he spoke, there was no anger in his voice, but rather something akin to pity. "Yes," he said. "Yes, it is our fault. And so it is *we* who will take full responsibility for fixing our mistake. There is no need for you to be involved any further. We are perfectly capable of finding Eden and returning her to safety. And when we have done that, we will take full responsibility for her. She needs to be raised as part of this family—her true family."

Cedar's face was a storm of emotion, and her voice was low and dark when she spoke. "You'll take *full responsibility for her? Part of this family?* I. Am. Her. Family. I'm all the family she needs."

"Rohan, this is hardly helpful," Riona said as she stepped between them. "Cedar, what he means is that we will help you with

Eden. We'll teach her about who she is and her place in our world. You won't have to worry about her."

"No. I'm done with this bullshit. Get the hell out of my house. *Now*."

"Cedar," Riona began, but the others had already started heading toward the door.

Nevan walked over to Riona. "It's her place," she said with an almost respectful glance at Cedar. "And she's right, we're just sitting here. We've got to get moving if we're going to track down Nuala before she gets too far." One by one, they left. Cedar slammed the door behind them and turned to face Jane.

"Holy shit, Ceeds," Jane said. "Who are those people? What kind of spell did that woman put on me? Is she a witch or something?"

"I don't know," Cedar said. She grabbed fistfuls of hair and pulled. "I feel like I'm losing my mind. But this is happening—it's real. And the magic is real too. Damn it, Jane, I need those people. They know Nuala, and I can't find Eden without them! But my mother says I shouldn't trust them, and I'm so angry and scared and confused. *What should I do?*"

Jane hugged her tight. "I don't know. I would have thrown them out too. But yeah, maybe you do need them. In any case, you're not going to find Eden if you drive yourself mad. You need to focus—and rest. Why don't you lie down for a bit, get some sleep. Then we'll decide what to do next."

Sleep was the last thing on Cedar's mind. But she nodded to Jane and went into her door-less room. She sat in the back corner of the walk-in closet, where she curled up into a ball and dissolved like a sand castle hit by a ten-foot wave. She writhed in pain, her mouth open in a soundless scream. Over and over again, she drew her knees up to her chest, trying to stem the flow from what she was sure was a fatal wound. *Eden's gone, she's gone, and it's all my fault.* Eventually, her voice clawed its way to the surface, and her moans and cries ripped through the air. Then Jane was there beside her, holding her together, and the two of them cried and clung to each other for what felt like hours. When Cedar finally lifted her head from her hands, she saw that Jane had fallen asleep on the floor beside her. She got up stiffly and covered her friend with a blanket.

She felt completely spent, but her mind was clearer than it had been all day. She picked up her phone and her purse and headed out the door. She stood still for a moment in the hallway, then went back inside and wrote a note for Jane saying she had gone out, and then another one for Eden.

> *Eden,*
> *Call me. Stay here. I love you.*
> *Mum*

She laid the notes on the table and headed back into the hallway and down the stairs. The fresh air hit her in the face like a splash of cold water. She looked at the time. It was already late afternoon.

She started walking downtown but reversed her course and headed in the other direction, toward Eden's school. She walked by the library on the way and went inside, but the memory of coming through the sidh with Eden made her stomach recoil, and she quickly retreated.

She dug out her phone and called Maeve. It rang several times, and she had already started formulating a message in her mind to leave on the voice mail when Maeve suddenly picked up.

"Cedar?" she asked, breathing heavily as if she had run for the phone. "What is it? Have you found her?"

"No, but we know who took her. Where have you been? Why haven't you called?"

"Someone *took* her? What do you know?"

Cedar recounted what had happened between Rohan and Jane, and the conclusion they had reached about Nuala. When she finished, there was a long silence on the other end of the phone.

"Dear God," Maeve finally whispered.

"Mum, they seem sure that Nuala has Eden, but they didn't say why, except that she wants Eden to open a sidh. Do you know anything more?"

"No, I don't. But we need to find out," Maeve answered. "Where are you now? Are you with them?"

"No," Cedar said. The fresh air had cleared the last vestiges of cobwebs from her mind, and she knew what she had to do. "They all left. Well, I threw them out. But they know Nuala; I can't do this without them. I'm going to call Riona. But first I'm coming over, okay? You said you have ways to find her, and I want to help."

"You can't, Cedar. I'm not at my apartment right now," Maeve said.

"Well, where are you, then? I can meet you anywhere," Cedar said, her voice rising in frustration.

"It doesn't matter. Look, I made it very clear what I think of you being involved with those people, but if you insist upon it, the least you can do is keep me informed of what they're doing. They may have *some* use," she said acidly. "If you find out any new information about Nuala, call me at once."

Maeve hung up, and Cedar stared at the phone in her hands. She sat down abruptly on one of the swings in the school playground, wondering if anything in her world was as it seemed. She leaned back on the swing and looked up at the sky, dotted with white, puffy clouds that seemed totally out of place on such a day.

Hang in there, Eden, she thought. *I'm going to find you.* Then she dialed Riona's number.

❦

It was getting dark when Cedar pulled up at the Fox and Fey. She walked around the back and was relieved to discover she could still see the descending stairs, even without Oscar's buoyant presence. She hesitated at the big wooden door, wondering if she should knock. Then she squared her shoulders and shoved her way inside.

She stood still for a moment as her eyes adjusted to the near darkness. She noticed a couple of clusters of people sitting in the corners of the pub but couldn't make out who they were. Then she heard a voice coming from behind the bar.

"Cedar, m'dear! Get yerself over here so I can pour you a drink."

She headed to the bar, where the friendly face of the barkeep waited for her.

"What's yer pleasure, then?" he asked.

"Just coffee, please. It's Felix, right?"

The old man grinned, a wide smile punctuated by two gold teeth and one black one, as he turned around and grabbed a carafe and a mug.

"You've got it right," he said. "Felix Dockendorff at your service, ma'am." He placed a steaming cup of coffee in front of her and plunked down a bowl of creamers and sugar. "How about some food, then? I make a mean fry-up."

"No, thanks," Cedar said, taking a creamer. Her stomach, already tied in knots, revolted at the thought of food.

He patted her hand and leaned forward, speaking in a voice just above a whisper. "Listen, I just want to say that I'm real sorry about yer troubles."

Cedar wasn't sure what to say, so she settled on, "Oh."

Felix nodded gravely and continued. "But don't you worry, m'dear. We'll fix things up right, don't you doubt it for a second."

Cedar stirred cream into her coffee and watched it swirl into beige. "Yeah. Speaking of which, do you know where Rohan and Riona might be? I called, and then I went by their place, but no one was home. That's why I came here; it was the only other place I knew to look."

"Aye, they're on their way here as we speak. Should be here any minute now."

Cedar thanked him and continued stirring her coffee. She wondered where he was from. He spoke with an odd sort of accent, but she couldn't quite place it. One minute he sounded as if he were from Scotland, the next from the American South. Maybe he had moved around a lot as a kid, she mused, but she thought it would be rude to ask.

The bar suddenly grew lighter and she saw the door open in the mirror behind the rows of bottles. Cedar recognized Murdoch and Anya from earlier, followed by Rohan and Riona, Dermot, and Molly.

Riona came over to hug Cedar. "Cedar! I'm sorry we didn't return your calls yet. We've been very busy, but I'm glad you're here."

"We need to talk," Cedar said without ceremony. She stood up and looked at Rohan. "I've had some time to think, and I hope you have too. There are a lot of things I don't understand, but the most important issue right now is finding my daughter."

She waited in case he wanted to say something, but when he remained silent, she continued.

"I don't want to hear any more talk about you taking responsibility for her. I'm her mother. No matter how important you think Eden is to you and your people, she's"—Cedar's voice broke and she paused to regain control—"she's a thousand times more important to me. But I do want your help. I *need* your help, and you need mine too. I know her better than any of you. You don't know her at all. So, with you knowing Nuala and me knowing Eden, maybe we can work together to find them."

She paused again, but still no one spoke, so she took a deep breath and soldiered on. "When we find her, she's staying with me, even if she is one of your people. But if you'll actually tell me who you are and why Eden is so important to you, I *might* be open to letting her get to know you, if she wants. But if I can't trust you, I'm not letting her get within a mile of you. And keeping me in the dark about what's really going on is not doing a whole lot to gain my trust. So…what's it going to be?"

She sat back down on the barstool and picked up her coffee cup, just for something to do with her hands. She stared at Rohan over the rim of her mug. She had said her piece, and the ball was in his court now. There was silence.

Finally, Nevan, whose presence Cedar hadn't even noticed, spoke up. "Makes sense to me," she said. Cedar felt a rush of gratitude toward her.

"Now wait just a minute," came another, more hostile voice, and Cedar bristled inwardly. Murdoch was striding toward the middle of the room.

"Don't go making any promises we can't keep," he growled at Rohan, ignoring Cedar completely. "That child's rightful place is with us."

Anya joined her husband's side. "I agree," she told Rohan. "Think about it, about what this could mean. She could be—"

Rohan cut her off before she could finish her sentence. "That's enough," he said. "I am aware of what the child means."

Cedar stood up again. "See? This is exactly what I'm talking about! What does she mean? How am I supposed to trust you if you know something about my daughter but won't tell me what it is?"

Rohan looked at her, and there was great sadness in his eyes. "Cedar," he said, and paused, "I am truly sorry for what has happened to you. It's…it's a tragedy, there's no other word for it. We will find Eden, but we can't tell you everything we know. There is too much at risk. It's best if you go home now. We'll contact you when we find her."

Cedar sat motionless as she processed his words and struggled to find her own to use as a weapon against them.

Riona looked at her husband. "Rohan, are you sure? None of this is her fault. I don't think alienating her is going to help anyone."

"She'll just get in the way," Murdoch argued. "Someone will have to keep an eye on her."

"Yes, but it's her daughter we're looking for. What's she supposed to do, just go home and do nothing? Would you?" Riona shot back.

"It might be safer for her that way," said a voice from the other side of the room, and Cedar recognized Sam from that morning.

She listened to them argue, but it didn't matter. They weren't going to keep her from finding Eden, or from getting answers. She cleared her throat and stood, ready to tell them that if they wouldn't help her, she would just do it on her own, when suddenly the back door to the kitchen swung open and all the oxygen in the room went out.

Everyone in the bar froze. Felix was the first one to speak. He addressed the ashen-faced young man with a headful of messy curls and unmistakable golden eyes standing in the doorway.

"Welcome home, Finn. Can I pour you a drink?"

CHAPTER 8

Cedar stood perfectly still, unable to move. Since Eden's disappearance, she had almost forgotten that she had been trying to find Finn, and now here he was, standing not ten feet away from her. She felt blood rush to her cheeks. Her body started to tremble, and for a few panicked moments she thought she had forgotten how to breathe. Then her lungs remembered and her heart started pounding, hard and fast, as if it were trying to escape the confines of her chest and leap across the room.

Finn was ignoring Felix's question and staring at Cedar. His face hadn't changed since the last time she saw him, only now it was filled with longing. His eyes bore into hers so intensely she had to look away. Cedar had imagined this scene a thousand times in a thousand different ways. She had imagined running into him on the street, or answering the door to find him standing there, or seeing him across a crowded art gallery in a foreign city. She had imagined what she would say to him—she would tell him how much she loved him and how sorry she was for whatever she had done to make him leave, and she would beg him for an explanation, for a chance to make things right.

But it had been years since she'd given up hope of ever seeing him again. Longing had turned into anger; despair into resolve. Life had turned into survival. Now, she had no idea what to say to him.

"They told me about Eden," he said, his voice a whisper. "I came to help. I got here as soon as I could. Cedar…I'm so sorry."

When she still said nothing, Finn looked at his father and said, "What are you doing? Why are you sending her away? She needs to know what's going on."

Rohan looked affronted. "Fionnbharr, this isn't—"

"You don't think I get a say in all of this?" Finn said. His cheeks flushed, and his eyes flashed. "Cedar is Eden's *mother*. She needs to know the truth."

Rohan crossed the floor to his son. "You don't understand."

"I don't understand?" Finn interrupted. His voice cracked through the room like a whip. "Who here understands her better than I do? My daughter has been taken, and Cedar needs to know why."

Perhaps it was the way he said the word *my*, or maybe it was his assumption that he understood her, but Cedar felt as though someone had thrown a switch inside her. She could hear the blood rushing in her ears and found her feet moving toward him. His face softened, and then tensed in confusion as she crossed the room. Her palm hit his cheek with a resounding smack, and she felt the pain of it shoot up her arm. When she spoke, even she was surprised by the hostility in her voice.

"*Don't*," she said. "Don't call her your daughter. You think you understand me? You think I'm still the same person you left?" She felt hot, angry tears prick her eyes and struggled to hold them back. "Don't you *dare* call yourself her father."

Finn's face twisted in agony. "Cedar," he whispered, the softness of his voice a sharp contrast to hers. "I didn't know. *I swear* I didn't know about her."

"And whose fault is that?" she demanded hotly. "I tried to tell you. I tried to find you. *Seven years of nothing*. I didn't even know if you were still alive."

"It was for the best," he pleaded. "I can explain everything. I'm sorry, and you're right, I don't know what you've been through, but trust me—it would have been worse if I had stayed."

"Trust you?" Cedar screamed, and then laughed sardonically. She was starting to feel quite hysterical. "Why would I trust you, Finn? You left me with nothing!"

"You had Eden," he said quietly. "She wasn't nothing."

"AND NOW SHE'S GONE!"

Cedar swayed on her feet, suddenly exhausted beyond belief. Someone placed a barstool under her and she sat down hard, and then promptly burst into tears. Riona and Nevan rushed over to her, but she hid her face in her hands and turned away from them. She felt so completely overwhelmed, so desperately alone in this room of strangers. She felt ashamed of her outburst, startled by the intensity of her anger. This was not the reunion she had dreamed of.

The awkward silence, punctuated only by her sobs and gasps for air, was finally interrupted by Murdoch, who said, "Enough of this nonsense. We've got to get on with it. Finn, why don't you take your girlfriend home, sort things out, and then meet us back here."

Finn seemed shaky on his feet too, but his voice was firm when he answered, "I'm not taking her anywhere until she's had some answers. And then it's up to her if she wants to go home or stay with us."

"Look at her, man!" Murdoch said, his face incredulous. "She's a bloody wreck! She'll only slow us down, and we don't have time to waste!"

"I agree with Finn," said a perky voice that belonged to Finn's sister, Molly. "It should be her decision!"

"This is bigger than just her," argued Anya. "We need to do what's best for us."

"But what if she can help?" Nevan asked.

"No, it's too risky," Anya shot back.

"Stop it!" Finn bellowed, throwing his words into the melee like a grenade. Everyone stopped talking and looked at him. "What's the matter with all of you?" he asked, seeming genuinely bewildered. "Have you learned *nothing* about humans in all this time?"

Rohan cleared his throat loudly, and Cedar looked up, her face a mess of tears and her nose running. Felix handed her some napkins, and she started wiping her face, keeping her eyes on Finn's father. He was gazing at Finn with a peculiar expression. "Murdoch is right," he said. "We don't have time for this, and there are certain things that are only for us to know for the time being."

Finn started to protest, but Rohan raised his hand and Finn kept silent, although the look on his face was defiant.

"However," Rohan continued, "there is a new element to consider now." He looked pointedly at Finn, as if to say *he* was this new element. "She can stay if she wants, but she is *entirely* your responsibility. And if this unfinished business between the two of you starts getting in the way, it will only make it more difficult for us to locate your daughter. Do I make myself clear?"

Finn nodded, and Rohan looked at Cedar.

She hesitated, and then nodded as well.

Several glances were shared around the room, and then Rohan said, "Now, could I speak to you in private, *son?*" and the two of them stalked off into the kitchen.

Felix refilled Cedar's coffee and handed it to her with a sympathetic smile.

"Quite a shock then, seeing him again?"

She let out the breath she hadn't been aware she was holding. "You could say that."

"Well, none of us have seen him in a long time, either," Felix said. "But it will be good to have him back, to be sure. I know you think he did you wrong, but he's a good man, young Finn is, and I've known him since he was a babe. He's not got a bad bone in him. Whatever he did, he had a good reason for it."

Cedar raised her eyebrows but said nothing. She sat in silence, half listening to the whispers and muted conversations around her. Finally, the two Donnellys emerged from the kitchen, both looking grim. Finn walked away from Rohan and slowly approached her, as if he was afraid she might spook and run if he came up too fast.

"I know you probably don't want to talk to me," he said, "but I can give you some answers if you'll listen."

Cedar looked at him standing there, so forlorn and yet so heartbreakingly beautiful, like a lost angel. She could feel her body responding to his closeness, even though he was standing three feet away, and she cursed the sudden warmth that flooded her veins.

"Yes, I want answers," she said. "Starting with who, or what, you people are."

"Do you remember when we were together, and I used to bring home books from the library about the Tuatha Dé Danann? Sometimes I would read some of the stories to you," Finn asked, looking hesitant.

She nodded slowly.

"You said you had read some of the stories before, in a book of your mother's you found as a child," he continued.

"Yes, but why? Are you saying…"

"I am one of the Tuatha Dé Danann. We all are."

There was a prolonged silence as Cedar stared at him, and everyone else stared at her, waiting for her reaction.

"You're telling me that you are a…Celtic god? Because that's… kind of crazy."

"It's the truth," Riona said. "I know it's hard to believe, but think about what you've seen and what Eden can do. Think about the staircase and what Nevan showed you she can do."

Cedar looked into Riona's somber, dark brown eyes. She certainly didn't seem delusional. There were so many of them here, watching her with a quiet confidence. She thought of everything she had seen over the past couple of days and willed herself to keep an open mind. *Logical explanations are not the only option anymore,* she thought.

"Okay," she said, trying to remember what she had read. It had been a long time ago. "So *if* you're the Tuatha Dé Danann, why are you here? Didn't they all go back to the land of Tír na nÓg?" Cedar tried to remember some of the stories she had read as a child. The Tuatha Dé Danann had ruled Ireland before the coming of the Celts, but had lost a great battle and had been relegated to Tír na nÓg, the Otherworld. Over the centuries, the Tuatha Dé Danann had developed into the "little folk" of Irish folklore.

"We did." It was Nevan who spoke this time. She had perched herself on a stool beside Cedar and was watching her intently. "You remember well. We used to live here, on Ériu, what you call earth. But then we were defeated by the humans. We were forced to leave and make our home in the Otherworld. But it wasn't so bad," she said with a small smile. "Tír na nÓg is indescribably beautiful, and we could visit Ériu by using the sidhe. Some of us spent quite a lot of time here, for a while."

"What do you mean, for a while?" Cedar asked. "You're here now."

"It's been a long time since our people have made regular visits here," Finn answered. His face darkened, and he glanced at his father, as if he was asking for permission to continue. His father's expression was carefully guarded, but he nodded slightly.

"There was a war in Tír na nÓg, and our side lost," Finn explained. "Those of us who survived escaped here. We were looking for help, and a chance to rebuild."

"Okay, so you're, um, ancient Celtic gods, but you're here, pretending to be humans," Cedar said, hearing how ridiculous her own words sounded. She wished Jane were with her.

"We're not gods," Riona said softly, "although we were once worshipped as such. We're a different race, you might say. And, yes, we've been trying to blend in."

Across the room, Molly grinned at her. "They say we're fairies now!" she said, putting her hands behind her back and flapping them like wings. Rohan shot her a look, and she dropped her hands back down to her sides, the grin sliding off her face.

Fairies, Cedar thought. *Eden would like that.* "What does this have to do with Eden?" she asked. "The thing she can do with the doors, is that because she's one of you, because she's half Tuatha Dé Danann?" Cedar forced herself to look at Finn, who looked nervous but nodded silently. At least she had her answer to that question. Only now she had about a thousand more.

"And Nuala?" she asked, turning to look at Rohan. "You said she put a spell on Jane. Is she a witch? Can you all do magic?"

"We are not witches and wizards, or fairies. This isn't some child's game," Rohan said.

"I didn't say—" Cedar started, but Riona interrupted.

"I suppose you might call it magic," she said. "But we're all different in our abilities. Nuala has a very rare gift. She has the ability of persuasion, let's call it. Even when she's not trying, she exudes a sort of charm that makes people trust her and want to do what she says. But her ability can be very, very powerful when she taps into a deep emotion or desire inside the person she is trying to persuade." She paused, searching for the right words to explain it. "She's like a very good salesman, in a sense, or a fortune teller. They're experts at reading people, at figuring out what they really want to hear. Nuala's gift is more than just good instincts, however. She can see inside a person and know his or her true heart. And that, combined with her gift of persuasion, means she can convince anyone to do almost anything, as long as there is a tiny kernel of desire inside that person, even if they don't admit to it to themselves. She just needs the tiniest of hooks, and she's got you."

"That sounds horrible," Cedar said.

Riona looked sad. "It is not a gift I would wish for myself or my children, no. Life has not been easy for Nuala because of it."

"So that's how she convinced Jane to forget what had happened—because Jane didn't want to be there in the first place," Cedar said.

Riona nodded. "More than that, she didn't want you to know what had happened, that she had been neglecting Eden. Her guilt was the only hook Nuala needed. But once Jane knew she was forgiven, everything came back to her."

Cedar could tell that the others in the room were getting restless. A few of them were huddled together, whispering. Even Nevan kept glancing toward the door. But Cedar didn't want to stop asking questions, not now that she was finally getting some answers.

"So why did Nuala take Eden? Why does she want her ability?" she asked.

Finn glanced uncertainly at his father, and Cedar wished he would stop doing that. It made her think he wasn't telling her everything. "We're not sure, but we think she might want Eden to open a sidh back to Tír na nÓg, so she can return."

"Why would she need Eden? If she wants to go back, can't she just go the same way you came?"

"That way is closed," Finn said. "Lorcan, who rules Tír na nÓg now, was tracking us. He was on our heels, and we couldn't risk him following us through. So my father sealed the sidh we traveled through, and it was the last one, in either direction. Eden is the only one among us with the ability to open the sidhe."

Cedar pinched the bridge of her nose, trying to keep everything straight. "So Rohan can seal a sidh, but none of you can create one? Then who made the one you came through?"

"He's dead," Rohan said.

Cedar waited, in the hopes of more information, but Rohan's face told her the subject was closed. "And if Eden opens a sidh to Tír na nÓg, Nuala will let her go?"

At this, Finn's body became very still. Cedar glanced at him and frowned. Finally, Rohan answered, "We don't know."

Cedar felt this sink in, slowly, painfully, like a boulder gradually settling to the bottom of her stomach.

"Now perhaps you can answer some questions for us," Rohan said. "You told us last night that Eden can't create a sidh to a place she hasn't seen before. Correct?"

Cedar nodded, the stone in her stomach lightening slightly. "I think so. I mean, we only tried it once, but it didn't seem to work." She looked at Finn. "She thought she'd be able to find you. She wanted to go wherever you were, but we didn't know where that was." She ran her fingers through her hair, feeling oddly relieved. Eden was still missing, but at least she was still in this world, *her* world. She wasn't out of reach—not yet.

Finn, seeming to sense her thoughts, reached out to touch her hand, but she withdrew it. "I'm sure she's okay," he said. "Nuala needs Eden. She'll be sure to keep her safe."

"Will Nuala put a spell on her like she did with Jane?" Cedar asked.

"She might try, but I don't think it will work," Finn answered. "My father and I both share part of Eden's gift—we can close but not open the sidhe. It makes us immune to the rest of the Tuatha Dé Danann. It's both good and bad, I suppose. Nuala cannot persuade us, and that's a good thing. And we can often help break

Nuala's spells on others, as my father did with your friend. On the other hand, Nevan can't communicate with us. Sam makes the most extraordinary music, but we can't hear it. We're just…closed. Murdoch's daggers can still stick us, though. We're only immune to the abilities that affect the mind or heart. But it does mean that Nuala won't be able to control Eden that way."

"Is it normal that Eden can both open *and* close the sidhe?" Cedar asked.

Rohan answered, his voice brusque and impatient. "I think that's enough questions for now," he said, breaking away from them abruptly to exchange words with Dermot and Anya.

Cedar turned back to her coffee, trying to make sense of this new reality while painfully aware of Finn's silent gaze on her back. He had returned, as she had always hoped he would, but he wasn't who she thought he was. He was a…she didn't even know what to call him. A god? A superhero? She thought of Zeus and Thor and all the other myths she'd heard and wondered if they were real too. She felt beyond stupid. She had been closer to him than she had ever been to anyone else in the world, and yet she had suspected nothing. *Nothing.* And now she was caught up in this world where, despite her protests, she knew she did not belong. She glanced at Finn over her shoulder, and he gave her a tentative smile. She looked away. She had to stay focused on finding Eden, no distractions.

"Okay, listen up," Rohan was saying in a loud voice. "Now that Miss McLeod here has had her history lesson, we can get on with finding the child."

"What's the plan?" Nevan asked. "We've already looked everywhere for Nuala, and all our allies have been alerted."

"Wait," Sam said. "We've been going about it the wrong way. We've been looking for Nuala, but we should be looking for what *she's* looking for."

Nevan scrunched up her nose, which made her look like a pixie more than ever. "What do you mean? What is she looking—ohh," she let out her breath.

"What? What is she looking for?" Cedar asked, confused.

"Of course! You said it yourself, Cedar. See, I told you she would be helpful!" Nevan said. "Eden can't open a sidh to Tír na nÓg unless she knows what Tír na nÓg looks like! Nuala's not stupid—she'll figure that out pretty quick, or Eden will tell her herself. So she'll be looking for a picture or some kind of depiction of Tír na nÓg. Right?"

"That's ridiculous," Anya said with a scowl. "How could she do that? No one knows what Tír na nÓg looks like except for us, and there aren't any pictures of it."

"You might be right, Anya," Riona said. "At least, I haven't seen any. Has anyone else?"

They all shook their heads. "We can't rule it out, though," said Dermot, who had come to stand beside Finn. "I mean, just because we haven't seen them doesn't mean they don't exist. Our people have been interacting with humans for centuries. Maybe someone else left something here, a photograph or a drawing. Would that work? A drawing?"

Cedar shook her head. "I don't know. The only things that worked were photographs—a wall calendar, actually—and images she saw on TV. I tried drawing a sketch for her of a place in Vancouver, but it didn't work. I think it would have to be a photograph, or pretty close to it."

"The kid's got a point," said Felix, who still stood behind the bar. "Here's my question: Is that ginger-haired bitch just lookin' for a photograph or drawing, or is there some other way she could show the wee girl what the place looks like?"

"Don't call her that," growled Murdoch. "We still don't know for sure she's got anything to do with this. And even if she did, you can't fault her for wanting to go home."

Felix cleared his throat. "Fine. If it'll make you shut yer mouth, I'll rephrase my question. Is *Nuala* looking for a picture, or is there some other way?"

"I could show her," Nevan whispered, a worried look on her face. Everyone looked at her.

"I could put an image of Tír na nÓg into Eden's mind. It's been over thirty years since I've seen it, but I can still see every leaf. Do you think Nuala has thought of that? What if she forces me to show Eden?"

Cedar was surprised by Nevan's words. She didn't look a day older than eighteen. How could she have been in Tír na nÓg thirty years ago, and have a clear memory of it?

"But you've tried to contact Eden, and it didn't work," Riona said reassuringly. "Her mind is closed to you, just like Rohan's and Finn's are." Nevan nodded, but the crease between her eyebrows remained.

"I have an idea," Finn continued. The others looked at him expectantly. He cleared his throat nervously. "What about Brighid?" he said.

Cedar didn't know who Brighid was, but apparently everyone else did, judging by their response. Molly smiled and said, "Ooo, yes!" while Felix snorted and Sam, who had been rubbing Nevan's neck, looked up and said, "You've got to be kidding."

"Look, I know she's chosen a different path than we have," Finn said, "but that's why we should talk to her. Maybe she knows something we don't or can at least point us in the right direction."

"Who is Brighid?" Cedar asked.

"You know, Saint Brigit!" Molly said, giggling.

"What?" Cedar asked, confused. Riona gave her daughter a smile. "I don't think Cedar is Catholic, dear." Then she turned to Cedar. "Brighid is one of us, a Tuatha Dé Danann. She is one of our Elders, one of the first who came to this world. However, she chose to leave Tír na nÓg many years ago; I think it was around the fifth century of your time. She said she preferred the company of humans to the company of gods. And she's lived here ever since, under various guises, of course, including a saint," she said, glancing at Molly. "We don't have much to do with her, however. She prefers not to involve herself in our affairs."

"Wait, she's *how* old? Don't your people…die?" Cedar asked, looking at Finn.

"We do," he said. "But not of old age. We can be killed by violence. We don't age, not physically, once we reach maturity. We stay that way forever."

"But…" Cedar looked back at Felix, with his grizzled white beard and toothy grin.

He laughed, showing his gold teeth. "I'm a healer by nature, but I can also whip up a right nice aging brew for those of us who want to blend in. I'm actually as young and virile as yer man Finn, here, and twice as charming," he said with wink.

Rohan interrupted. "Enough questions, I said. Finn, go ahead and call Brighid."

"Speaking of charming," Murdoch muttered.

Finn blushed and gave Murdoch a dirty look. "She was fond of me for a while," he said to Cedar. "But nothing ever happened between us. She knew my heart belonged to someone else." Their eyes met for a heartbeat before he looked back at the group. "I'll give her a call. I'm sure she'll be willing to help."

Finn disappeared into the kitchen, and they all sat in silence, waiting. A few minutes later, he came back out, looking nervous.

"Well?" Murdoch demanded.

"She says she'll tell us what she knows about depictions of Tír na nÓg. She wouldn't say more on the phone, but it sounds like one exists and she knows where it is." He hesitated and looked at Cedar. "She wants me to go see her in New York. And she wants me to take Cedar with me."

"Why me?" she asked.

Finn's cheeks reddened, but he held her gaze. "She says she wants to meet the woman who nearly drove me mad."

Blood streamed down Maeve's arms and dripped off her elbows. She ran her hand through her hair distractedly, leaving red streaks in the disheveled gray. The butchered remains of a cat lay on the floor in front of her. She was in the small workshop in the front yard of her house in the country, just outside the tiny town of Chester. It was the home Cedar had grown up in, and though Maeve had an apartment in the city so she could be close to her daughter and granddaughter, she still kept the country home for weekend get-aways—and for the memories it held.

Maeve picked at the entrails, moving them around the floor for the dozenth time, examining them as she consulted faded charts and diagrams stained with bloody fingerprints. She shuddered, not at the gruesome display in front of her, but at the thought that she might fail, that she might not find Eden in time. *Like a lamb to the slaughter*, she thought, looking into the cat's sightless eyes. Then she shook her head sharply. She needed to stay calm, to think clearly. She breathed deeply, trying to push her fear down, but it clung to her like a desperate lover. Nothing she tried was working as it should. She shuddered again and rolled a strand of cat intestine between her fingers, wondering what on earth she could try next.

Cedar's betrayal had cut her like a knife, but she had not been entirely surprised. Despite all Maeve's warnings, Cedar had loved

Finn with all her heart, and she loved him still. Maeve could see the anguish of it on her face whenever anyone said his name. Cedar had chosen him once, and now she was choosing his people over her own mother, even though she had only known them for a day.

"You're not one of them, Cedar, and if you have to learn your lesson twice, so be it," Maeve muttered. And maybe there would be a silver lining to all this. If Cedar was with them, she could keep Maeve informed about their movements, helping her stay one step ahead of them.

She looked at what remained of the cat and sighed. She had not used her skills as a druid for many years, and she had grown rusty. The Ogham sticks had told her nothing about Eden's whereabouts, nor had the runes. She had spent the entire night in the woods surrounding her country house, communing with the earth and the trees, begging them to speak to her, to help her find the child. Silence had been the only response.

She cursed herself for not anticipating this, for not doing more to keep Cedar and Eden away from these people. Nevertheless, Cedar had made her choice, and now it was up to Maeve. She had to find the girl, and find her before they did. And then she had to discover a way to protect her from them—forever.

CHAPTER 9

Cedar hated taking the red eye. Usually she couldn't sleep on planes, but she was so exhausted she managed to doze for nearly the whole flight from Halifax to New York. She was glad, because it meant she didn't have to talk to Finn. For the past seven years, she had been desperate to know why he had left, but now that he was sitting next to her, she was terrified of finding out. It was easier to ignore him.

When they got off the plane, she called her mother. Maeve sounded tense, and Cedar assumed she was still upset that she had chosen to accept the help of the Tuatha Dé Danann. Maeve listened quietly as Cedar filled her in. Then she asked several questions, but brushed off Cedar's own questions with more promises to tell her more later.

Cedar hung up, frustrated, and she and Finn hopped in a taxi and headed into the theater district. The last time she had been to New York they had been together, on a spur-of-the-moment road trip. They had been sitting around on a Friday night, debating which movie to go to and bemoaning the lack of cheap theaters in Halifax. Finn had reminisced about a great hole-in-the-wall movie theater he had been to once in New York that showed classic films around the clock. Cedar had never been to New York, and as he told her about it, her eyes had started to twinkle, a cheeky smile spreading across her face. He knew her well enough to know what she was thinking.

"Really?" he asked, starting to grin. "It's...seven o'clock."

"Which means," Cedar started counting on her fingers, "if we leave in an hour we can be there by ten in the morning, spend the day seeing the sights, go see a show or something, spend the night, and drive back on Sunday. It will be perfect!"

And it had been. They had crammed as many touristy things as they could into one day and collapsed in exhaustion at the Banana Bungalow hostel in the wee hours of the morning on Sunday. After breakfast at the greasiest spoon they could find, they had started the fifteen-hour drive home. It had been one of the best weekends of Cedar's life.

Now, seven years later, Finn made a few attempts at conversation as they rode through the city, but Cedar's answers were so stilted he soon gave up. They spent the rest of the ride in silence. When the cab pulled up in front of the café where they were meeting Brighid, Finn paid the fare and they got out. Cedar stood for a moment under the awning before following Finn inside. She told herself she didn't care about him anymore, but that didn't lessen her desire to break this other woman's legs, goddess or not. She told herself she was being juvenile, that of course Finn had dated other women since her. Maybe he was even seeing someone now. It didn't matter, she told herself. All that mattered was finding Eden. She quickly silenced her inner dialogue and walked into the café, where Finn was waiting for her just inside the door.

"This won't take long, don't worry," he said. "We'll just ask her our questions and then we'll decide what to do next." He turned and searched the room, stopping when his eyes rested on a woman in the corner. The woman saw him, too, and stood up to greet them. She was tall, with black hair and a regal bearing not unlike Riona's. But this woman was designed to stand out. She had dramatic, prominent cheekbones; dark, deep-set eyes that framed a long, straight nose; and a full mouth that was stretched into a wide, expansive smile. When she held out her arms in welcome, several folds of silky black material fell from them. Under her flowing top, she wore tight leather pants and platform shoes, adding another three inches to her already impressive height. She had an ageless beauty, and she could just easily be twenty or fifty. Cedar couldn't tell.

"Fionnbharr," Brighid said, wrapping her arms around him and kissing him on both cheeks. "You came."

"And you," she said, taking a step back and looking Cedar up and down. "You must be Cedar." She clicked her tongue and made a *hmm* sound that Cedar couldn't interpret. "Well, she's certainly attractive, I'll give you that," Brighid said to Finn.

"Er, yes," Finn said, holding out a chair. "Cedar, this is Brighid," he said.

"So I gathered," Cedar said dryly as Brighid settled herself dramatically into the proffered chair. Cedar pulled out her own chair and sat down across the table. A young woman appeared with a pot of coffee and took their breakfast orders.

"Brighid is one of the leads in the musical *Jezebel* here on Broadway," Finn explained once the server had left.

"Seriously?" Cedar asked. Finn and Brighid looked at her. "I mean, I guess I just didn't expect that's what someone like you would be doing. No offense. I've heard the show's great."

To Cedar's surprise, Brighid threw back her head and laughed. Her voice boomed across the café, and several people turned to stare.

"Well, you're probably right," she said when she had stopped laughing. "I've done a great many things, some important, some not. But the nice thing about being around for as long as I have is that you get to try a bit of everything." She gave Finn a sly look. "Well, *almost* everything."

Finn blushed but smiled. "You don't need to make Cedar jealous. She hates my guts, and rightfully so."

Brighid raised an eyebrow at Cedar. "Really?" she said. "Well, isn't that a shame. He's a very nice boy, you know. He was absolutely miserable when he had to leave you. Sulked in a corner of my flat for a week. Or was it a month? At any rate, you shouldn't be too hard on him. He's very useful to have around. And now that the cat's out of the bag, well, you should really give him a second chance."

Finn cleared his throat and leaned across the table. "Brid, on the phone you said you'd be able to help us—that you know where we can find an accurate depiction of Tír na nÓg."

"Mmm, yes, well, I must say I'm surprised that none of you have one."

"Have one what?" Finn asked.

"A painting," she said. "I suppose you haven't been away long enough to want one for sentimentality's sake." Turning to Cedar, she explained, "I only get back to Tír na nÓg once every couple of centuries or so. It's good to see the old place, but I must say I prefer the company here. It's a beautiful country, though—I'll give you that. Far more spectacular than anything you'll find here, and believe me, I have seen the world. At any rate, a few years ago I commissioned a painting of the place—well, of one of my favorite little nooks. One of my lovers was a rather well-known landscape artist at the time. I'm no shabby artist myself, of course, but it was much more romantic to have it painted for me than to do it myself. And he was good—very good, in fact—once I had described the scene in detail and given him a few sketches. When he was done, I gave it the finishing touches, and I swear I could have almost walked right through it into Tír na nÓg. I couldn't really, of course—I still had to use those silly sidhe, but the likeness was remarkable."

"Do you still have it?" Cedar asked. "The painting?" She was thinking of the picture she had hastily sketched for Eden, and how it hadn't worked. But if this painting was as lifelike as Brighid said, maybe it really would help Eden open a sidh to Tír na nÓg.

Brighid inspected her nails. "Well, no. That was…oh, I suppose it was a couple hundred years ago, now that I think of it. So it's been a little while. I was loath to let it go. I was almost as fond of it as I am of Fionnbharr here." She reached out a smooth hand and patted Finn's cheek. "But Deardra had done me a great favor, and that's what she wanted in return." She shrugged. "I won't bore you with the details of what she did for me, but let's just say that after that I could hardly refuse her anything she wanted. And I suppose another artist will always come along sooner or later."

"Who is Deardra?" Cedar asked.

Brighid looked at her in surprise. "Haven't they told you anything?"

"Deardra is, well, I suppose you'd call her a mermaid," Finn answered quickly.

"A *what*?"

"I think you'd be surprised by how many of your legends and fairy tales are based in truth," he said with a small smile. "Only we call them the Merrow, not mermaids. Deardra is their queen." He turned to Brighid. "I'm surprised she was willing to help you," he said.

She smiled back at him. "Well, I seem to have successfully removed myself from the stigma of being Tuatha Dé Danann, at least in her eyes. The Danann and the Merrow aren't enemies, per se, but neither are they the best of friends," she explained to Cedar.

Cedar pinched the bridge of her nose and willed herself to just go with it. "Okay," she said. "So the painting is with this Deardra. Is this common knowledge? Would Nuala know?"

They were interrupted by the arrival of breakfast. Cedar took a large gulp of coffee and nibbled on the edge of her toast. Her appetite had been remarkably diminished these days. Brighid and Finn tucked into their plates, both piled high with bacon, sausage, eggs, hash browns, fried mushrooms, and buttered toast. One of the benefits of being forever young and beautiful, Cedar supposed.

Brighid shrugged. "I wouldn't say it's common knowledge, no. But I don't know who Deardra may have told." A peculiar expression crossed her face.

"What is it?" Finn asked.

"I had the impression that there was something else I wanted to tell you, but it's slipped my mind. Oh, well, not to worry. I'm sure it will come back to me if it's of any importance."

"So where can we find Deardra?" Cedar asked, impatient.

"Finn knows the way, don't you, dear?" Brighid answered calmly.

He nodded and stood up. "Let me make a few calls," he said, and walked out of the café and onto the street. Cedar could see him through the window, and wondered why he had chosen to make his calls outside.

"So this is quite a pickle you've gotten yourself into, isn't it, my dear?" Brighid asked her.

"Excuse me?" Cedar said.

Brighid waved her hands airily. "Oh, I'm not talking about your missing daughter, although that *is* tragic. I mean what are you going to do about Finn?"

"I'm not really thinking about my love life right now," Cedar said through gritted teeth.

"One should *always* be thinking about one's love life," Brighid said.

Cedar thought it was time to change the subject. "What can you tell me about this guy named Lorcan?" she asked.

"Ah, well, there's a cheery topic of conversation." Brighid's nose wrinkled with disgust. "Lorcan is the worst of us, I'm afraid. He's old, very old, though not one of the Elders, or else he would have gone back with them. They told you about that, yes?" Cedar shook her head. "The Elders, of which I am one, were the first to arrive here in Ériu. We lived, we loved, we prospered, and we got our asses handed to us by those damned Milesians—you call them the Celts now, I suppose—and then relegated to Tír na nÓg. We were always at war those days, it seems. First with giants and half giants and then the Sons of Mil came from over the sea and thought they'd rather well have our lovely green isle. Don't get me wrong, Tír na nÓg is quite lovely, I assure you, but I, for one, didn't want to spend all eternity there. And neither did the other Elders, apparently, because after a few years—or was it a few hundred? I can never keep the time straight—they decided to call it a day and went back to the Four Cities, our true homeland. Unfortunately for everyone else, only those who are originally from the Four Cities can ever return there. I'm afraid Tír na nÓg hasn't been quite the same since the Elders left. Things went downhill very quickly. Which brings us to Lorcan. He is, in a nutshell, ruthless. Also, delusional. He has never accepted the fact that our people were defeated in war. He still believes this world should belong to the Tuatha Dé Danann. He and I are at the opposite ends of a spectrum, you could say. Some think I love humanity too much and have sought to re-create myself in its image, and maybe they're right. But Lorcan's hatred for humanity is unparalleled. All he has ever wanted is revenge and retribution for the insult he feels was done to our people. There are others who feel the same way—too many, to be sure—but they don't have the power that Lorcan does, and are easier to keep in check."

"What kind of power does he have?" Cedar asked.

"Almost every kind," Brighid said. "That's the problem. He's like a sponge. His natural ability is to absorb the powers of others at the moment of their death, when their spirits are leaving their bodies. As long as he is close by, the powers of the dead attach themselves to him."

Cedar stared at her, aghast.

"It didn't used to be so bad," Brighid said. "It was very rare, incredibly rare, in fact, for someone to die in Tír na nÓg during our centuries of peace. Oh, once in a while a hothead would go pick a quarrel with some giant or warrior and get himself killed for his trouble, but by the time we brought his body back to Tír na nÓg, his spirit and power had already left him, and there was nothing for Lorcan to absorb. So it's a rather useless gift, really, when there is peace."

"But then the war came," Cedar observed.

"See, I knew you weren't just a pretty face," Brighid said, beaming. "When the Elders left, Lorcan started stirring up trouble, small acts of rebellion against the High King. A death here and a death there, and his power began to grow. The more powerful he became, the more trouble he was able to cause. He started building an army of supporters, telling them they would take back the world they had lost, exact revenge on their conquerors—everything they had ever dreamed of. So the High King had no choice but to go to war against him. It was all very dramatic, from what I've heard."

"From what you've heard?" asked Cedar.

"Well, it's not as if I were there myself, is it?" Brighid answered. "No, I only heard about the whole mess after I met your Finn." She sighed dramatically. "Sometimes I think it's a shame I've kept myself so separate. I would have liked to say good-bye to my sisters before they returned to the Four Cities. But, here we are."

"How did the war end?" Cedar could see Finn looking in at them through the window while he talked on the phone, and she wanted to get as much information as possible out of Brighid before he returned.

"Apparently, it went on for quite some time, several years, I believe. Tír na nÓg was almost destroyed." Brighid shook her head. "I suppose it ended when he killed Brogan, the High King. He was after the king's gift, of course."

"What was the king's gift?" Cedar asked.

Brighid looked surprised. "Don't you know? Goodness, child, I know they're not telling you everything, but I thought they would have told you this. He, too, had the ability to open the sidhe."

Cedar thought of Eden, her ability to effortlessly swing open the door to any place she could picture in her mind.

"The king? How is that—"

"It's very rare, of course, especially nowadays. There used to be sidhe all over the place for those of us who wished to travel back and forth between the realms. But when the Elders left, they closed all the sidhe, and only one Tuatha Dé Danann with that gift remained—Brogan."

Cedar wanted to ask Brighid to slow down, to let what she was hearing sink in so she could try to make sense of it. But she saw Finn pocket his cell phone and head toward the café door, and she still had so many questions. "So did it work? Did Lorcan get the king's power?"

"No, and I'm sure we're all grateful for that. We don't know why it didn't work exactly, but the assumption is that this particular gift, because it controls the passage between the worlds, can only go to someone worthy, someone who won't abuse it. Lorcan, of course, is far from worthy. So it's a gift he cannot take through the death of the one who owns it." She sat back in her chair, a strangely satisfied look on her face.

Before Cedar could ask another question, Finn arrived and threw some bills on the table.

"Let's go," he said to Cedar. "We have another plane to catch." He gave Brighid a suspicious look. "What were the two of you talking about?" he asked.

Brighid stood up and enveloped him in what Cedar thought was a far too intimate hug. "Just girl talk," she said, and gave his rear a squeeze.

"Why don't you come with us, Brid?" Finn asked as he tried to disentangle himself. "Deardra is much more likely to cooperate with you."

"Oh, I doubt that," Brighid said vaguely. "Besides, I have a show tonight. So go get 'em, tiger," she said with a wink. "Keep an eye on him for me, will you, dear?" she said to Cedar.

Cedar ignored this and simply said, "Thanks for your help. Good luck with your show tonight."

Brighid beamed back at them. "My pleasure, my dears! Have fun!"

Cedar and Finn left the café, Cedar shaking her head. Finn grinned at her, "She takes a bit of getting used to, but she's all right."

"I wasn't…I mean, yes, she does take some getting used to, but I was thinking of something else," Cedar said as they got into a cab and headed toward to the airport. "Why does she call you Fionnbharr? I heard your father call you that too."

"That's what you were thinking?"

"No. I'm just curious."

"Well, it's my name, I suppose. My real name."

Great, Cedar thought. *I didn't even know his real name.*

"The names from our homeland are difficult to say with the human tongue, and they draw too much attention. So most of us have taken on more ordinary names for our time here."

Our time here. So he would be leaving again.

"Where are we going? Where are these Merrow?" she asked, changing the subject.

"Ireland," Finn said. "Some of the others are flying over from Halifax. They'll meet us in Dublin. You've never been to Ireland, have you?"

"No," she said. "My mum traveled there for a while, though, before she had me. I've always wanted to visit." Cedar had never dreamed she would still be living in Nova Scotia as an adult. Not that she didn't love Halifax. She found the small city quaint and the history fascinating. But when she had left for university, she'd figured she would never be back. She had wanted to travel, see the world, experience other ways of living and being. She had interned at Ellison West while in design school in Vancouver and, ironically enough, had been offered a job at Ellison East when she had graduated. So she had returned to Nova Scotia, determined to put in her time and then get transferred to one of the agency's other offices in Toronto or Montreal, maybe even New York or London. Then Eden had come along, and she had realized that a stable income and a helpful mother were more important than seeing the world, at least for the time being. She still harbored dreams of spending a summer in Europe with Eden when she was older, or even home-schooling her for a year while they traveled through South America in a caravan. But for now, she was stuck. She hadn't been outside the Maritimes since Eden was born.

"Speaking of mothers…" Finn began, and Cedar tensed. He noticed, and his brow furrowed. "I was just going to say that my mother gave me something to give to you."

He reached into his pocket and pulled out a long silver chain. Cedar stared at it.

"Your mum is giving me a necklace? Why?"

Finn glanced at the back of the cabbie's head and lowered his voice. "It's more than a necklace," he said as he handed it to her. She took the chain in her hand it. It was delicate but of good quality. Hanging from the chain was a large stone, about the size of a silver dollar, set in an ornate silver frame. The frame was designed with the same swirling, twisting patterns Cedar had seen on the door of the Fox and Fey. She brushed her thumb over the stone, which was the color of onyx. Its surface was gritty, like a fine layer of sand had settled there. When she moved it, it glittered slightly in the light, as if the grains of sand were the dust of diamonds. She was, for a moment, mesmerized.

"It's beautiful," she said. "What is it?"

Finn reached into his pocket again and pulled out what appeared to be an old-fashioned pocket watch. He flipped it open, and Cedar saw that instead of clockwork, the gold frame held a large round stone similar to the one embedded in the necklace.

"They're called starstones," he said. "This set belongs to my parents. My mother insisted we take them in case we become separated. They're connected, so we can communicate and see each other if we need to."

In response to Cedar's silence, he said, "You don't have to use it. She just asked me to give it to you."

"Your parents don't have cell phones?" Cedar asked, and then regretted her sarcastic tone. She had never held anything more beautiful.

Finn didn't look offended. He smiled and said, "They do, and they use those most of the time, but these are a kind of tradition among our people. And they do come in handy. They were used a lot more when our people were traveling between this world and ours, but they sometimes use them here. It beats long-distance roaming fees."

Cedar started to smile, then stopped herself. "Why did you tell me your parents were dead?"

He looked at her mournfully. "I'm so sorry. I just...there are rules for my people. Rules I'm not very good at keeping. One of the main ones is that we're not supposed to get close to humans. I knew if I told you about them, you'd want to meet them. You wouldn't understand that I couldn't tell them about you. So it just seemed best to pretend they didn't exist."

"And you thought I'd never find out? That you and I could live in the same city as your parents and they'd never know about me? How—" Cedar cut herself off abruptly, clenching her teeth together. His rationale made sense, of course, now that she knew the truth. Of course he didn't want his parents to know he was dating a human. Well, they were stuck with her now, at least until she had Eden back.

"It doesn't matter," she said. "How do these starstones work?"

To her surprise, Finn blushed. "Each pair is activated by a particular song," he said. "The person who wants to use it needs to sing the song in order to activate the stone. It's simple to learn, though. Shall I sing it?"

She looked away. "If you want."

Finn cleared his throat and took a breath. Then he began to sing, and Cedar bit her lip as she felt her heart ache and tears spring to her eyes. She stared out the window as he sang, his voice rising and falling as effortlessly as an eagle coasting on the winds. It was a beautiful song, but made almost unbearably so by his tender voice, which she remembered so well. Finally, she could take it no more. Without looking at him, she whispered, "Stop. Please stop." He fell silent, and she could feel his gaze on her.

"I'll take the necklace," she said after a moment. She forced herself to look at him. "Thank you."

Finn wordlessly put the pocket watch away and looked out his window. Cedar closed her eyes and laid her head against the back of the seat, thinking of what Brighid had said: "You should really give him a second chance." Cedar huffed. *Easy enough for her to say. She's probably never been abandoned or betrayed. She has no idea what I've been through.* She thought about the rest of what Brighid had told her, and then straightened up and opened her eyes, breaking the silence.

"Brighid told me that opening the sidhe was the gift of the High King," she said. "She also said he was killed by Lorcan."

Finn looked at her cautiously. "He was."

"So, is your family part of the royalty over there? How did Eden end up with this gift if it's so rare?"

Finn was silent for a moment. Then, looking out the window again, he answered, "The ability to open the sidhe is given to someone who is worthy of it. That person was our king. Now, apparently, that person is Eden."

ȣȣ

Nuala. Nuala. Maeve's consciousness reached out as far as it dared. *Are you there? Can you sense me? I'm not here to harm you. Let me speak to you. Let me help you.*

Maeve could feel Nuala's consciousness, faintly at first, and this only after hours in her self-imposed dream trance. She tried to speak to Nuala, tried to touch her mind so they could communicate, like the Tuatha Dé Danann and their druids had done for centuries. But there was nothing but stony silence. Maeve felt her thoughts bouncing off Nuala's closed mind like a child off the walls of a bouncy castle—repeatedly, and without harm, but without any luck at breaching the wall. Nuala was alive; that was all she could determine.

After Maeve awoke from the trance, she sat still for several long minutes. There was one other person who might be able to help her, but she was unsure if she could reach him, or if he would even respond to her.

She did not even know if she would be able to handle seeing him again, but then she thought of Eden, and her resolve hardened. With shaking hands, she began to mix the tea again, this time making it stronger, so her sleep would be deeper and longer, and her consciousness able to travel farther.

She was going to attempt contact with Brogan, the High King of the Tuatha Dé Danann, who had once been her lover, and who had been dead for twenty-two years.

CHAPTER 10

They were close. Nuala could feel it as she walked hand in hand with Eden down an empty country road in the west of Ireland. It was Saturday afternoon back in Halifax but already evening here in Ireland, and the sun was hanging low in the sky over the ocean.

Nuala hated human technology as a rule, but she had to admit that Google Earth was very convenient when traveling with a child who could open sidhe if she knew enough about where she was going. That, of course, was the problem, and one Nuala had not anticipated. She had thought it would be easy to get the girl to open the sidh to Tír na nÓg. At first she had thought Eden was lying to her when she'd insisted she couldn't do it because she didn't know what Tír na nÓg—or Fairyland, as Nuala had called it—looked like. The Internet had been of no help; none of the human artists' depictions of her homeland had been even close to accurate. Nuala had tried to draw it, but that hadn't worked either. Finally, she had sought out help.

Eden was dragging her feet, so Nuala led them to the top of a small hill, where they sat on the grass, facing the sunset.

"Why couldn't we stay in New York City?" Eden asked. "I liked that Brighid lady."

Nuala pulled a chocolate bar out of her bag and handed it to Eden. "Because I told you, we need to go see the mermaids."

"Mermaids aren't real," Eden said, but she sounded uncertain.

"They are, and I'll prove it to you," Nuala said. "It's too late to go see them now. It's hard enough to find them in the daytime, let alone at night. But first thing in the morning, we'll go down to the coast and I'll introduce you to one: the Mermaid Queen." She gave Eden a playful nudge. "And then maybe you'll believe me when I say you're a fairy princess."

Eden didn't answer, her mouth full of chocolate and caramel.

Nuala lay down on her back and crossed her hands behind her head. This was the land her ancestors had conquered millennia ago, the land where so many of them had died in battle with other ancient races and, eventually, humans. She closed her eyes and tried to feel their power seeping up through the ground. *Why did you think this place was worth fighting for?* she asked them. There was no answer.

She glanced over at Eden, who had mimicked her and was now lying on her back and looking at the sky. This child was the key to her escape, she was sure of it. She remembered Lorcan's edict during the waning days of the war.

Bring the child to me, alive, and you will be richly rewarded. All will be forgiven. Just bring me the child.

Eden was not the child he had meant, but she was a worthy substitute. It would be enough, and Nuala was desperate to return home. All would be forgiven, and the power and status she had once taken for granted would be returned to her at last.

The sooner they got there, the better. She stood up and brushed the grass off her legs. "Let's go," she said. "There's a village down the road where we can stay the night. Then it's off to see the mermaids."

❧

Nuala had to drag Eden out of bed the next morning. The child seemed more and more exhausted as time went on, and Nuala wondered if opening and closing the sidhe sapped her strength. Eden had created several over the past couple of days, as Nuala strived to keep herself and the girl away from the others while she gathered information and planned what to do next. Fortunately, Eden's ability made it rather easy to stay one step ahead of the others, who must have noticed her absence by now and put two and two together.

Nuala and Eden headed back up the same dusty road they had walked the night before, but then veered off onto a small track that looked as though it had been made by animals, not people. The track led through a sparse and rocky field, dotted with the occasional scraggly bush. At last, they came to an outcropping of rock. In front of them stretched the ocean as far as the eye could see, still black and ominous in the early morning light. "Stay away from the edge," she warned Eden.

Nuala peered down. About fifty yards directly below them, a rocky beach ran along the coastline for a couple hundred yards before meeting the vertical sides of the cliff. A woman dressed in a sheer white gown walked along the beach. She was pacing back and forth, from one end of the beach to the other, moaning such a mournful tone that Nuala felt the hair on her arms rise. On a small island of rock several yards from shore was a battered old hut, big enough for two men, at most, to move around in. Nuala had heard the stories. Long ago, an aging fisherman had struck up a friendship with one of the Merrow, and this hut is where they would meet and get drunk together. There were no such friendships now, not since the Merrow queen had been betrayed by a human lover. Now the Merrow hid themselves from humans, all past affections forgotten.

Nuala swore as she saw Eden leaning over the cliff's edge to get a better look. She yanked her back by her belt. "Are you stupid?" she said. "Are you trying to get yourself killed?"

Eden looked at Nuala in surprise, her face crumpling.

"Oh, don't start crying," Nuala snapped. "I just don't want you to get hurt."

"Is that the mermaid?" Eden sniffed. "Where's her tail?"

"How the hell am I supposed to know?" Nuala said with a scowl. "I suppose we'll have to go down and find out. And Eden, whatever I say to Deardra, just go along with it, okay? We need her to help us so you can get to your father, but I might need to make some things up. So it's best you don't say anything. Got it?"

Eden nodded, and Nuala hoped the kid would keep her mouth shut. She was nervous about meeting Deardra. The Merrows' minds were not susceptible to Danann abilities such as hers, and there was bad blood between the races. Nuala knew she would have to resort to old-fashioned diplomacy, something that had never been her forte.

"I don't want to go down there!" wailed Eden.

"Don't worry. Brighid said there's a rope here somewhere that should carry us down." Nuala groped around until her eyes fell on a single golden thread that seemed to grow out of the rock. She grabbed it and spoke the words Brighid had taught her.

"I mean no harm to the sea, or to those who dwell therein. I seek only to find, and not to take. If my words prove false, may I be buried forthwith beneath the waves, never to taste the air again."

When she finished speaking, the rope grew thicker and sturdier in her hands. She told Eden to climb onto her back and wrap her hands around her neck. Clinging to the rope, she backed up and took a tentative step off the edge of the cliff, looking for a foothold. Eden screamed as all of a sudden they started dropping. But it was a controlled drop, and Nuala realized there was no need to climb down. The golden rope was dangling them out away from the rocks and gently lowering them to the beach below. When their feet touched the rocks, the rope receded to the top of the cliff. Nuala set Eden on the ground and turned to find the white woman standing only a foot away. Eden stared at her, eyes and mouth wide open. The woman's gown was made out of sheer white fabric that clung to her wasted body as if she had just emerged from the ocean. Her skin was even paler than the dress, and tinged slightly with green. Her eyes were bloodshot, so much so that the whites were almost completely red, and her hair was the color of the deep purple sky Nuala and Eden had reclined beneath the previous night. It fell in a series of tangles and knots down the length of her back.

Nuala was unsure of the proper protocol, so she simply asked, "Deardra, Queen of the Merrow?"

The woman looked at them both. Then she spoke in a rasping voice that grated against Nuala's nerves like a steel block being dragged across a cement floor. "It has been many years since the Tuatha Dé Danann have deigned to visit these shores."

"Yes, it has been," Nuala said uncertainly. "I bring greetings from my people. I am Fionnghuala. This child is Eden. As you know, many of our people have been exiled from our home, and we seek a way to return. This child has the ability to take us there, but first she must see where we are going. Therefore, I have come to you on behalf of my people to request that you show this child the painting of Tír na nÓg that was given to you by our Elder, Brighid. We do not wish to take it, only to look at it. You will have our gratitude."

"The gratitude of the Tuatha Dé Danann is worth as much to me as their excrement," rasped the woman. Nuala struggled to keep her expression passive, while inside she seethed at the insult.

"There is, however, something I desire that has much more value to me than your gratitude," Deardra continued.

"And what is that?"

"The closed-mindedness of your race has probably not prevented you from noticing that I stand here on this shore instead of in my rightful place in the waters."

Nuala pursed her lips together, and Deardra continued. "I am not too proud to admit that I was a fool," she said. "You are no doubt aware that I once took a human as my lover, and have paid dearly for it." The look on Deardra's face was murderous. "This man stole from me the cohuleen druith, and without it I cannot enter the water. Return it to me, and I will do as you ask."

"I share your distaste for humans," Nuala said. "I am sorry that you were so betrayed, but not surprised. Tell me where I can find this man, and I will see to it that he pays for his betrayal."

"There is a village two leagues to the northeast, called Doonacuirp. He'll be an old man by now, and I would slit his throat myself if I could leave this cursed shore."

"Why can't you leave?" It was Eden who spoke, and Nuala hissed at her to be silent. Deardra squatted to face the girl, who stepped closer to Nuala.

Deardra reached out a long green nail and lifted a lock of Eden's brown hair, then let it fall. "Because, little one, if I leave these shores for any reason the Merrow will choose a new queen, and then I will be at her mercy. And Deardra is at no one's mercy."

She stood up and came so close that Nuala could see the hundreds of red veins crisscrossing the queen's eyes. "So it seems we can make some use of each other. His name is Seamus Kilpatrick. Bring me back the cohuleen druith stained with his blood, and I will show you your homeland." Then she turned and, wringing her hands and moaning, walked away toward the other end of the rocky shore.

Nuala was strong, stronger than any human, but even she was growing weary of carrying a fifty-pound child as she trudged for miles through the Irish countryside. Perhaps it was the incessant whining that was taxing her strength, not the weight.

"Are we there yet?" Eden grumbled for the umpteenth time.

"I thought I told you to shut up," Nuala said. The cheerful, pacifying facade she had tried to maintain over the past couple of days had completely unraveled. "Do you want me to make you walk?"

"No," Eden muttered against her back. Nuala wished she could just dump the child somewhere while she dealt with Deardra's ex-lover, but Eden had started complaining about how long this was taking, and asking about her father, and crying for her mother. Nuala didn't want to let her out of her sight in case she found a door somewhere and decided it was time to go home.

At last, they arrived at Doonacuirp. Eden slid down off Nuala's back. "I'm hungry," she whined.

"We'll get food later," Nuala said. "First we have to find this cohuleen druith."

"What is it?" Eden asked.

"Didn't your useless mother teach you anything?" Nuala said. When Eden's bottom lip started to poke out, she quickly added, "If I tell you, will you stop whining?"

Eden nodded, and Nuala rolled her eyes and said, "Yeah, right. I suppose you would call it a hat of sorts."

"Is that why her hair is so messy? Because she lost her hat?"

"No, I don't think so," Nuala replied tersely. "It's important to them. It's a part of their bodies, like wings are for birds. Taking away a Merrow's cohuleen druith removes her tail and leaves her stranded on dry ground. I can't believe Deardra was stupid enough to get so close to a human that he could take it from her."

"Why'd he take it?" Eden asked.

"I don't know and I don't care," Nuala said. "Stop asking questions."

She picked up the pace, dragging Eden behind her. She was confident the task wouldn't take long. There was nothing stopping her from bewitching the whole village if she had to. They walked along the main road until they came to a small general store. Nuala pushed the door open, and the young man at the counter looked up. His jaw was slack as he stared openly at her. *Pathetic,* she thought.

"Tell me where I can find Seamus Kilpatrick," she said, not wasting time on pleasantries.

The young man's eyes glazed over and he said, "Old Stumpy? You'll be finding him down at the pub, I reckon, havin' his lunch. Eats there every day, so he does."

"Where's the pub?" Nuala asked.

"Just down the road," the man said, pointing.

She spun on her heel and left the store, dragging Eden by the hand. "Can we get some lunch too?" Eden asked. "I'm starving!"

"I said, later!" Nuala hissed. She saw the sign for the Slug and Lettuce up ahead. She could hear Eden sniffling as she trailed along behind her, but ignored it.

They stepped through the door and into a crowded room. More than one set of eyes lingered on them as Nuala led Eden toward the bar through a maze of tables and stools. Great barrels of ale and other brews sat behind the bar, and a large orange cat rubbed itself against Eden's legs. Eden bent to pet it while Nuala ordered the barman to point out Old Stumpy.

"Aye, he's just in the corner there, the gent with the hat and cane," the barman said, his head tilting in the general direction but his eyes not leaving Nuala. "What's a young filly like you doin' looking for a weathered ol' chap like him, eh? Come pull up a stool and I'll pour you a drink on the house."

Nuala ignored him and headed in the direction he had indicated. Eden, looking mournfully back at the cat, trailed in her wake. They stopped at a table in the corner, where two old men sat together over bacon sandwiches and pints of beer. A cane leaned against one of the wooden chairs. Nuala looked at the man in the chair.

"Seamus Kilpatrick?" she asked. The man looked up at her and started, then recovered himself sufficiently to tip his hat to her.

"The very same," he said in a soft, kind voice. Nuala leaned down and put her lips next to his ear as his companion gaped openly at both of them.

"If you want to live, you will take me to the cohuleen druith that once adorned the head of the Queen of the Merrow," she whispered. It was an unsophisticated threat, she knew, but she didn't have time to search his heart for his deepest, most hidden desires. Everyone wanted to live.

"Aye, aye, all right," the old man said, slowly rising to his feet and grabbing his cane. Without saying good-bye to his companion, he shuffled through the pub and out onto the street, Nuala and Eden trailing behind him. They walked through the main part of town and up a dusty side road until they came to a small house with peeling green paint and empty window boxes. "This way, this way," he said, as he opened the door and went inside. Nuala's nose wrinkled and Eden sneezed when they stepped inside the house. The acrid smell of pipe tobacco hung thick in the air.

"Where is it?" Nuala asked, impatient.

"'Tis in the safe," he said. He went to the corner of his bedroom and pulled a torn and dirty afghan off a small safe that sat on the floor. Nuala watched as he spun the dial back and forth until it clicked. He reached inside and pulled out a simple wooden box. With effort, he stood up again, holding the box.

"Show it to me," Nuala said. Eden sat on the floor and watched.

The old man lifted the cover off the box. He put his hand in, and when he pulled it out, it looked as if it were covered in red paint. So fine was the fabric of the cohuleen druith that it clung to his flesh like a second skin. Nuala could see the knots and veins in his hand through the deep red sheen.

She reached out and swept the fabric off his hand like a cobweb. He watched, wordlessly, as she took the box from him and let the cohuleen druith fall back into it. "Deardra sends her regards," she murmured.

Then the old man spoke, and although he had given her the cohuleen druith without resistance, his eyes were sharp and canny. "I'll be givin' you this because I value my life, and I see that yer a woman to be reckoned with. But you should know what kind of a creature you'll be givin' it to. I was enchanted by her, to be sure, and I'll take the blame for gettin' to know her as I did. I had a wife, and three fine children, and when I wouldn't go to live with her under the waves, leavin' my children to starve, she killed them all. And so I did go with her then, lest she kill my brother and his children too. I became her lover, and when my chance came, I stole what's in that box yer holdin' as payment for my wife and children's lives. I thought maybe she would die from the lack of it, but since she sent you, I can see I was mistaken, and more's the pity. And though you may spare the life of an old man, I can be certain she will not."

Nuala glanced down at Eden, who had curled up into a ball on the floor and was staring blankly at the wall, not listening anymore. Nuala prodded her with her foot.

"Eden. Go outside."

Eden looked up at her, but didn't move.

"I said, go outside. Wait for me there."

Nuala bent down and hauled Eden to her feet. She opened the door to the small house, being careful not to let Eden touch it, and then deposited her on the front walkway where she could see her out of the corner of her eye. Eden didn't seem inclined to escape, or even move. She just sat back down on the dirt path and resumed staring at nothing. Nuala frowned and resolved to get some food into the girl as soon as this was over.

She slid the box into her bag and turned back to the man, moving out of Eden's line of sight. "Humans and greater beings such as the Merrow are not meant to be together," she said, looking at him impassively, "as you have no doubt learned. The result is always the same." With one smooth movement, she drew a small silver knife from under her jacket and swept it across the old man's neck. As he crumpled to the floor, she quickly retrieved the cohuleen druith and held it to the gash. She was amazed at the amount of blood the weightless material was able to absorb. When she had soaked up enough, she put the cloth back into the box and the box into her bag.

"Let's go," she said to Eden as she stepped out of the house and closed the door behind her. Normally, she would have disposed of the body more thoroughly, but the sooner they got back to Deardra, the sooner she would no longer have to worry about covering her tracks from humans ever again.

❦

The sun was once again beginning its descent into the ocean when they returned to the shoreline and the moaning, pacing queen. Nuala had risked a stop at the general store on their way out of town to buy some food for Eden, who had devoured two apples, half a box of crackers, a hunk of cheese, and a bottle of milk. Not relishing the thought of carrying the lethargic child the six miles back to Deardra, Nuala had simply flagged down a passing car and told its owner to give it to them. After crawling into the backseat, Eden had promptly fallen asleep. Nuala glanced at her in the rearview mirror. The girl's long eyelashes rested on her cheeks, and her mouth hung slightly open. Her dark hair was tangled and matted and her face was smudged with dirt where she had tried to push her hair out of her eyes. Her pants, which had once been pink, were now a mottled gray.

I have stolen a child, Nuala thought to herself.

You are taking her home, answered a stronger voice inside her. *She will not be harmed; Lorcan needs to keep her alive if he wants to use her gift. She'll be treated well. She doesn't belong here, not in this world, with that human woman and a father who has become too much like the humans he so loves. Someday she will thank me…and in the meantime, we will both be where we belong.*

Her thoughts turned to Tír na nÓg and she drove faster, jostling Eden in the backseat as the car bumped along the dusty road. Soon she recognized the trail that led to Deardra's shore and pulled the car over. She half considered letting the child stay asleep but quickly rejected the idea. The young sidh-maker could disappear from her grasp with no more effort than it took to open the car door. She lifted Eden into her arms. The child snorted softly and squirmed but stayed asleep as Nuala maneuvered them through the path to the cliff's edge. She found the golden thread again and muttered the words of peace. Then she wrapped it around one hand, and held Eden closely to her with the other. The thread had lowered them about halfway down the cliff when without warning Eden let out a bloodcurdling scream and started to flail her arms and legs. Nuala almost lost her grip on the girl and on the golden rope as Eden thrashed and convulsed, her legs kicking at Nuala repeatedly.

"Eden, stop!" Nuala shouted. Eden kept on flailing, and Nuala had to tighten her grip so hard she was sure she would break the girl's ribs. When her feet touched ground, she let go of the rope and released her hold on Eden, who fell onto the rocks and looked up at Nuala in wide-eyed horror. Then she scrambled to her feet and ran toward the ocean's edge, screaming.

"Eden!" Nuala called after her. What had gotten into the child? "Eden!"

Suddenly Deardra was beside Eden and had knelt down in front of her. "Hush, child," she said as she held out a large fan-shaped shell. "It is not as it seems. You are safe here on my shores." Eden's eyes were still wide and her breathing heavy, but she had stopped running. Nuala walked slowly toward them, trying to stay out of Eden's line of sight lest she start screaming again.

Eden took the shell and turned it over. "What is it really?" she asked.

Deardra smiled. "Very good, child. It, too, is not as it seems." She touched the shell, which filled with a clear pink liquid that smelled like strawberries. "Drink," Deardra said. "It will calm you, and clear your mind."

Nuala watched as Eden tipped up the shell and drank, licking her lips. When she looked back up at Deardra, her eyes were sparkling and her cheeks flushed. "Can I have some more?" she asked with a shy smile.

Deardra laughed. It sounded like a poorly tuned violin, and Nuala winced. "Perhaps later, child. Right now your friend and I have business to attend to."

Nuala pulled the box out of her bag but did not hand it over. "I have done what I promised to do. Will you show the child Brighid's painting?" she asked.

Deardra looked at the box hungrily. "For sixty years I have paced this shore," she rasped. "Now I will rule the sea again. Yes. I will show this child the painting, but not tonight. The painting is in my home under the waters, and I must go and reclaim my throne before I can safely escort you there."

Nuala felt the blood rise to her face, and she struggled not to lash out at the woman in front of her. "And when," she asked through gritted teeth, "will this be? We do not have the luxury of time, I'm afraid."

Deardra looked indifferent. "You have been exiled for many years now. One more night should make no difference. Come back at first light and you shall have what you desire. And now, give me the cohuleen druith."

Nuala could see that she didn't have a choice, although she knew there was a very good chance the other Tuatha Dé Danann would give in and ask Brighid for help if their other sources turned up nothing. She had tried to convince Brighid to forget about the painting's existence, but Brighid was one of the Elders, who had come from the Four Cities. She was not easily bewitched, and Nuala had needed to satisfy herself with convincing Brighid to forget their conversation.

"Where can we spend the night?" she asked Deardra, who was waiting for an answer. "I do not wish to take the child back to the human village." Eden, energized by the shell drink, was jumping from rock to rock a little way down the shore.

"You may stay in the hut," Deardra answered. "You will find it most comfortable."

Nuala looked at the hut surrounded by the icy Atlantic waters. It looked far from comfortable, and it seemed like a better idea to climb back up the cliff to sleep in the car.

"All is not as it seems," Deardra reminded her, and Nuala nodded, not wanting to offend the Merrow by refusing her hospitality. Then Deardra held out her hand for the box, and Nuala gave it to her.

The queen's eyes glittered as she lifted the blood-soaked cloth from its wooden nest. At her touch, the cohuleen druith rose into the air and settled over her matted purple hair, weaving together with the strands until her hair fell smooth and silky down her back, neither purple nor red, but the ever-changing colors of sunset. Her skin lost its green tinge and became as pure as the whitest sand on a Caribbean shore. The red veins in her eyes drew back, unveiling bright turquoise irises flecked with gold. Under the sheer white gown her body plumped, her wasted breasts filling and rising and her hips forming lush hills and valleys where there was once only brittle bone and taut skin. She let out a peal of laughter that no longer grated on Nuala's nerves, but instead made her feel refreshed, as if she had just had a cool drink of water. Even Eden had stopped her makeshift game of hopscotch to stare at the transformation of the Merrow queen.

Without a word to either of them, Deardra turned and sprinted for the shore, peeling off the white gown and throwing it into the air. When she reached the water's edge, she leapt into the air, twisted, and disappeared without a splash or a ripple into the water. The last thing Nuala saw was the flick of a golden tail.

"That was so cool!" Eden squealed as she ran over to where Nuala stood watching the waves. "Wasn't that cool, Auntie Nuala?" Nuala looked at her sharply. She hadn't told Eden to call her that, and it made her uneasy. Maybe it was just the effect of whatever it was Deardra had given the child, who was still bouncing up and down on the balls of her feet.

"What are we doing now?" Eden asked as she bounced.

"We spend the night in that," Nuala said, nodding toward the decrepit hut that looked far from hospitable.

Eden stopped bouncing and wrinkled her nose. "How do we get there? I'm not a very good swimmer."

"I don't think we'll have to swim," Nuala said, walking down the shoreline. "The Merrow were once renowned for their hospitality, if you could find them." She took off her shoes and tentatively placed a foot in the water, bracing herself for the sharp pain of bitter cold. Instead, she found the water quite warm. When she pulled her foot out again, it was dry.

"Let's try walking there," Nuala said, holding out her hand to Eden, who was giving her an uncertain look. "Come on, it'll be fine," she said. "I won't let you drown." Eden was not visibly cheered by this, but took Nuala's hand all the same and stepped into the water. Nuala kept expecting the water to get deeper, but it stayed at Eden's waist level even though they couldn't see the bottom. It felt comfortable, like wading through a warm bath. Reaching the rocks where the hut was perched, Nuala helped Eden climb up before pulling herself up behind her. Eden started to open the door to the hut, and Nuala roared, "Don't touch it!" Eden froze and looked back at her in bewilderment.

"I just meant that you should save your strength. The place where we're going, where your father is, it's quite far away, and it might take a lot of energy to open the door between here and there. So I don't think you should even touch any doors until then, just in case it uses up more of your strength."

Eden pouted, but she stood back from the door. Nuala opened it. Inside, the hut looked just as it did from the outside: wooden, bare, decrepit. Suddenly, Eden reached down and pulled on a handle that was sticking up out of the floor.

"No!" Nuala screamed, flinging out her arm to grab the girl.

"Ow! You're hurting me!" Eden cried in pain as she dropped the handle.

Nuala kept hold of Eden's arm. "I told you not to touch any doors."

"I just wanted to know where it went!" Eden yelled back at her.

Nuala bent down and lifted up the handle, opening the trap door just big enough for one person to squeeze through. Getting on her hands and knees, she peered down.

CHAPTER 11

A delicate ladder led down to what looked like a large glass room, where there should have been only rocks. Nuala told Eden to climb down first, and then she followed her, closing the trap door above them. As soon as Eden's feet touched the floor, the glass room filled with an eerie, rippling light, like the color of sunlight reflecting on the sand beneath calm, shallow waters. Large, plush cushions lay clustered around the floor in deep shades of purple, blue, and green. Bowls of fresh fruit and large shells filled with clear, fragrant water stood on a pedestal in the center of the room. The glass bubble was surrounded on all sides by water, and even the ladder seemed to rise up into the waves. It was like being inside the world's lushest, most exotic aquarium, instead of under a pile of rocks in the North Atlantic. Outside the glass walls, brightly colored parrotfish swam past, darting between the waving strands of sea grass and towers of coral. Eden pressed her face against the curved glass, oohing and ahhing over the schools of tiny damsel-fish, squealing in delight as a giant sea turtle swam by, and star-ing in wonder at the curling arms of an octopus tucked in a coral cave. The room was warm, and light shone through the waves, casting moving designs on the floor, even though Nuala knew it was now dark outside. She admired the magic of the Merrow, who had created such a beautiful place, and closed her eyes to take in the soothing sounds of rolling waves and rustling sea grasses. After a moment, Nuala walked up behind Eden and gently laid her hand on the girl's shoulder.

"See, my dear?" she said softly. "When you listen to Auntie Nuala, everything turns out just right."

Eden sighed with pleasure, and then sank down onto a cushion to stare at the spectacle around them. Nuala placed a bowl of fruit and a goblet of water next to her, and then retreated across the room to watch the girl.

Auntie Nuala, she thought, snorting slightly. This girl was her ticket out of this mundane hellhole. Rewards, a royal pardon, they would all be hers for delivering the child. But there was no reason why she should stop there.

∽

Nuala awoke at first light. She had slept at the bottom of the ladder as a precaution, but Eden had not attempted to escape. She was still asleep, slumped over on the same pile of cushions she had been sitting on the night before.

Nuala gently prodded the girl awake. "It's time, Eden. It's time to go see your father." Eden blinked at her and stretched, then sat up.

"Now?" she said with a growing smile.

Nuala nodded. "First, we'll visit the mermaids, and they'll show us a really lifelike picture of where your father is. Then you'll be able to take us there. I bet he's so excited to meet you."

Eden's smile faltered, and she looked at her fingers.

"What's wrong?" Nuala asked. "Aren't you excited too?"

"What's my father like?" Eden asked.

Nuala paused before answering. The child couldn't possibly be getting cold feet at this point. "I've known him since he was born," she said. "He's very handsome and strong. He loves music. He can play any instrument ever created, and he makes songs so beautiful you want to listen to them forever. He's strong-willed, some would call him stubborn, and sometimes reckless. He asks a lot of questions, just like you. And he loves you very much."

"My mum said he didn't even know I was born," Eden said, not looking up.

"I told you before, that's because she didn't tell him," Nuala said. "She wanted to keep you away from him. But he knows now; as soon as I found out about you, I told him. I'm trying to bring the two of you together. He's so sorry he hasn't had a chance to get to know you. He wants to make up for all that lost time."

"How do you know him?" Eden asked.

Because I was supposed to marry him, Nuala thought, trying to keep the bitterness from showing on her face. When the small group of survivors had escaped to Ériu, one of their priorities had been to rebuild their numbers, and that meant procreation. Nuala had had several lovers in Tír na nÓg. The relationships had never lasted, however, because the men grew suspicious of her power and began to question whether they loved her of their own free will, or if she had enchanted them. Nuala, in turn, could never know for certain if their affections were real or a result of the charm she unconsciously exuded. In Tír na nÓg, Nuala had tried to suppress her ability, and had never used it to gain power for herself. She'd had plenty of friends and a good reputation among the Tuatha Dé Danann. But intimate relationships had been more difficult. When Finn was born, they had all waited and watched to see if he would, as expected, inherit his father's immunity to Nuala's power. It would be the perfect match—both of them would be able to rest in the knowledge that their affection for each other was real and uncoerced.

Except Finn did not love her, despite being the only person in both worlds who could do so freely. Nuala's insides burned at the thought. Instead, he had paid her the ultimate insult by choosing to be with a human, a fact he had managed to conceal from the rest of the Tuatha Dé Danann for over two years.

Well, look where that's gotten you now, she thought bitterly. *Your human pet can't stand you, and your daughter is about to be far beyond your reach. Oh, I'm sure you'll see her again—standing beside Lorcan as he slowly guts you just to listen to you scream.* Her face tightened in determination. She wasn't going to return to her old, passive self, trying to hide her ability to win trust and acceptance from others. Lorcan was no sidh-closer; he would be as susceptible to her ability as any other person. If she played her cards right, there would be no limit to her power.

"Nuala?" Eden asked, and Nuala focused her eyes back on the girl and forced herself to smile.

"Our families have been friends for a long time. C'mon, let's go," she said, starting to climb the ladder.

After walking back through the impossibly warm, dry water, they climbed gingerly over rocks slippery with dew and mist. The morning was cold, and the sky was obscured by a thin layer of clouds diffusing the sun's early rays. They reached the spot along the shore where Deardra had left them the day before. Nuala realized she had no idea how to contact Deardra or let her know they had arrived. She wondered if they should have waited in the hut. Eden was starting to shiver, and Nuala hated standing here so exposed. She knew it was only a matter of time before some of the other Tuatha Dé Danann went to see Brighid. Then they would descend on these shores where they had once ruled, but hopefully they would be too late.

Brighid had said this painting was as accurate a depiction of Tír na nÓg as her own memories, which were flawless. Once Eden set eyes on it, they would be gone, leaving the others behind with the humans they so desperately wanted to protect. *Let them stay,* she thought. *They've chosen their side, and I have chosen mine too.* Still, she looked up at the cliff top behind them with unease. She reached down and put a hand into the water. "Deardra?" she called. Nothing.

"Can we go back to the glass room now? I'm freezing," Eden said through chattering teeth.

Nuala got down on her knees and pulled her hair back into one hand. Crouching as low as she could, she touched her lips to the water, wincing as she tasted the salt. "Deardra?" she said again.

She stood up and wiped her mouth. For a moment she wondered if she would need to involve Anya, who, with her ability to control the ocean, would be able to push back the water and expose the Merrow kingdom in an instant. Anya regarded the Merrow with suspicion, as did most of the Danann. It would be easy enough to convince her to fight against them—after all, Nuala possessed the ability to convince almost anyone of almost anything—but getting her involved would complicate things, and Nuala had encountered enough complications on this quest.

Just as she was starting to strategize on how she could separate Anya from the others and bring her here, there was a disturbance over the water. A small whirlpool formed about ten feet offshore. It spun and twisted, and then out of it rose Deardra—not the haggard, spurned woman who had roamed the shore for sixty years, but a queen of the Merrow in all her beauty and majesty. As the whirling water carried her to shore, her golden tail separated into two smooth, pearl-white legs, and she stepped out of the water to greet them.

"What happened to your tail?" Eden asked before Nuala had formed some proper words of greeting.

Deardra smiled and bent to pat Eden on the head. "Sometimes I wish we kept our young," she said. "Your curiosity is refreshing, little one."

"What do you do with them?" Eden asked, but Nuala interrupted her.

"Greetings, Queen. We give you our thanks for your excellent hospitality. You were, of course, quite right. The hut is certainly not what it first seemed."

Deardra nodded graciously. "And I, too, am grateful for the service you have given me, and will reward you as you have requested. There are many rooms in my palace below the waves, and adorning one of them is this painting you wish to see. I cannot bring it above the waves, for the touch of air would ruin it. But I can take you to it, and you may consider yourselves fortunate. Not since the Son of Lir have we welcomed one of your race into our home."

"You are very gracious," Nuala answered, "but Manannan mac Lir possessed a certain affinity for the water which we do not. We cannot breathe without air."

"I shall remedy that," Deardra said, and without warning she stepped forward and kissed Nuala on the lips. It was a slow, lingering kiss, and Nuala could feel tendrils of heat rising in her body. She opened her mouth to take a breath, and then realized it was not Deardra's mouth on hers that was preventing her from taking in air. She pulled back, eyes wide, and Deardra smiled. "My pleasure," she murmured, and nodded her head toward the water. "You'll find you can breathe quite easily once you're below the surface."

Nuala took a step toward the water, then turned and looked pointedly at Eden. "Yes, yes, she'll be right behind you," Deardra said, bending down to give Eden a quick peck on the lips. "No need to panic," she said to the child as she led her toward the water's edge. "You'll be able to swim in my kingdom as well as you can walk in yours."

Nuala took Eden's other hand, and together the three of them disappeared beneath the waves.

CHAPTER 12

Cedar was fighting to stay awake. More accurately, she was fighting to avoid falling asleep on Finn's shoulder. They were crammed together in the backseat of a rental car, with Rohan and Riona in the front. In the van ahead of them were Anya, Murdoch, and Oscar, as well as Felix and Molly, the others having stayed behind in Halifax. They had flown through the night, arriving in Dublin just as the sun was beginning to rise. Her head kept nodding, but then Eden's face would appear in her mind and a fresh jolt of adrenaline would jerk her upright.

"Cedar, sleep, dear," Riona said. "It's a four-hour drive, and you might as well take advantage of it."

"I slept on the plane," Cedar muttered.

"Not enough," Finn said.

Cedar looked at him in annoyance. "Don't the People of Danu need to sleep?" Finn raised his eyebrows at the title. "I looked you up online," she said in response. "Tuatha Dé Danann means the People of the Goddess Danu."

"Yes, well, don't believe everything you read," he said.

"I haven't read anything about you specifically, though, although I suppose I don't know any of your real names, do I? Except for Fionnbharr," she said, stumbling over the pronunciation.

"Riona *is* my real name," Riona said from the front seat. "And Rohan's isn't too far off. It's Ruadhan. He really has less gray, though," she said with a smile, reaching over to ruffle the hair at the nape of his neck.

"Right, you don't really look this way either," Cedar said.

"I do," Finn said. "One of the perks of actually being young is that it's okay to look that way. But you're right about the rest of them, for the most part." He grinned. "Felix got his old fisherman look off a postcard he saw in a gift store. In reality, he's... well, let's just say I hope you don't ever have the pleasure of seeing him in his true form. He makes the rest of us look like trolls."

"Yes, well, he does have a flair for the dramatic," Riona said. "Most of us just appear to be an older version of ourselves. Felix is the only one to completely reinvent his appearance."

"And what's his real name?" Cedar asked.

"Toirdhealbhach," Finn answered. "It's a bit of a mouthful."

"No kidding," Cedar said. "So, when we find this painting, how are we going to destroy it? Is it just like a normal painting?" Cedar was quite sure that nothing she encountered on this trip was going to be "normal."

"We're not going to destroy it," Rohan said from the front, his first words since they had started driving.

"What are you talking about?" Cedar asked. "We *have* to destroy it before Eden sees it!"

She looked at Finn to back her up. He remained silent.

"What?" she demanded.

"We can't destroy it," he said. "We need it. Right now Eden is our only hope of ever getting back to Tír na nÓg. She's the only one who can create the sidhe, and she'll need to see that painting."

"Are you insane? Eden has been kidnapped by one of *your* people, who's trying to use her to return to some all-powerful psychopathic mass murderer in your world. The painting is the only way she can get there. If we destroy it, Nuala won't be able to use Eden. She'll let her go!"

"We don't know that," Rohan said. "Like you said, for all we know, this is the only route to Tír na nÓg in existence. We cannot risk destroying it—not if we ever want to go back."

"We can make another one! Brighid commissioned that painting; can't you just do the same after we have Eden back?"

"It's Brighid's power that makes the painting so close to reality," Rohan said, his passionless voice contrasting with Cedar's. "We have no guarantee that she would help us create another one."

"You haven't even asked her!" She saw Rohan glance at Finn in the rearview mirror. "What was that, your 'Hey, Finn, keep your dog on a leash' look?" she snarled. "I know there's some sort of bigger battle-of-the-gods thing happening here. I get it. I know you don't care what I think, but I *need* to get my daughter back. I need to keep her safe, and she's not going to be safe with that picture floating around, no matter who has it. I'll destroy it myself if I have to."

None of them answered her, and it felt pointless to continue tirading against the silence. She bunched her jacket up against the window and shoved her face into it, too upset to sleep but too tired to think straight. She closed her eyes and imagined what it would be like to see Eden again, how tightly she would hold her. *I found your father, Eden*, she thought. *But now I can't find you. Must I always be without one of you?*

༄

She awoke to the sound of tense voices. The car was stopped on the side of the road, and Finn and his parents were standing outside, talking with Murdoch and Felix.

"It might just be a local," Riona was saying, "or a traveler who ran out of gas."

"Not bloody likely," Felix growled. "We need to be prepared for the worst."

Cedar got out of the car and walked over to them. "What's going on?" she asked.

Finn answered. "We're here—close to where Deardra lives. But it looks like we're not alone." He nodded his head down the road, where another car sat abandoned.

Cedar was instantly awake, panic coursing through her veins. "Nuala," she said. "She got here first."

"We don't know that for sure," Riona said soothingly. "Why would Nuala need a car if she has Eden with her?"

"Eden wouldn't know how to bring her here, would she?" Murdoch asked. "She'd have to drive at least part of the way."

"I don't know," Cedar said, looking wildly around them. "I've been thinking about it...and, well, you can find a satellite image of almost anywhere on earth online, and photos too. If they have Internet access, they can go anywhere Nuala wants. I think Riona's right. Why would they need to drive?"

"Standing around isn't going to help. Let's go. Everyone on alert," Rohan said.

Cedar continued to survey the area as she followed the others down a narrow path through a field. They had driven from Dublin to the west coast of the island. A long way off, Cedar could see a round tower and some tiny white dots she took to be sheep. Behind them was field after field of grass and stone, not a tree in sight. In front of them were more fields, but she could see the ocean stretched out in the distance.

"Where are we?" she asked Finn, who was walking behind her and bringing up the rear of the group.

He gestured back toward the road. "We're nearest to the village of Staddle, if you can even call it a village. Cluster of houses, really. The closest actual village is Doonacuirp. The people in these parts are few and far between."

Despite the cool breeze, the sun was shining. Cedar lifted her face to it, willing it to warm her and give her strength. Finn touched her arm. "Let's let the others get a little bit ahead," he said, standing still for a moment as the rest of the group moved ahead of them. "I sketched you doing that once, lifting your face to the sun. Do you remember?"

"I remember," she answered, thinking of the tin of memories she had thrown away. She glanced at the retreating back of Felix, who had been walking in front of her.

"Cedar, don't you see that I had good reasons for not telling you the truth about who I am? You wouldn't have believed me," Finn said.

She looked at him incredulously. "Did I really seem that fragile to you? I believe you now, don't I? I've been exposed to impossible things every day for the past week, and I haven't flipped out or run away screaming. I've believed it, because as crazy as it sounds, all of it makes sense." She glared at him. "Is that why you left me like that? Because you thought I wouldn't believe you? You didn't even give me a chance!"

Finn reached out to put his hands on her shoulders, but she twisted away. "I tried to tell you!" he protested. "I told you magic was real. I thought if I could at least convince you of that…but you wouldn't listen. I wanted to tell you everything, and I would have, but like I said, there are rules—"

"Rules?" Cedar said, her voice carrying over the empty landscape. "*That's* your excuse? Since when have you cared about rules?" Her voice thickened and grew quiet, but lost none of its ferocity.

"You *lied* to me, Finn, the whole time we were together. It was nothing but a charade to you—but it was real to me. Now everything has changed, and not just because of Eden and the sidhe. I don't know who you are anymore."

Finn's expression darkened. "You don't know what you're talking about," he said. "You have *no idea* what I have done to protect you, what it has cost me. You've known nothing but peace your entire life. I have been at war since I was two years old." He exhaled loudly in exasperation. "Open your eyes, Cedar! This isn't just about you! It's not even just about Eden! There are millions of lives at stake! So forgive me if I didn't completely turn my back on my own people and let them all be damned."

"If yer done shoutin' at each other, we should be moving along," Felix called from several feet ahead. The others had stopped and were waiting for them, well within hearing range. She hurried to catch up, her face burning, and they walked the rest of the way in silence.

When they stopped again a short time later, they were standing at the edge of a tall cliff overlooking the ocean. Everything about the place seemed profound to Cedar—the silence, the hugeness of the sky, the ocean that divided the world. A dilapidated hut sat perched on a pile of rocks off shore to Cedar's right, the only visible indication that humans had ever set foot in this part of the world. Cedar could see more green fingers of land jutting out into the water around the shoreline, and she felt something very old and deep stirring inside her. This was where gods and giants, warriors and fairies had lived, loved, and fought for millennia. The looks on the others' faces told her they were having similar thoughts. This land had once been theirs. She felt very small, standing among these ancient beings and gazing out at the vastness of the ocean.

"Why Halifax?" she asked Felix, who was standing beside her. "When you escaped from the war, why did you choose Halifax?"

"It's where the sidh took us," he answered, still staring out across the water. "And so we stayed." His voice was somber, and had lost the folksy accent he affected as part of his old man persona. "There are other reasons, of course. It's complicated. But one of them is because Ireland would be the first place Lorcan would look for us if he found a way to open another sidh. It was best to stay hidden, somewhere he wouldn't think to look for us."

Cedar saw Oscar waving at her, and she waved back. Felix went over to speak with Riona, and Oscar came over to stand next to her. "Hey," he said. "Ready to meet the Merrow?"

Cedar shrugged, trying to act more casual than she felt. "Oh, you know, I meet magical creatures every day. Mermaids are no big deal."

"Ha!" Oscar laughed. "I've never met them either. Mother has a few choice names for them, none of which are fit to be said in the presence of a lady," he said with a mock bow.

Cedar raised her eyebrows. "All that matters is that they can help us," she said. "How do we find them?"

"You'll be doin' no such thing, I'm afraid." Felix had rejoined them, Riona by his side.

"The Merrow are on even worse terms with humans than they are with us," Riona clarified. "They won't talk to us if you're with us. I'm afraid you'll have to stay up here while the others go down and talk to Deardra. It will take some careful diplomacy to convince her to give us the picture. Having a human among us won't do us any favors."

Cedar's stomach twisted painfully. "No way. What if that car really does belong to Nuala? What if Eden is down there? I *have* to go," she protested.

"We can handle it, Miss Cedar," Felix said, his voice gruff and accented once more. "If your wee one is there, we'll bring her back, but you'll be best helpin' us by stayin' out of the way, if you don't mind me sayin' so."

"But Eden won't even know who you are!" she said. "If there's any chance of her being down there, I need to be there too."

"Cedar, listen to me," Riona said. "I hate to put it so bluntly, but if Eden has been here, she's probably already seen the painting, and they'll be gone. There's nothing you can do. And if she hasn't been here yet, we need to get that painting before she sees it. The Merrow won't even show themselves if they sense a human's presence. If you want to help Eden, you have to keep out of sight."

Cedar closed her mouth tightly and stared out over the ocean. Riona placed a gentle hand on her shoulder. "We might not be too late," she said. "I'll stay up here with you. Let's just wait and see what happens."

Finn came over and kissed his mother on the cheek. He gave Cedar a long look and then joined the others, who were already climbing down a golden rope that led over the edge of the cliff.

The vegetation was sparse and there was no place to hide, so Cedar settled down on her stomach and peered over the edge, her heart racing. She watched as the others descended one by one and gathered in a small knot at the base of the cliff. Riona lay beside her. Together, they looked on in silence.

The Tuatha Dé Danann approached the water slowly and stopped at its edge. Anya and Rohan stood side by side in front. Behind Anya stood Murdoch and Oscar, and behind Rohan were Felix, Finn, and Molly. Cedar glanced over at Riona and saw that her eyes were trained on her daughter.

"Why are Oscar and Molly here?" she whispered. "Aren't they a bit young?"

Riona's forehead creased, but she didn't take her eyes off the group below. "When you live forever, or for centuries, at any rate, 'young' doesn't mean quite the same thing. Once you pass thirteen of your years in our world, you are expected to shoulder the responsibilities of an adult, but you may also partake in the pleasures. Besides, if there is to be another war, they will need to know how to gain allies. Now watch," she whispered.

Cedar looked back down at the shore. Anya knelt and placed her hand in the water, and then stepped back and stood beside Rohan. For a moment, it seemed like nothing was happening. Then there was a disturbance beneath the waves and a large bubble floated out of the water and hung in the air before them. The bubble appeared to be empty, but a voice came from it, clear enough for Cedar and Riona to hear it. The voice said, "Who calls on our queen?"

Anya stood perfectly still as she answered, "I am Aine, water warden of the Tuatha Dé Danann. With me are Ruadhan, Fionnbharr, Mallaidh, Muireadhach, Osgar, and Toirdhealbhach. We wish to speak with Queen Deardra concerning a matter of some urgency."

The bubble hovered for a moment longer, then disappeared once more beneath the waves. At once, a dozen Merrow rose to the surface. They were beautiful, with skin as white as pearls and long, flowing hair that spread out in the water around them. Though the color of their hair varied widely, they all had strands of red woven throughout their tresses. The Merrow in the center swam forward and walked onto the shore, her tail separating into two long legs. She stood before the Tuatha Dé Danann, clothed in nothing but her long hair and a delicate circle of pearls and gold that rested on her head. She addressed Anya formally.

"Well met, Aine, water warden," she said, "and your companions also. It is not often that I am inundated with so many visitors from the Tuatha Dé Danann."

Cedar held her breath, straining to hear the Merrow's words.

"Others have come before us?" Anya asked.

Deardra tilted her head in what may have been a nod. "Are the Tuatha Dé Danann so disorganized? A small party arrived yesterday on your behalf. I have already given them what you seek."

Rohan stepped forward and addressed Deardra. "Did this party consist of a woman and a child?"

"Of course. And a delightful thing the young one is," Deardra answered with a small smile. "They are still here now, if you wish them to join your group for your journey home."

When Cedar heard this, a cry escaped her lips and she started to scramble to her feet. Riona yanked her back down fiercely and hissed at her to wait.

On the beach, Anya's voice shook as she spoke. "I am afraid you have been deceived, Queen Deardra. They are not a part of our group, nor are they ambassadors or messengers from the Tuatha Dé Danann. The woman is a traitor, and she has stolen that child. The child's father is here." She waved a hand, and Finn stepped forward. "We have been searching for them. The woman, Fionnghuala, wishes to use the child to reignite the war in our world, and to bring it to these shores."

Deardra looked at Anya carefully. Cedar wished she could see the expression on her face more clearly.

At last, the queen spoke, and there was an icy edge to her voice. "This is why I choose not to involve myself and my people in the affairs of the Tuatha Dé Danann," she said. "You are like beasts or humans, always fighting among yourselves, never speaking with the same voice. I do not even know who among you is your leader. Is it you?" she spat at Anya. "Or is it the child?"

She smiled as the others exchanged glances. "Just because I don't *care* about your affairs doesn't mean I don't *know* about your affairs. I should think you would want the girl to return to your world, given the prophecy you all cling to so desperately."

"And what do you know of our prophecies?" Rohan asked, taking a step forward and lowering his voice.

"I know the words the poet Cairpre mac Edaine spoke as he abandoned your land with the rest of your Elders," said Deardra. "'The dyad that should not be will rise from the ashes and purge the land of the coming poison,' blah, blah, blah. You certainly *are* the ashes, I'll give him that. And I *did* hear you'd managed a human-Danann hybrid. I'm assuming that is the child whom my maids are entertaining. I should have known. She doesn't come across as one of the Tuatha Dé Danann. As I said, I found her quite charming. Perhaps it is an improvement on your race to breed with humans."

From her view above, Cedar could see Finn shifting his weight from side to side, and his hands twitching. "What prophecy?" she whispered to Riona. "What are they talking about?" Riona merely put a finger to her lips and continued looking intently below.

Suddenly, Finn moved so that he was directly in front of the Merrow queen. "My daughter is being held captive against her will and mine, and she is in your domain. Give her up at once, or you will be an accomplice to this act of villainy."

"I do not take sides in your war, Danann," Deardra said, her lips curled back over her pearly teeth. "I will do as I please in my own domain and with those who have entered it."

"She is just a child!" Finn said, the muscles in his face straining and constricting his voice. "She was taken by someone who would use her to see this whole world destroyed!" He was trembling from head to foot. "You said you were fond of her. Will you do nothing to help her?"

Deardra stared at him through narrowed eyes. Then she opened her mouth slightly and slowly exhaled.

"There," she said, waving her hand toward the water behind her. "I will leave her for you to fight over. We are not of this world, nor are we of yours, and your troubles do not concern us." She turned and looked out over the water, and the others followed her gaze.

Cedar cried out as she saw Nuala's and Eden's heads break the surface of the water outside the ring of Merrow, close to a small rocky island that held a ramshackle hut. Their hands were flailing in the water, and they both coughed and spewed seawater back into the ocean.

"Eden!" she cried, starting to scramble to her feet again. Riona yanked her down, and Cedar's knee connected painfully with the rocks underneath her. She struggled to stand up again, but Riona's grasp was unmovable. "Let go! She can't swim!" Cedar pleaded.

"You cannot be seen!" Riona hissed back. "Anya will help her. You *must* stay hidden."

But it was Nuala who held Eden afloat as they both gasped for air. Nuala's eyes fell upon the shore, and then several things happened at once. Rohan and Finn started to run along the shoreline toward Nuala and Eden, moving so quickly Cedar could barely follow them with her eyes. Murdoch pulled a handful of small silver daggers out from the inside of his jacket and followed on their heels. Oscar stood transfixed for but a moment, and then pulled out his own long dagger and took off after his father. Felix and Molly followed close behind. Anya held out her arms toward the ocean and started chanting in a loud voice words Cedar did not understand. Deardra stepped in front of her. "These are *my* waters!" she said.

Then Nuala, still holding Eden afloat in front of her, took a deep breath and shouted, "Tuatha Dé Danann! The Merrow are your enemy! Attack them!"

Rohan and Finn spun around to face the others. "No!" Rohan roared. "She lies! Close your minds to her! *Nuala* is the enemy!"

Everyone on the beach stopped as if momentarily stunned. Each face was creased in concentration. Cedar held her breath and looked over at Riona, who had the same look of paralyzed torment on her face as the others. Below, Oscar whirled about and flung his dagger down the beach toward Deardra. Cedar watched it fly through the air for an impossibly long time, as if the laws of gravity did not apply. Then it connected with its target, sinking itself hilt-deep into Deardra's bosom. The queen's mouth opened but no sound came out. Then she collapsed at Anya's feet, a pool of violet blood forming around her and running into the water. Instantly, the water near the shore started to seethe as dozens of Merrow rose to the surface, hissing and screaming in tortured, high-pitched voices.

Meanwhile, Riona had regained control of herself and was watching the scene below with a look of horror on her face. More and more Merrow swarmed to the surface, and the water churned and started to rise, turning into a giant wave that towered over the rocky beach. Anya lifted her hands into the air once more and started chanting. The wave stopped cresting and started to recede, taking the still-screaming Merrow with it. Then one of the Merrow gave an order, and immediately the others started emitting loud, forceful bursts of sound that almost pierced Cedar's eardrums. She saw Anya crumple as if she had been shot. Felix and Molly rushed to her side and tried to pull her back, away from the Merrow's invisible projectiles, but they, too, stumbled as the Merrow continued their onslaught. Cedar watched as Molly disappeared in a thick cloud of smoke that hung close to the ground, obscuring Anya and Felix from view.

Farther down the beach, Oscar was continuing his attack on the Merrow. His dagger out of reach, he was wielding melon-sized rocks with unwavering precision, cracking the skulls of at least a dozen Merrow before a spear sank into his side beneath his raised arm. Murdoch roared with rage and threw his entire handful of short daggers at once, each of them finding a target in a Merrow throat before dislodging themselves and soaring through the air, dripping with purple blood, back to their owner.

Riona looked at Cedar. "Stay here!" she commanded. Without another word, she turned and made a running leap off the edge of the cliff. Cedar screamed and scrambled to her feet. Riona was falling, her arms outstretched, but then she twisted in midair and in a burst of feathers transformed into a hawk, screeching as she dove to join the melee below. Darting at the eyes of the Merrow, she danced through the air, avoiding the spears, tridents, and deadly bursts of sound being flung at her. Anya had emerged from the cloud that was Molly and was advancing toward the water's edge, while Murdoch continued his assault on those brave enough to stick their necks out of the water. Anya raised her arms once more and the water started to push back, exposing dry land underneath. Rohan was dragging Oscar's limp body behind a large rock close to the cliff's base, and Felix was running toward him with a speed that did not belong to a man of his apparent age. Cedar looked around for Finn but couldn't see him. Then she looked back at the ocean and saw that Nuala was fighting the turbulent waters, moving herself and Eden slowly toward the rocks beneath the hut.

"No!" Cedar screamed. "She's getting away!" She ran over to where she had seen the others climb down a thick rope, but all that was left was a thin golden thread. She put her hands around it, but it was no thicker than a strand of sewing thread. *How did they do it?* she asked herself. She grabbed the thread again. "Help me!" she yelled at it. "I need to get down!" Still it remained limp in her hand. Tossing it aside, she slid onto her stomach and without another thought lowered herself over the edge, searching for a toehold. She tried to remember what she had learned during her weekends of rock climbing while at university, but this was a far cry from those excursions, with their safety harnesses and anchors and belayers. The rock face was almost perfectly vertical, and Cedar knew one false step would send her plummeting to the rocks below. But she merely tightened her grip and searched for the next hold.

Suddenly, she heard a cry coming from one of the Merrow, louder than any of their screams thus far.

"Human!"

Cedar froze. She knew she was completely exposed. There was no possibility of hiding or climbing back up to the top. Then she cried out in pain as something hard hit the small of her back. A trident clanged off the wall just inches from her head. Barely clinging to the rock, she turned her head and almost released her hold in terror.

Beside and above her loomed a creature more terrible than anything she had ever seen. Its body, as large as the cliff she clung to, was covered in green scales and large, round, pulsating suckers. Claws as long as her arm extended from each of its dozen fingers. Instead of a mouth, the creature had a swarming mass of tentacles, as if it were in the process of swallowing a giant octopus. Two golden eyes protruded grotesquely from atop its head, and a pair of dragon wings unfurled from between its shoulder blades. A harpoon struck it in the neck but the weapon just glanced off, as if it had hit the rock wall. The creature turned its eyes on Cedar, and she screamed, her fingers losing their grip on the rocks. A tentacle shot out and wrapped around her, but instead of devouring her or thrashing her against the rock as she had expected, the beast lowered her to the ground. It set her in a crevice in the rock wall and rolled a large boulder in front of her. Then it turned and, with a deafening roar, moved its massive body toward the screeching Merrow.

Cedar stared after it in horror, shocked to still be alive. Then she remembered why she had been trying to climb down the cliff in the first place. *Eden.* She hoisted herself up and over the boulder that was blocking her way and ran as fast as she could down the beach, ignoring the stabbing pain in her back where the Merrow had struck her. She watched as Nuala and Eden reached the island and rested for a moment on the rocks, both of them panting. Then Nuala stood and dragged the girl to her feet. Eden's eyes were wild with terror. Cedar sprinted the last few feet to the shore and started to wade into the water. "Eden!" she called as loudly as she could. "EDEN!"

Eden turned her head in the direction of the sound and screamed back, "Mummy!"

"Eden, I'm coming! Hold on!" Cedar yelled as she tried to run through the water.

"Stop!" Nuala raised a hand toward Cedar, and she felt herself immobilized.

It's just a spell, she told herself. *You can move. You want to move!*

Nuala yanked Eden back against her side. "We can go now, Eden. We can go to Tír na nÓg, where your father is waiting for us. You've seen what it looks like, now all you need to do is open the door!"

"Mummy!" Eden screamed again, trying to get out of Nuala's grasp.

"No!" Nuala screamed back at her. "We are going home! You open that damn door or your mother will drown."

Eden sobbed hysterically while Nuala dragged her up the rocks and to the hut's door. "Open it," Nuala hissed.

Cedar fought against the fog in her head. *Think about Eden. You have to get to her.* "Eden, don't!" she yelled, and felt her body start to free itself.

She saw Eden reach for the door, which was barely hanging onto its hinges, and push it open.

"Why isn't it working?" Nuala yelled. "You stupid child!" She slapped Eden's face. "I said open it!"

"I'm trying!" Eden screamed back.

"We don't have time for this!" Nuala said. "Just get us out of here!"

Cedar had almost reached the rocks when Eden opened the door for a second time. "Eden! Eden! Come to me!" she cried out in desperation.

Eden spun away from the open door and started to run toward her mother, but Nuala caught her by the hair and jerked her back. Then Nuala looked Cedar in the eye and said in a low but clear voice, "You will stop trying to find us. You will forget about her. You never had a daughter."

Cedar fell to her knees in the water as her thoughts turned as thick as cold molasses. She looked up just in time to see Nuala and a small child disappear into the hut. There was a glimmer of pink, and then the door slammed shut behind them. The sound of screaming was all around her, but she stayed on her knees in the shallow water, staring at the door and wondering what she was supposed to be doing. Then everything around her fell silent. The next thing she knew, Finn was splashing toward her and pulling her to her feet. Rohan stormed past them and into the hut. His curses filled the silence and sent a chill down Cedar's back.

"Cedar, where is Eden?" Finn shouted, though she was only inches away from him. She stared at him, her brow wrinkled. "Who?" she asked.

CHAPTER 13

There was a monster…did you kill it?" Cedar mumbled as Finn pulled her back onto the shore. She stumbled across the rocks, her arm firmly encased in his grip.

"I'll explain later," he said. "Right now we need to get out of here."

She ducked and screamed as a giant eagle swooped down toward them. He pulled her in close.

"Shh! It's okay!" he said. "It's just Riona. The rope has disappeared so she's going to lift us up to the top of the cliff."

Cedar closed her mouth tightly to keep herself from screaming again as she felt the eagle's bony talons close around them like a cage. It lifted them into the air and, seconds later, deposited them gently onto the same grassy bank where she had witnessed most of the battle. Finn immediately lifted her into his arms and started running toward the car. "I can walk!" she protested, but he ignored her. She saw Murdoch settling Oscar's limp form into the back of the van.

"Is he…?" she asked Finn as he helped her into the car's back seat and climbed in beside her. Rohan, who was already in the driver's seat, started the car, and they turned onto the dusty road.

"Dead? Yes," he answered. "And Molly is badly wounded, but she should be all right once Felix can tend to her. Anya probably has a concussion, but she's too proud to admit it, and too distraught to let Felix even look at her. And now we have a new enemy, thanks to Nuala."

"Where are we going?" she asked. Cedar felt as if she, too, had taken a hit to the head. She tried to focus, to remember what was going on, but her thoughts stumbled around in her head like a drunkard after last call.

"Away from here," Finn said. "Someplace where we can lay low and figure out what to do next." His face was pale and his eyes bloodshot. "Nuala and Eden are gone. We couldn't hear their Lýra anymore. Did you see them go through a sidh?"

"Nuala…" Cedar murmured. "Yes, she was on the rocks by that hut. She went into it. And then…I don't remember."

Finn's mouth grew tight and he put his arm around her, drawing her close. She was too tired to resist, and leaned into him.

"I think I might be in shock," she said.

"That doesn't surprise me. Felix can help you once we stop."

"Riona can turn into a bird."

"Yes."

"And there was a giant monster, but it helped me. What was it?"

"Uh, that was me."

She rubbed her temples, certain she had misheard him. "That was…you?"

"I'm what you would call a shape-shifter. My mother has that ability as well. We can take the shape of any living being. One of the benefits of being a firstborn child is that we sometimes end up with more than one ability."

Cedar shuddered at the memory.

"I'm sorry I frightened you," Finn continued. "It's a good form to take on when warring with creatures of the ocean. I was just trying to protect you."

"You did," she said, her words slurring slightly. Her head ached, and she put it into her hands. She felt untethered, like a balloon released into the sky. She wanted to hold onto something, but her thoughts kept slipping out of her grasp and floating away.

"Sleep, Cedar," Finn said, his voice wavering. "We'll take you somewhere safe, and we'll figure out how to fix this."

She closed her eyes, rested her head against his chest, and fell asleep listening to the steady beating of his heart.

Two hours later, they pulled up in front of a small cottage surrounded by thick trees. Finn gently nudged Cedar awake and they went into the cottage, where the others were already crowding into the front room. Oscar's body was wrapped in a cloth, lying on the floor in front of a smoldering fire. Anya was hunched over it, her moans filling the room. Felix carried Molly in and set her on the sofa, placing her head in Riona's lap. Angry red welts covered her face and arms. Felix started pulling what looked like packets of dried herbs out of the small bag he wore around his waist.

"Logheryman!" he said. "I'll be needin' some hot water, and a clean cloth. And some whiskey, if you've not drunk it all."

Cedar looked around. Logheryman, she supposed, was the sinewy old man standing in the corner of the room, watching them all with a haughty expression. Instead of answering Felix, he walked out of the room.

"Where are we?" Cedar asked Finn.

"At the house of a friend," Finn said. "This is like a safe house for us. Logheryman is a cousin of ours."

"You mean he's another Tuatha Dé Danann?"

"Not exactly. He's a leprechaun. Our races are distantly related, but the leprechauns were permitted to stay on Ériu when our people were banished. The humans believed if you could catch a leprechaun it would make you rich, so they wanted as many around as possible to increase their chances."

"Is it true?"

"No one's ever caught one," he grinned, "so who knows?" Then he grew somber again. "How are you feeling?"

"Foggy," she said. "I just need to wake up a bit more, I think." There was a horrible feeling in the pit of her stomach, a vast emptiness, as if someone had removed all her vital organs. "I feel awful about Oscar and Molly." She looked around the room again. "Where's Murdoch?"

"Outside, I think. Tearing down trees," Finn answered.

"He can do that?" Cedar asked. Now that she was listening for it, she could hear crashing and breaking sounds echoing from outside the cottage.

Finn nodded.

"Can Felix do anything for Oscar?" she asked.

He looked grim. "No. Oscar was dead before he could get to him. Even Felix's grandfather, the great healer Dian Cecht, could not bring the dead back to life."

Logheryman came back into the room carrying a tray laden with a steaming kettle, a folded white cloth, and a half-full bottle of amber liquid. He didn't look like he'd be that hard to catch, but by now she knew better than to make any judgments based on appearances. He placed the tray on the floor beside Felix and retreated to the other side of the room.

Just then, the door flew open with a loud crash and Murdoch burst into the room. His clothes were ripped and the palms of his hands were bleeding, but he didn't seem to notice. He advanced on Cedar, his eyes wild. "You!" he snarled. "You did this! It's your fault my son is dead!"

Finn stepped between Murdoch and Cedar, his hands raised and palms outward, "Murdoch, just wait—"

"I'm sick of this! I'm sick of you and your human pet always getting what you want! I told you she would cause nothing but trouble! I told you she would slow us down! If we had gotten there sooner, this wouldn't have happened!" Spit flew from his mouth when he spoke, and Cedar cringed at the fury in his eyes. The two men were standing only inches apart, both with their fists clenched and the tendons in their necks strained and protruding.

"This isn't her fault!" Finn protested.

"Like hell it isn't!" Murdoch bellowed.

"It's mine!" Finn shouted back.

"Finn, this isn't—" Riona began, moving toward her son.

"IT IS!" he yelled, and she stopped in her tracks. "This is all my fault, everything that has happened. None of this, not Oscar or Molly or even Nuala doing what she did, none of it would have happened if I had just followed the damn rules. Eden wouldn't even exist. It's my fault. I accept that, and I will do whatever I can to make up for it. But I don't regret what I did. I don't regret being with Cedar. I'll never be sorry Eden is alive. And part of fixing this, of making things right again, is finding her and keeping her safe."

"It's rather late for that now, isn't it?" Murdoch said with a sneer.

"I don't believe that," Finn said. "There *has* to be another way to get to Tír na nÓg. There has to be a way to find her or to communicate with her somehow. Maybe she'll escape; maybe she'll find a way to come back. We can't give up hope! We just have to keep trying."

"And risk more lives? More of our children? Why is it that your child is worth so much, and mine so little?" Murdoch said, gesturing at the body by the fire. "Tell me that! You're just fooling yourself. Lorcan's got his hooks in her now, and she's beyond our reach. Well, good riddance, if you ask me. That bastard child of yours has brought us nothing but trouble."

"Don't be stupid, man," growled Felix, who was laying long strips of cloth over Molly's burns. "Yer in grief, and we understand that. Oscar was like a son to many of us. But now you're talkin' nonsense. If Lorcan has his hooks in her as you say, then soon he'll be doing what he's always wanted. He'll use her power to send his whole blasted army here and kill every man, woman, and child with human blood in 'em."

Murdoch spat angrily. "And who would miss them? Maybe Nuala's right. Why should we sacrifice our own children to save theirs? We need to be thinking of ourselves, protecting ourselves, not them!"

"And do you think he'll let you live?" asked Riona angrily. "Just because you're not human? I don't remember him being kind to the rest of the traitors in Tír na nÓg. We're all in the same danger. We need to stop fighting each other, and figure out how to fight Lorcan! Finn is right. There must be another way to save Eden."

"What makes you so sure she's still alive?" Murdoch said, staring hard at Riona.

"You know very well he can't assimilate her ability. He couldn't take Brogan's power after he killed him, so he won't dare risk killing Eden. He needs her alive, and that means we still have a chance to rescue her." Riona turned and looked at Cedar. "I'm sorry, Cedar, this must be so upsetting for you."

Cedar looked back at Riona, conscious that all eyes in the room were on her, but unsure of what to say. She had tried to follow the volley of conversation, but her mind was still sluggish. She felt foolish, like a child trying to join an adult conversation. Finally, she asked the only question she could think of.

"Sorry," she said, "but who are we talking about?"

Riona looked nonplussed. "We're talking about Eden, of course," she replied, "about what will happen to her now."

Cedar waited for further explanation, but Riona just sat there, looking at her expectantly. Finally, Finn spoke up.

"I was going to mention it, but I thought it might wear off. Cedar doesn't seem to remember Eden. She said she saw Nuala go into the hut. But I think Nuala must have spoken to her and made her forget...about Eden."

There was another silence while the group absorbed this unexpected news. Then Murdoch snorted. "Well, that makes things a bit easier then, doesn't it? Wasn't it you, Rohan, who wanted her to go home and stay out of this? Maybe now she will."

"That's enough, Muireadhach," Rohan said from where he was standing by the window.

"No, that couldn't have happened," Riona said. "How could she forget Eden?" She looked at Cedar. "You don't remember your own daughter? Not at all?"

"I don't have a daughter," Cedar said. She didn't understand what they were talking about, or why Riona was having a hard time believing her.

Felix started cursing, and Molly moaned, "Oh, no, Cedar."

"I think it's fitting," mumbled Anya, who still sat huddled over Oscar's body. "We've lost our son, and now she's lost her daughter." She looked up at them all, the rage in her eyes intensified by the flickering reflection of the fire. "My husband is right. This is her fault. Maybe she got what she deserved." No one dared argue with her, so pitiful she seemed there on the floor, hunched over her son's dead body. She turned away from them and resumed her mourning.

The eerie sound of Anya's keening sent a shiver up Cedar's spine. Something was wrong, incredibly wrong. She felt disembodied, as though she were watching events unfold at a distance.

"You *do* have a daughter," Finn said to her. "*Our* daughter. Nuala has just used her power to make you forget."

She shook her head. "That's ridiculous, Finn." Her cheeks reddened. "I think I would know if I had a child. I don't understand why you keep saying I do. Is this some kind of joke? Or another lie?"

"No!" Finn exclaimed. "You have to believe me. It's Nuala who is the liar. She planted this in your head. But you can fight it! *Think*, Cedar. Why else would you be here? You flew from Halifax to New York and then to Ireland *to look for Eden*. That's what all of this is about! Why would we lie about that?"

Cedar felt her hackles rise at this question. She looked up at him, incredulity spreading across her face. "Are you kidding me? You've done nothing but lie to me ever since we met. I'm just a human, remember? Every time I turn around I'm discovering some new piece of information you've withheld from me."

"That may be, Miss Cedar, but you're discoverin' all the same, are you not?" Felix said. He stood up from where he had been kneeling beside Molly. "Not as fast as you'd like, I dare say, but I can tell you this for certain: you know a far sight more about us than any other human ever has or possibly ever will, save for our druid friends. And it strikes me that *you* might be the one withholdin' information."

"What?" Cedar asked. "I'm not withholding anything."

"Whether you remember her as your daughter or not, from what Finn has told us, you were the last of us here to see Eden and Nuala," Felix said. "I believe it might be worth your trouble, and ours, if you would tell us exactly what you remember."

Cedar felt mutinous and was about to ask why she should tell them anything, but then she glanced at Oscar's body on the floor, and saw Molly lying mottled on the sofa, and her anger lessened. She looked around at the faces in the room. There was so much power here, and yet every face was tinged with despair. Whatever they were up against, it was enough to cause dread among this race of gods. The room was cold, and she crossed her arms and hugged herself as she tried to remember.

"I remember the battle, and seeing Nuala. I ran down the beach. Everyone else was fighting, and I was afraid she was going to get away. She was climbing up the rocks. There was someone with her, a child. The child was screaming, fighting her. Then they went into the hut."

"Who went in first?" Rohan asked, his voice low and urgent. "Who opened the door?"

Cedar closed her eyes, trying to reconstruct the scene in her mind. "The child, I think."

"Did you see inside the hut?" he asked. "Did you see what it looked like?"

"There was a lot of screaming. The kid—a girl, I think—opened the door. It looked dark inside. And then they were screaming and fighting again, and I fell down in the water. I don't know why. Then the girl opened the door again, and it was like a light had been turned on inside. It was pink. It looked like a little girl's bedroom."

Immediately, the air in the room lightened, as if someone had infused it with oxygen and sunshine. Riona started sobbing and laughing at the same time. Rohan looked shaky on his feet as he walked over to rest a large hand on Cedar's shoulder. "Okay," was all he said, nodding at her. "Okay."

Cedar looked around in bewilderment. Molly, whose burns were rapidly healing, stood up and hugged her. "We still have a chance then. She's still here," she said.

Cedar looked at Finn for an explanation. His eyes were bright and his arms trembled slightly as he followed his sister's lead and wrapped Cedar in a tight hug. She pushed him away and stood back, glaring at him with suspicion. "What's going on?" she asked.

"What you saw, that's not Tír na nÓg," he said. "I don't know why it didn't work, but there's nothing that looks like a human girl's bedroom in Tír na nÓg. It was probably Eden's room. Is it pink?"

"How would I know what her room looks like?" Cedar protested.

"It *is* pink," Molly said. "I saw it when we were there the other day."

"Then we should go. Now!" Riona said. "She might still be there!"

Rohan looked at Murdoch, as if he were trying to gauge the other man's state of mind. Murdoch held his gaze, his internal struggle written on his face. Then he nodded and said, "I'll call Nevan. I'll tell her to take Sam and Dermot and get over to Cedar's apartment as soon as they can."

Logheryman, who had been standing silently by the front door, cleared his throat. When he spoke, it was with the voice of a much younger man, almost a boy, and Cedar wondered if his voice or his appearance reflected his true age, or neither.

"Forgive the intrusion," he said, "but I believe I may be able to offer you some assistance." He waited for a response, and when there was none, he continued.

"My limited understanding of your situation leads me to believe that the sooner you return to your, er, temporary home, the better. Am I correct in this assessment?"

"Spit it out, ye damn leprechaun," Felix growled.

Logheryman folded his weathered hands and inclined his head toward Felix. "As you wish. I happen to have in my possession several pairs of thousand-league boots, which I would be pleased to loan you for a brief and specified period of time. You may find them useful in catching up to your quarry, who always appears to be a few steps ahead of you."

"And what's yer price?" Felix demanded.

Logheryman shrugged as if payment was but an afterthought. "What does any self-respecting leprechaun want?" he asked in his unnaturally high voice. "Gold."

Rohan stepped forward. "We don't have gold," he said. "Something you know very well."

Again, the leprechaun shrugged. "You may not have it on your person," he conceded, "but it is well known that the Tuatha Dé Danann had access to vast amounts of wealth hidden on Ériu during the centuries in which they still counted kings and queens among their friends. You need not trouble yourselves by fetching the gold for me. All I ask is that you show me where those stores are, and the boots are yours. That is, unless you would rather enjoy the hospitality of British Airways and arrive back home, mmm, sometime tomorrow afternoon?"

Rohan looked like he wanted a third option that involved wrapping his hands around the leprechaun's neck.

"A moment, please," he said to Logheryman. He stalked off into the kitchen, and the rest of the Tuatha Dé Danann followed him as if by some secret signal. Not sure what do to, Cedar hung behind. The leprechaun smirked at her.

"This, my dear, is why I deal with the Tuatha Dé Danann but rarely. You always know where you stand with them." He gave her a significant look. "Beneath."

"So how do these boots work?" Cedar asked, trying to change the subject. She didn't need to be reminded of her status among the Danann.

"They work rather splendidly, if I do say so myself. Slip them on your feet and you can travel a thousand leagues in a single step."

"How far is that?" Cedar asked. She wasn't trying to be cheeky, but the leprechaun seemed to take it that way. He rolled his eyes.

"About three thousand miles, if you must think in such mundane terms. But this is magic, my dear, not geography. And it's also a one-time offer. I'll tell the boots where to go, and that's where they'll take you. Once you arrive, they will become ordinary boots until they are returned to me. The magic does not reside in the shoe, you see, but in the shoemaker."

The others returned from the kitchen and Rohan said, "All right, Logheryman. We'll direct you to a store of gold in return for the use of these boots, provided you can ready them immediately."

"Mmm." Logheryman put a finger to his lips. "One store of gold will get you precisely one pair of boots."

"There are nine of us, in case you haven't noticed, not that I expect you know how to count," snapped Murdoch. "You think you need nine stores of gold?" He looked around the cramped, dingy cottage. "What would you even do with it?"

"I hate to be the one to point this out, but there are now only eight of you. And what I do with my gold is no one's business but my own," Logheryman replied, seemingly unperturbed. He looked at Cedar and winked. "Perhaps I have a great dragon in the cellar that sits on it and keeps it warm."

"I've been in your cellar and there's nought there but cobwebs and whiskey," Murdoch said. He turned to Rohan. "Even if we do make this bargain, who's to say the boots won't end up drowning us in the middle of the Atlantic?"

"We accept," Rohan said to Logheryman. "Finn, Murdoch, Anya, and I will take the boots and travel back to Halifax that way." He held up a hand to stop Logheryman's inevitable question. "Yes, that means we will direct you to four stores of gold. Riona, you stay with Molly and Cedar and catch the next flight you can find."

"Wait. Cedar comes with us," Finn said.

"We don't have time to argue about this," Rohan said. "We need to get our best warriors after Nuala, and she's not one of them."

"It's fine, I really don't mind waiting," Cedar said.

"I'm not letting her out of my sight," Finn argued. "We don't know what else Nuala may have told her to do. If I leave her…"

"I'll stay," came Anya's voice from the back. "I'm not much use for fighting right now. Besides, I want to bury him here, in the old country."

Rohan glared at Finn, but nodded curtly after a moment. "So be it. Logheryman, bring us the boots," he demanded.

"Not quite yet. I have one other minor condition," Logheryman said.

Rohan stiffened but said nothing, waiting.

"It's a delicate matter, of course, because I do not wish to imply that the Tuatha Dé Danann could ever be duplicitous in their dealings with lesser folk. However, it would put my mind at ease if you would make use of the goblet of Manannan mac Lir while sealing this agreement. Am I correct in assuming it is in your possession even as we speak?" Logheryman raised a grizzled eyebrow at Rohan.

Cedar had no idea what the goblet of Manannan mac Lir was, but she could sense the Tuatha Dé Danann's offense.

"You doubt my word, leprechaun?" Rohan's voice was low and icy.

Logheryman didn't seem threatened. "Not at all, Rohan Donnelly," he said, stressing Rohan's human name. "I simply prefer to do business this way."

Rohan gave the leprechaun a stony look, but then pulled something out of an inner pocket of his coat. It was a small, plain silver goblet that looked more like a child's toy than anything an ancient being would use to seal contracts.

"You have maps, I presume?" Rohan asked Logheryman.

"Old and new," Logheryman chirped. He stepped out of the room and Cedar could hear his footsteps going down the stairs to the cellar.

While he was gone, Cedar turned to Felix and asked, "Does anyone in your world ever help anyone else just for the sake of it?"

Felix made a face. "A fair question, Miss Cedar, and the fair answer would be no. Now I've a question for you. I reckon I'd be in my rights to say yer unfamiliar with the goblet of Manannan mac Lir, yes?"

"Shocking, I know," Cedar answered dryly, "but yes, you're right. What does it do?"

"Tells the truth," he said. "Or, rather, it tells if *you're* telling the truth. Watch." He took the goblet from Rohan and said, "My given name is Felix Dockendorff." Instantly, the goblet shattered and fell in clattering pieces onto the floor. Cedar gasped and took a step back.

"Told a lie, then, didn't I?" Felix said. "Now we'll try for the truth. My given name is Toirdhealbhach MacDail re Deachai."

Cedar watched in amazement as the shards on the floor reformed themselves into the goblet. Felix picked it up and handed it to her. She ran her hands around it. There was no evidence it had been lying in pieces only moments ago.

"Now you try it," Felix said, watching her carefully. "Tell the goblet you've not got a daughter."

Cedar stared at him, then down at the goblet. She felt her pulse quicken. What if this small cup in her hands confirmed what everyone had been saying? What if they were right, and she did have a daughter she couldn't remember? She shuddered. She felt as though she were being played somehow. But if they were right, if she couldn't even trust her own memories, it would mean she couldn't trust herself. And then she would have no one.

She handed the cup back to Felix, shaking her head. "I can't."

"I'll do it." Finn strode over to them and took the cup from Felix. Before Cedar could protest, he said, "Cedar McLeod does not have a child."

The cup shattered and fell to the floor in pieces.

Cedar watched them fall as if in slow motion. She heard them clatter as they hit the floor, but felt strangely removed from the sound. Without knowing why, she bent down and picked up the shards, turning them over in her hands, examining each one as though it might dissolve into powder if she held it too tightly. She cupped her hands in front of her and whispered into them, "I have a daughter." Then she handed the perfectly whole goblet back to Finn and, without looking at him, walked out of the room.

CHAPTER 14

Maeve had met Brogan when she was seventeen years old. During her childhood, her grandmother had told her stories of fairies and leprechauns, of the mighty High Kings of Ireland, and of the great warrior Fionn mac Cumhaill. She had told her how Fionn and his followers, the Fianna, were going to awaken someday from their enchanted sleep to defend Ireland in its hour of greatest need, and free the north from what she called "those damned left-leggers." Maeve's mother had rolled her eyes and said, "Don't be putting your republican ideas in her head, Ma. It's naught to do with her. She's a Canadian now."

But the stories had stuck in Maeve's head. In high school, she had written papers on Irish mythology and other aspects of Irish history and culture. For her graduation gift, her parents and grandparents had chipped in to send her to Ireland for the summer. She was to stay with her mother's cousin and his family in Cork. Her grandmother had squeezed her hands and told her she wished she were young enough to go with her back to "the blessed isle."

Maeve had spent the summer traveling around the island with her new friend, her second cousin Siobhan. That's when she first saw Brogan. He was sitting on top of the ancient burial mound of Newgrange as the sun was beginning to set and the clouds were becoming rimmed with orange. Although Maeve and Siobhan were chatting animatedly as they approached, he did not appear to notice them coming. When they saw him, both girls stopped and simply stared. He looked to be tall and lean, with fair skin and dark, curly hair. He wore a black leather jacket, the collar turned up, over a tight white T-shirt. He sat on the hill with his chin resting on one hand, a brooding expression on his face. Siobhan whispered, "He looks like James Dean," and seemed about to swoon. Maeve saw the similarities, but James Dean had been just a boy in comparison. This was a man, or something more than a man. He was, without a doubt, the most exquisite creature she had ever seen. Turning, he looked at them. The setting sun glanced off his fair skin, giving him the appearance of an angel, or a ghost. He smiled at them and stood.

"He's coming this way!" Siobhan squealed under her breath, and Maeve shushed her.

"Ladies," the angel-man said, nodding at them.

"H-h-hi," Siobhan stammered. Maeve stood silent, transfixed. His eyes were dark and unfathomable, framed by thick black brows. His jaw was shadowed with stubble, and when he smiled at them the most incredible dimples indented his cheeks. His lips looked like they would refuse to take no for an answer, and Maeve found herself wondering what he would taste like.

"We didn't mean to interrupt you," she said in a quiet voice.

"Not at all," he said. "Is this your first time to Newgrange?"

"Yes," Siobhan injected enthusiastically. "Do you come here often?" She moved slightly in front of Maeve and thrust out her considerable chest. Maeve frowned, but didn't try to put herself back in the man's line of sight.

She thought she saw the corner of his mouth twitch as he answered, "Mmm, once in a while. I have relatives buried nearby. I come to visit their graves."

"Oh, I see. Well, perhaps you could show us around!" Siobhan stood there beaming at him. Maeve looked past both of them to the hill looming in front, and wondered what kind of people were buried here. How interesting it would be to have relatives interred so close to such an ancient site.

She noticed he was holding out his hand to her. "Brogan mac Airgetlam," he said. She took his hand and shook it. His grip was gentle but firm, and she could feel calluses on his palm. She felt slightly light-headed at his touch, but then mastered herself and smiled back at him, enjoying the way his eyes lit up when she did. Though nothing compared with him, she herself was not lacking in beauty. She was tall for her age, and had hearty curves that complemented the bouncing red curls that spilled down her back to her waist. In contrast, Siobhan was unremarkable save for her impressive bosom. Apparently, she also had a weaker constitution, for when Brogan reached out and shook her hand, she fell to the ground in a dead faint.

Once Maeve and Brogan had revived her and Siobhan had mumbled something about not eating all day, the three of them climbed to the top of the hill to watch the sunset. Later that night, at Brogan's request, Maeve made her apologies to Siobhan at their youth hostel and met him for a drink, not returning to her cousin until daybreak.

That night was the first of many spent together over the next several years. He never stayed around long, usually just a night or two, maybe a week at most. At first, he refused to tell her what he did or where he lived, instead making her guess, laughing at her theories about spies and secret missions as he trailed soft kisses down the length of her spine. When she returned to Nova Scotia to start college, he promised to visit her as often as he had in Ireland, and he was true to his word. She gave up trying to find out more about him and, truth be told, enjoyed the intrigue of having a mystery lover. She tried dating college boys, but they were so inferior to her

Brogan that she soon gave up on them as well, and just waited for him to make his next appearance.

He told her the truth on the morning of her twentieth birthday. They were lying in her bed, listening to the sputter of the coffeemaker in the next room. He rolled over so that he was looking down at her, and she reached up to cup his face, marveling at the beauty of it.

"I have a gift for you," he said.

"Do you, now?" she said coquettishly. "Am I going to have to guess what it is?"

"You've been guessing since we met," he answered. She raised her eyebrows.

"My gift is the truth," he said, "about who I am and where I come from."

Maeve sat up, pushing her thick red curls behind her shoulder. She felt her pulse quicken with excitement and anticipation.

"Let me guess one more time," she said, trying to suppress her nerves with lighthearted banter. "You're the great Fionn mac Cumhaill, awake at last to help Ireland in her hour of great need."

A shadow crossed his face, and she wondered if she had somehow offended him with her insouciance.

"And if I were?" he asked softly. "Would you believe me?"

She considered his question carefully. Would she? She had always been of the mind that her grandmother's stories must have some grain of truth to them. There was no reason to believe fairies and gods were not real just because she herself had not seen them. However, Maeve had long since learned not to voice such opinions at the dinner table, lest her parents start crossing themselves and saying prayers for her salvation.

She took Brogan's face in her hands again and looked him straight in his eyes. "I would believe anything you told me, my love."

He kissed her then, and said, "I am not Fionn mac Cumhaill, but my father knew him, and saw him die. I am afraid he will not be awakening to help the Irish anytime soon." Then he told her the most unimaginable things: that magic was real, and the stories she had grown up on were true, or at least had their basis in reality, and that he was one of the Tuatha Dé Danann of Tír na nÓg, a descendent of the great Nuadu Airgetlam who had ruled the Tuatha Dé Danann during their conquest of Ireland many thousands of years ago. He told her how he loved all humans, but her most of all. And she believed him.

It was shortly after that, the year she finished college, that he asked her to study the druidic arts. He found her a mentor, one of the world's few remaining druids, and bought her a secluded house in the country that overlooked the ocean and bordered a small forest. Eagerly, she took her vows, left her friends and her family, and spent all her time studying, training, and waiting for his visits. It was a lonely life, with only her druid mentor for occasional company. As time went by and she progressed in her studies, even his visits became less frequent.

But it was all worth it for the ecstasy of her days and nights with Brogan. He would sometimes not appear for a month, but other times he didn't seem to be able to stay away for more than a few days. Now that he had told her his secret, he created a sidh in the cellar of her house so he could come and go with ease. He placed an enchantment on her that prevented her from going through the sidh without him. It was for her own safety, he said. Some of his people were not as accepting of humans as he was, and he did not want her to stumble through the sidh and into danger. And so he came and went, and although she begged him to take her to Tír na nÓg with him, he told her the time had not yet come, and she needed to concentrate on becoming a fully trained druid before they could consider such things.

Things continued this way for three more years. Then Maeve started to notice a change in him. Not a physical change; he was still frozen in time, his face and body as full of youth and beauty as they had been on the day they met. But his eyes, once light and clear, were now often dark and clouded with worry. Something was weighing heavily on him, yet all he would say was that things in Tír na nÓg were changing, that a threat brewed among his people. He stopped looking at her the way he used to, with undisguised lust and adoration. She would make jokes about getting older while he remained virile and handsome, but he didn't take the bait and assure her that she was as beautiful to him as ever. She began to look for invisible wrinkles and nonexistent gray hairs hiding among the red. His visits became less frequent, and she could not tell if it was because he desired her less or because trouble in his homeland kept him away.

She had just celebrated her twenty-fourth birthday when he told her he would not be coming back.

She cried and screamed, and threw a jar of rare herbs at him, which he caught effortlessly and placed gently back on the shelf.

"My place is with my people," he said.

"Your place is with me!" she argued, her face ugly with tears.

He did not respond to this, but said, "There is a war brewing in Tír na nÓg. I must concentrate on keeping our people from tearing one another apart. We have never had a civil war in Tír na nÓg. It would be the death of our entire race, of that I am sure."

"But why does that mean you can never see me again? Won't you promise to come back when this is all over?" she wailed.

"It may be many years, decades, even centuries, before everything is settled. I do not wish for you to spend the rest of your life waiting for me."

"You mean you don't want to come back to an old woman," she said bitterly.

"Maeve." He spoke her name with intimacy but also with authority. He owned her, and they both knew it. "You have great fire in your spirit, but you and I have allowed it to be quenched by your love for me, your dependence on me. You have the makings of a great druid, and you will have power that only a handful of mortals in the last century have enjoyed. Use your gift, and make a life for yourself. My life is in Tír na nÓg, with my people…and with my wife."

There was a horrible, empty silence as Maeve absorbed what he had just said. "Your…wife?" she repeated after a long moment, barely able to utter the words.

He nodded slowly and without apology, but did not meet her eyes. "Fidelity is not a strong point among my people, nor is it completely expected. But my wife's family will be important in the coming war, and to aggravate them would be unwise."

"This whole time, you had a wife. And children?"

He shook his head. "Not yet. Do not blame yourself, Maeve. I've already made sure you will be taken care of. You will lack for nothing."

"I don't want your charity," she spat. She looked him in the eye, her chin thrust out in challenge. "Tell me you don't love me."

He looked at her sadly. "Love is but one factor among many. It is the cause of wars and of peace. I do love you, in my own way. I regret causing you pain. I've enjoyed our time together, but now it is over."

"Will you never speak to me again, then? What about the dream-speech?" she asked, referring to the way they had begun to communicate through her self-induced trances and dreams.

Again, he shook his head. "No. I cannot afford any distractions. You will do best to forget about me. You will not see me again."

He was true to his word.

❦

Sitting alone in the workshop Brogan had built for her four decades ago, Maeve lifted her glass, which was smoking slightly and giving off a pungent odor. She toasted her long-lost lover, drank the potent brew, and then sat in the armchair in the corner, wrapping a blanket around her. She thought about him and tried to picture him clearly, even as she felt herself losing consciousness. She remembered how he had smelled of sunlight and mountain air, how intoxicating it had been to be around him, even after years together. She remembered the way his black curls would fall into his eyes, how the touch of his hands had brought fire to the surface of her skin. She cried out to him in her mind's voice, "Brogan, Brogan, come back to me! I have such need of you. After all I have done for you, will you not come to me now?"

She waited, feeling herself pass through the veil of reality to a place where time had no meaning, where death was but another sidh to be opened. She walked through a gray cloud that pressed heavily against her chest, calling and calling to him for what seemed like hours. Finally, she reached the ocean and, without thought, stepped onto the water. She kept walking and calling until she crossed the vast expanse and landed on the shore of a distant country, where she fell to her knees. She could not stand again, so great was her exhaustion. Instead, she curled into a fetal position and continued to moan his name. "Brogan…Brogan… Brogan…"

She did not know how long she lay there, but after some time she felt a hand on her shoulder. Strong arms picked her up and set her on her feet. Raising her head, she looked into the eyes of the one she had been seeking. "You came," she whispered, as her eyes devoured him.

"Maeve," he said simply. "What madness has brought you here?"

She felt a pang in her stomach. He was not glad to see her. Then she straightened herself and answered, "The madness of a mother who loves a child. Eden is in trouble. Do you know who—"

"I know who Eden is," Brogan said, smiling slightly.

"I need to find her," Maeve said. "Nuala has her, and is taking her to Lorcan."

Brogan's face looked just as she remembered it—young, flawless, and heartbreakingly beautiful. But where a moment ago it had been soft and warm, now it was hard and tight. He took a step toward her, and she drew in a small involuntary gasp.

"She doesn't belong there, Brogan. I know who she is, but please, she's just a child. I love her as if she were my own flesh and blood. Don't take her from me."

Brogan's pale hand touched Maeve's wrinkled cheek. "Maeve, you are stronger than this. You loved me too much. There is nothing I can do from this side. I have neither the power to take her nor to save her."

"No," Maeve said. "I refuse to believe that. You have the power to appear to me now. You were the most powerful of them all. Surely there is something you can do."

"I can give you knowledge," he said. "It is all that is within my power to give." He closed his eyes, as if gathering himself. Maeve just watched him, her gaze lingering on the lines of his neck as he tilted his head back, eyes still closed.

"She is still in Ériu. She is home. Her home. But she is not alone. Fionnghuala is with her, as you say."

"She's home," Maeve breathed. Perhaps Nuala had reconsidered and was willing to let the girl go.

"But she is in greater danger than you realize," Brogan continued. "Lorcan will not let her live. He will kill her the minute he discovers who she is."

"No!" Maeve protested. "He needs her alive; all your people say so. He killed you and yet couldn't take your gift—*Eden's gift*. If he wants to reopen the sidhe, he has to keep her alive. Doesn't he?" She looked at him and waited for him to agree, trying to ward off the panic she could feel rushing toward her.

He shook his head, and she ached to reach up and wrap one of his curls around her finger. "That is what my people believe, but they believe a lie. It was a well-intentioned lie, but a lie nonetheless. Lorcan *can* kill her, and *can* take her ability. He could have killed me and taken mine."

"Then why…?"

"I was far away from Lorcan when I died. It happened when we were ambushed by fifty of his warriors, with orders to take me alive. Ruadhan and I slew them all, but I was mortally wounded. Before I died, I told Ruadhan to spread the word that Lorcan had killed me yet failed to assimilate the gift of the sidhe. He has been a faithful friend to conceal my secret for so long." He looked urgently into her eyes. "You must stop them, Maeve. Stop Fionnghuala. You are more powerful than you realize. Eden must not reach Lorcan or her death will be the first of many."

Maeve was staring at him in shock. "Why? Why did you do it?"

"To protect you, all of you. Don't blame Ruadhan. It was my decision to conceal the truth," Brogan said, his face agonized. "I hoped it would show our people that Lorcan was unworthy of the gift, that it would undermine his claim to the throne and give others the courage to stand against him. I did not foresee this." He shook his head and started backing away.

"Wait!" Maeve called after him. "Stay, please, just a while longer. I have so much to ask you. Let me be with you for a moment more."

By now, Brogan was several paces away, and the outline of his form was beginning to fade. His voice, when it came, sounded as if he were standing right next to her, his lips tickling her earlobe as he lifted a lock of hair to whisper in her ear. "You must go back now. Save the child. Tell Fionnghuala the truth about my death. I knew her well, and she is not beyond hope. She is starting to grow fond of the child and may listen to you." His voice started to fade as his body disappeared. She could not be sure whether it was his voice or her own imagination that whispered, "Maeve...I love you still..."

She tried to follow him but her legs refused to obey—some unknown force held her feet fast to the ground no matter how much she strived to move forward. Finally, she cried out in frustration and took a step in the opposite direction, and found she could move quite freely that way.

It was enough. "Eden," she gasped, remembering what Brogan had told her. "Wake up," she said to herself. "Wake up!" She shook her head violently and slapped her cheeks until they stung. She let loose a cry of anguish, then stepped back over the water and began to run as fast as her sixty-seven-year-old legs would carry her. She had to find a way to wake from this dream before it was too late. She ran and ran until she thought her heart would explode. Then she felt herself falling through nothingness, without even a breeze to slow her descent.

She awoke with a gasp. She sat perfectly still for a moment as the physical world rushed back to her, and then she glanced at the clock. She had been asleep for most of the day. Was she too late? She grabbed her purse from the desk and hastily locked up and ran to her car. Then she peeled out of the gravel driveway, leaving behind nothing but dust and memories.

CHAPTER 15

I hate you! *I hate you!*" Eden was hysterical, pummeling Nuala with her fists. Nuala was breathing heavily. Their escape from the Merrow and the Tuatha Dé Danann had been too close, too sloppy. She ignored Eden's screams and looked around. Then she swore loudly. She was surrounded by pink: light-pink wallpaper with tiny white polka dots, a deep-pink carpet, and a poster of a pink unicorn on the wall. They were in Eden's bedroom.

"You brought us *here*? We have to get out of here. Now," she said, grabbing hold of Eden's wrists.

"No!" Eden roared back. "I don't want to go! I want my mum!"

"Listen to me! I know you're scared, but that's why we have to go. All the fighting you saw, that's what will keep happening if you stay here. That's what we're trying to get away from. You won't need to be afraid in Tír na nÓg. There's nothing scary there—no fighting, ever. Just magic and peace and music and happiness. And don't forget about your father."

"I want my mum," Eden said stubbornly.

"Of course you do. But your mum doesn't want to go to Fairyland. She wants to stay here with the monsters and the people doing all the fighting. I want to get you somewhere safe. Your mum can come if she wants—you just need to go first to show her how wonderful it is. It's not like you're leaving her behind. You're just opening the door for her. Without you, we're all trapped in this horrible place. You have to be brave enough to take us to Fairyland, Eden. We can't do it without you."

Eden didn't say anything, which Nuala took as a good sign. At least the girl had stopped screaming. "Let's talk about what happened. Wasn't the Merrow kingdom amazing?"

Eden nodded.

"What was your favorite part?" Nuala asked.

"I liked the candies that turned my hair different colors," Eden said with a small smile.

Nuala smiled back. "I liked that too. And did you like the big picture of Tír na nÓg, er, Fairyland?"

Eden nodded. "I thought I could jump right into it, like in *Mary Poppins!*"

"I know!" Nuala tried to sound enthusiastic. "I thought that too. Can you still remember what it looks like?"

"Uh-huh," Eden answered. "I think so."

"I know there was a lot going on when you tried to open the door to Fairyland the first time. Don't feel bad that it didn't work. Let's try again, okay?" Nuala said.

Eden sighed audibly, then walked over and opened the bedroom door. Nuala's breath, which she had been holding, came out in a snarl when the open doorway revealed only the austere hallway of the apartment.

"What happened?" she asked Eden, fighting to control her anger.

Eden was looking through the door, confused. "I don't know," she answered. "I really don't!" she insisted at the skeptical look on Nuala's face.

"Try again. Think harder." Eden closed the door and then opened it again, with the same infuriating result. "Damn it!" Nuala screamed. She was so close, so incredibly close, and there was no way she could turn back now. The Tuatha Dé Danann would accept no apology, they would show no mercy, especially not after what had happened to Oscar. They would hunt her down, even if it took the next several centuries to do so. Spending centuries in hiding was not a prospect Nuala relished. Why hadn't it worked? She had seen the painting with her own eyes; it had looked as real as any photograph. Was the girl trying to trick her?

"You're doing something wrong!" she hissed at Eden.

"No, I'm not! I'm doing it the same as I always do it!"

"Don't play games with me! Don't you want to see your father? He's not going to wait forever, you know! Try again!"

"No!" Eden yelled, and ran out into the living room.

Nuala ran after her. "You little bitch!" she screamed at Eden, who cowered behind the sofa.

"I hate you!" Eden screamed back. "Leave me alone!" Then she looked up and her eyes brightened. "Gran!"

Nuala twisted around to see Maeve standing in the doorway of the apartment. *Damn*, she thought. She knew this might happen. This was the worst place in the world they could be. Now she would have to kill the old lady. In less than a second, she was holding Maeve by the throat.

"What are you doing here, druid?" she hissed.

"Here…to…help…you," Maeve gasped.

Nuala dropped her hand, and Maeve fell choking to the floor. Eden darted out from behind the sofa and threw herself into her grandmother's arms. Maeve cradled the girl in her lap, still struggling to regain her breath.

"Really?" Nuala asked dryly. "You're here to help *me*?"

"I'm here to give you information," Maeve said, getting back to her feet and pulling Eden behind her, "not to fight you. I'm here alone. No one else knows you're here."

"And how exactly did *you* know we were here?" Nuala asked.

"I have just dream-walked with Brogan mac Airgetlam," Maeve said, looking her in the eye. "And he begs you not to sacrifice the life of this innocent child. He says that Lorcan will kill her the moment he realizes who she is."

"Lorcan needs her alive," Nuala spat. "She will be well treated."

"She won't! It's a lie!" Maeve said. "Brogan told me the truth about what really happened in Tír na nÓg. Brogan was killed in an ambush, not by Lorcan. Lorcan *could* have killed him, *could* have taken his power."

"Do you think I'm stupid, druid? Do you think I can't see what you're trying to do?"

"I speak the truth!" Maeve insisted. "The story you've been told was planted by Brogan and Rohan. After Brogan died, Rohan spread the word that Lorcan had killed him, but had failed to assimilate Brogan's power."

"And why would Rohan spread such a lie?"

"To stop the war. Brogan and Rohan thought your people would be less likely to follow Lorcan if they believed that he was unworthy to receive the gift of the sidhe. Obviously, they were wrong."

Nuala stared at the plump, frazzled woman. Maeve had some nerve coming here, but she didn't believe her story. Nuala had heard from Rohan himself how Brogan and Lorcan had fought, how the king had fallen. She had heard of Lorcan's rage when he had discovered he could not have the one power he so desperately wanted, which was now beyond his grasp. And then there was Lorcan's edict, his promise of a pardon and rewards for anyone who brought him the child. She knew taking Eden to him would make up for her part in the rebellion. She knew how badly he wanted to reopen the sidhe. He would not risk losing that power by killing the girl.

"You're lying," she said to Maeve. "You think you can trick me? Are you that great a fool?"

"No!" Maeve cried. "I'm telling the truth! You will deliver her to her death! I can help you. There is another way!"

"Why would you want to help me if you think I'm trying to kill her?" Nuala said through clenched teeth.

"She can't open the sidh, can she? That's because she still hasn't seen Tír na nÓg, not really. I know a way that might help, a druid way. The others won't suspect that I would help you, or even know that I can. But you have to swear to me that once she opens the sidh, you will leave her behind in our world. You'll have what you want—you'll be home."

Nuala considered Maeve, who was trembling almost as much as the child who clung to her leg. "What is this druid way?" she asked.

"A dream-share. I can link your subconscious minds, so Eden will be able to see the images of Tír na nÓg in your mind, in your memories."

"That won't work with her," Nuala snapped, impatient and still suspicious. "Mind powers don't work on the sidh-closers."

Maeve shook her head frantically. "This is different! It's a potion, one I've used before. There's no reason it wouldn't work."

Nuala glanced down at Eden, who was watching the exchange with large, frightened eyes. She didn't trust Maeve, but she had run out of ideas.

"Fine," Nuala said. "How do we do this dream-share?"

Maeve relaxed visibly. "Thank you," she said. "We'll need to go to my workshop at my house in the country. I have all the supplies I'll need there. And it's very private."

Nuala went over to the girl and lifted her up by the arm. Eden squealed, and Nuala saw Maeve's face crease with worry. "Eden. Open a sidh to your grandmother's house," she said.

"Wait," Maeve said, looking uncomfortable. "We'll need to drive, if I am to come with you. I'm unable to cross through the sidhe. It's an old enchantment, one Brogan placed on me. I have tried to lift it, but cannot." Nuala glared at her. "I am not trying to trick you, I swear it! I swear it on Eden's life!" she said.

Nuala narrowed her eyes at her, but then nodded. "So we drive. *You* drive. I'll sit with the child. I don't think I need to warn you about what will happen if you betray me."

Maeve nodded and said, "Just let me gather some food for Eden. She looks half-starved and dead on her feet."

Nuala waited impatiently while Maeve stuffed a bag with food. An hour later, they pulled up in front of the old house. Nuala had been there before, the day after she had taken the child, in the hopes that Eden could open the old sidh in Maeve's cellar. This was also where she had first set foot on Ériu soil, many years ago. She hated the place, despite all its picturesque charm, its white siding and dark-green shutters and gables. It was situated at the tip of a finger of land that jutted into the bay between Mill Cove and Halfmoon Cove. From the veranda, one could look out into Mahone Bay, past Little Fish and Big Gooseberry Islands, and into the ocean, and imagine a world beyond. To Nuala it represented the worst decision she had ever made—leaving the splendor of Tír na nÓg.

She had been naive, yes, but she had also been deceived. She had never met a human before, but she had heard the stories—tales of handsome, mighty warriors who could kill a wild ox with their bare hands, and who wrote poetry, sang, and gave counsel to the wise. She had heard the women were breathtakingly beautiful, and that to see one was to instantly fall in love. When the time had come to choose sides, she had rallied with the king to prevent Lorcan from waging war on the humans. She snorted in derision at the thought now. She couldn't believe she had been so wrong, so entirely misled. The humans she had encountered after fleeing through the sidh with Rohan and the rest of their small group of survivors were nothing like those in the stories. Instead of epitomizing valor and beauty, they seemed to revel in pettiness, sloth, and greed. They were pathetic, weak, ugly, and unexceptional in every way.

Eden was asleep when they arrived. Nuala shook her awake, and the girl looked around the yard, sleepy and confused.

"Where are we?" she asked.

"We're at the country house," Maeve answered. "You haven't been inside this building before, have you?" The older woman sounded almost chipper when speaking to Eden, but whenever the girl's eyes left her, her face crumpled back into lines of worry. "This is where I do my work," she said as she led them toward the small shop in the yard. She waved her arms in front of the door and muttered incantations under her breath before letting them in.

"Wow," Eden said, looking around. Along one whole wall of the shop was a long, low table. Above the table were several shelves filled with dozens of dark, carefully labeled glass jars. In one corner was an oversized armchair with colorful blankets draped over the arms. In another corner stood an old desk and a double-stacked bookshelf, filled with various gramaryes, books of herb lore, and several volumes of Irish legends. Nuala walked over to the bookshelf and ran her fingers along the spines of the *Lebor na hUidre*, the *Book of Leinster*, and the *Lebor Gabála Érenn*. She paused at this last one, the *Book of Invasions*, which she knew told the stories of the coming of the Tuatha Dé Danann to Ériu and their great deeds, and also of their defeat at the hands of the Milesians. *We have disappeared from history,* she thought, *but not for long. They will know our names again soon enough.*

"Gran, what do you mean, this is where you do your work? I didn't know you had a job," Eden was asking Maeve. Nuala was surprised when the woman answered truthfully.

"Well, I'm what you might call a magician of sorts," she said.

Eden gasped. "You are?"

Maeve smiled at her. "Mmm hmm. I'm a druid, which is a little different from the magicians in your stories. But I can do some magic. Like making the world's best peanut-butter sandwiches." She opened the bag she had brought and started slathering peanut butter onto bread. She handed the sandwich to Eden, and then started pulling jars from the shelves.

"What are you doing?" Eden asked through a mouthful of peanut butter.

"I'm making a tea for you to drink," Maeve said. "It will help you sleep. Then when you wake up, Nuala will go back to her home and you can go back to yours. How does that sound?"

"Good," Eden said, and then resumed eating.

"Tell me how it works," Nuala demanded.

"You'll enter the sleep state on equal footing," Maeve said, mixing and measuring various substances into a small pot. "Sometimes the two dreams blend together to form a new, shared dream. Other times one dream will dominate the other. It's impossible to predict. As you drink the tea, concentrate as hard as you can on your memory of Tír na nÓg. Once you enter the dream state, you should be able to direct your consciousness to the thoughts and memories you'd like Eden to share."

"How long will it last?" Nuala asked.

"Also difficult to predict," Maeve said, "but it shouldn't be more than a few hours." She lowered her voice. "You'll need to be in constant physical contact while you're in the dream state together. To break this contact could be very dangerous. The person who is sharing the other person's dream wouldn't be able to find their way out of the dream. I don't want to frighten Eden, so I'm going to ask you to just hold hands while you drink the potion and sit down.

Once you're asleep, I'll bind your hands together so there will be no chance of the contact breaking."

"And what's to stop you from killing me once I'm asleep?" Nuala asked.

"Because it would kill her too," Maeve said, handing each of them a cup.

CHAPTER 16

Cedar stood in the middle of a child's bedroom. She walked carefully around it, picked up the porcelain figure of a unicorn and set it back down, ran her hand along the frilled curtains, then finally sat on the flowered bedspread, a small pink-and-brown stuffed rabbit in her hands. She had just traveled three thousand miles in a single step, in a blur of wind and color, but somehow seeing this little girl's bedroom in her own house was by far the bigger shock.

So they were right. They had all been telling the truth. The apartment was empty, save for her and Finn and Rohan. As soon as they had arrived on the shores of Halifax, Rohan had called Nevan, who was already at Cedar's. Eden and Nuala were not there, she told him, but it looked as if they had been. Nevan had also tried to contact Maeve using telepathy. There had been no response, so she had gone to Maeve's apartment, only to find it empty. Rohan had insisted on visiting Cedar's place himself, and Cedar and Finn had gone along with him. He stood in Eden's room now, watching Cedar closely.

"Is this what you saw through the sidh?" he asked.

She nodded, unable to speak. "We're going to meet up with the others," Rohan said, turning to leave. He paused then, and said to Finn, "Why don't you stay here with Cedar for a while. Your mother says, well, she is quite sure you can help her remember." He gave Finn a significant look, and Finn nodded back, his eyes on Cedar. Then Rohan left the two of them alone.

After he was gone, Cedar looked up at Finn, who was standing in the doorway, watching her.

"What kind of a person am I," she whispered, "that I could so easily forget that I have a daughter?"

A tortured expression crossed Finn's face, and he sat down next to her. He took the stuffed rabbit from her hands and examined it, holding it up to his face and breathing in the scent.

"Nuala's power is very great," he said. "There are few of us who can resist her. Don't blame yourself."

She shook her head. "Nuala's power only works when she can tap into something true. They told me that's what happened with Jane. So it must mean that deep down inside, I don't…want…" She couldn't continue, but let the horrible truth hang in the air between them.

Finn wrapped his arms around her and pulled her to his chest. She didn't resist. She was too tired, too in need of comfort. "No," he whispered. "This is not your fault. I'm the one who left. I did everything wrong, Cedar. I left you alone, with good reason to hate me, to raise a child who reminded you of me every single day. It's not that you didn't want Eden. It's that you didn't want that constant reminder of me, of your pain. Don't you see the difference? You love her deeply—anyone can see that."

Cedar closed her eyes and breathed in slowly. Finn smelled just as she remembered, a mixture of honey, lime, and black pepper. Then she smelled something else familiar, and sat up and looked around.

"What is it?" Finn asked.

"Lavender," Cedar said. "I remember this room smelling of lavender." She reached under the pillow and pulled out a small sachet of dried flowers. She held it to her nose and inhaled.

"You're remembering!" Finn said. He hugged her again. When he moved to let go, she held on to him.

"Wait," she said. She tried to relax her body as he held her in his arms. She closed her eyes again.

"I remember…looking for something. I remember feeling panicked and…desperate."

Finn pulled her even closer. "Yes," he said, resting his chin on the top of her head. "You were looking for Eden. Finding her was all that mattered to you." Then he gently tilted her face up so he was looking her in the eyes. "It's all that matters to me, Cedar. Finding Eden, and being with you. Putting our family back together. Believe me, please—it's the only thing that has ever truly mattered to me."

Cedar met his gaze and felt something stir deep within her. It felt like a breath of wind coming in from the ocean, and it filled her with longing for something she couldn't quite grasp. She tried to hold on to it, but it slipped through her fingers, drifting away. As it passed, she saw in her mind a faded picture of a small girl with wild brown hair and eyes…eyes the same as those peering at her now. "Eden…" she whispered, determined to hang on to the fleeting memory.

The picture was starting to solidify in her mind when the sudden sound of shouting interrupted the silence. Cedar jumped, and the image of the girl dissolved into nothing.

Finn stood up first, and together they ran out into the hallway toward the shouts, which were coming from outside the front door. Cedar reached for the knob, but Finn pulled her behind him. "Wait," he said. Then he opened the door to find a very irate woman with purple bangs yelling at someone Cedar didn't recognize.

"You're like what, twelve? I don't know who you are, but I am Cedar's best friend and if she's in there, I'm going to talk to her! Don't think that I'm scared of your voodoo or whatever the hell it is you people can do!" Jane stopped her tirade when she noticed Finn standing in the doorway.

"It's all right, Brian," Finn said to the young man in the hallway. He looked at Cedar and explained, "Rohan thought it would be best if one of us stood guard."

"Ceeds, where the hell have you been?" Jane said once she had elbowed her way inside. "I've been calling you. And then I come over to check on you and this frakkin' young punk tells me I can't come in!"

Cedar gave Jane a hug, feeling ridiculously relieved to see someone from the "normal" world. She tried to look apologetic when she said, "I'm sorry, Jane, I should have called. I told you I was going to be away."

"You didn't say 'away,' you said 'busy.' There's a big difference. And I've never known you to be so busy that you couldn't answer your phone. You didn't even call in to work! Don't worry—I told everyone you were sick. So? Did you find her?" Jane asked.

"Um, no," Cedar said, looking sideways at Finn. "But we're getting close."

Jane turned her attention to Finn. "Is this…?"

"Yes. Jane, this is Finn. Finn, Jane."

Jane narrowed her eyes at Finn, who blinked and said, "I'm going to talk to Brian for a few minutes. See how guard duty is going." He stepped out into the hallway, closing the door behind him.

"I'm sorry for not calling," Cedar said again. "Things have been insane."

Jane shrugged and sat down beside Cedar. "I'm just glad you're okay. You are, aren't you? They haven't brainwashed you or anything?"

Cedar laughed nervously. "No, nothing like that."

"Good," Jane said. Then she leaned closer. "Holy crap, Ceeds, Finn is smokin' hot. I'm just saying. But what's going on?"

Cedar faltered as she tried to answer. "Um, well, apparently he's been living overseas all this time. But he came back to help," she finished lamely.

"Uh-huh," Jane said with a skeptical look. "Is it totally weird to see him again?"

"You could say that, yes," Cedar said with a small smile. "So, how are you?"

"I'm all right. Same old. But who cares about me? Are you sure you're okay? What have you been doing?"

Cedar thought about everything that had happened over the past couple of days—everything she could remember anyway—then shook her head. "I'm going to have to tell you later. I can't think straight right now."

Jane grabbed her hands and said, "You're going to find her, Cedar. I saw what Eden can do, and she's one smart kid. All she needs is a chance and a door, and she'll be back here with you. Right?"

Cedar nodded mutely.

"How's your mum holding up?" Jane asked.

"You know, I really have no idea," Cedar said, frowning. She tried to remember the last time she had talked to Maeve. "I spoke with her yesterday morning, I guess. But she wouldn't tell me where she was, or what she was doing. We tried to call her tonight, but she's not answering her phone."

Jane wrinkled her nose. "That's weird. I mean, as if you don't have enough to worry about."

Cedar tried to remember her recent conversations with her mother, but they seemed hazy to her. She wondered if they had spoken about Eden, and that's why she couldn't remember them clearly. "I just know that she's always hated Finn," she told Jane. "She's angry that I'm letting him and his parents help me."

"Seriously?" Jane said, her face the perfect picture of indignation. "You're her daughter. *She* should be helping you, no matter who else is. Jeez. She should at least be here with you. Although if I had someone who looked like Finn in my apartment, I wouldn't want my mother around either."

Cedar smiled despite her exhaustion.

"No offense, but you look like the walking dead," Jane said. "When was the last time you slept? Do you want me to stay here with you, or to come back after Finn leaves?" She looked at Cedar knowingly. "*If* he leaves?"

"No, no, I'm good," Cedar said, shaking her head. "Really, thank you, but I'll be fine. I'm just going to go to bed."

"Mmm hmm," Jane said, unconvinced. "Well, I'm going to call you tomorrow, and answer the damn phone this time, will you? I love you. Now go to bed." Jane gave Cedar a tight hug and let herself out.

Cedar leaned against the back of the sofa and closed her eyes. Her head was swimming, but she couldn't give in to her exhaustion yet. There were still too many mysteries, too many unanswered questions. She thought about her mother. *She's hiding something, something big, but do I even want to know? Can I handle any more revelations?* She shook her head to snap herself out of it. Yes, she could handle it. She was determined to find out the truth—all of it.

Her thoughts were interrupted by Finn's reappearance. He lifted her up by her arms and stood her on her feet, saying, "You need some sleep."

She frowned. "I don't want to sleep. I want to figure this out. Can we go back into the girl's room? I think I was starting to remember something before Jane showed up."

They stood together in the center of the pink room, and Cedar tried to recall the image of the girl. Nothing happened. She picked up a copy of *Little House on the Prairie* from the dresser, examining the cover. "I loved this book as a child."

When she looked up, she was surprised to see that Finn was grinning.

"Do you remember meeting when we were kids?" he asked.

Cedar stared at him, shocked. "We met when we were kids? When?"

He grinned at her. "You were ten years old, and scrawny as a barn cat. Not that I was much better. Remember how Nevan told you we escaped from the war in Tír na nÓg? The escape route we found was a sidh that happened to be in the cellar of Maeve's house, the house where you grew up. That's how she first got wrapped up with all of us. We weren't properly introduced, of course, but I saw you there when we first arrived."

"*What*? There was a sidh in our cellar? Did my mum know about it?" Cedar searched her memory, trying to remember a group of strangers emerging from the cellar, but nothing came to her. How could she have forgotten something like that?

Finn opened his mouth to respond, but it looked like he was struggling to form words. He closed his lips and frowned, then tried again. Finally he said, "She did, but you wouldn't have noticed it. The sidhe can be hidden. The way Eden opens them, with an actual door—it's not the way it was done before."

"Done before. By the High King, you mean," Cedar said.

"There were many sidhe once, all over the place," Finn said. He looked ill, as if he were trying not to throw up. Then he seemed to recover and said, "You should know the truth about why I left."

Cedar felt the familiar pang in her stomach and looked at her feet. "I know why you left," she said. "You're a god, or some kind of superbeing, anyway. I'm only human. It's pretty simple, isn't it?"

"No," he said forcefully. "It's not simple. Listen to me." He placed a hand on her shoulder, and she turned around, still looking at the floor.

"If I had stayed with you, they would have killed you," he said.

This made her look up. "Who would have killed me?"

"My people. Nuala, specifically."

"Because you're not supposed to be mixing with humans?"

"It's complicated, but yes. We couldn't risk exposure. If we got close to humans, they might begin to suspect, or we might be tempted to tell them the truth. But we're social beings, to put it mildly, so we were bound to slip up occasionally. That's where Nuala came in. She would be dispatched to make the human forget about whichever one of us had broken the rule. Sometimes it worked well. Even if the humans began to suspect something was up, they often didn't want to believe what their mind was telling them, so it was easy to convince them they had imagined everything, including their friendship or encounter with one of us. But other times…" He trailed off, looking at Cedar with worry.

"If she couldn't make them forget, she would just kill them," she finished for him.

He nodded. "We don't have any proof, and Rohan never endorsed it, not outright, but neither did he explicitly forbid it. We just never talked about it. Sometimes humans would just go missing, and if we asked her about it, she would shrug and say, 'They're not a problem anymore.' Her attitude toward humans was the fewer of them, the better. It's inexcusable, I know. I can't imagine what you must think of us."

Cedar pressed her lips together, saying nothing.

"I didn't want that to happen to you," he said, his eyes full of pleading. "It's my fault, I know. I knew the risk I was taking the first day we met; when we met again as adults, that is. I didn't think it would go anywhere. I didn't think it was possible I could love you so much. And I tried to be careful. I changed shape every time I left your place so they wouldn't see me coming and going. I had as little to do with my people as I could so I wouldn't have to lie to them so much. But then Nuala saw us together once, at the busker festival, and she could see your heart even if she couldn't see mine." He looked away, sorrowful lines marring his beautiful face. "She could see how much you loved me, how happy you were, and she hated you for it. Everyone thought she and I were meant to be together, but I didn't love her. I didn't even *like* her. When she found out, I knew she wouldn't settle for just erasing your memories. She wouldn't be able to handle the insult that I had chosen a human over her. She would want you dead."

Cedar picked at a loose thread on her shirt, trying to make sense of what he was saying. "So why am I still alive?" she asked.

"Only because of my father's position within our community," he answered, "and my mother's compassion, I suppose. I begged them to forbid Nuala to go near you. Finally, they agreed, but in return I had to swear an oath that I would leave you, that I would never contact you in any way or leave any trace of where you could find me. The break had to be absolute."

"It was absolute," Cedar agreed. She rubbed her temples, remembering the excruciating pain of those first few weeks, and the numbness that had followed.

And yet she could feel the anger she had been holding onto slip away, withdrawing like a slow tide. It was being replaced with a swirl of new emotions—horror that Nuala had dispatched other humans so cavalierly, relief that her own life had been spared, guilt over the way she had been treating Finn, when he had just been trying to protect her, and something else—a small shoot of hope that was breaking through the hard soil of her heart.

"I thought about you every single day," he said. His voice was quiet but strained, as if he longed to pack as much meaning as he could into each word. "Each day, I wondered where you were and what you were doing, if you were married, if you had a family. But I was forbidden to contact you, or even to watch you from afar. They thought that if enough time went by, I would forget about you; I would get you out of my system, come back and marry Nuala, and start producing offspring to further my race. But my people have long memories, and after seven years my feelings for you are as strong as they were on the day I last saw you."

Cedar could feel the tiny shoot of hope in her stirring, reaching. But she was afraid—afraid to give it air or room to grow.

"It doesn't change anything, does it?" she asked. "The rules still apply. You're still Tuatha Dé Danann, and I'm still human."

Finn put his arms around her. She stayed there, perfectly still. "Everything has changed, Cedar. Everything," he said. "The rules don't apply anymore. You already know about us, you know the truth about me. We have a child together, and we can have a life together. I never stopped loving you. But I need to know that you forgive me. Please forgive me for leaving you."

She reached up and rested her hand on his cheek. He leaned into it and closed his eyes. She had held onto her pain for so long, first as a way to hang on to him, and then as a way to protect herself from being rejected again. She saw herself clearly for the first time in years. She didn't want to be like that anymore, running from what she felt, trying to shut down the best parts of herself because they reminded her of him. She wanted to be whole again and happy and free. She wanted to believe him, to trust him—but first she had to trust herself, and let go.

"Yes," she whispered. "Yes, I forgive you."

As soon as the words left her mouth, his lips were on hers, one hand tangling in her hair and the other wrapping around her, pulling her close. She closed her eyes and felt the hurt of the last seven years dissolve away under the gentle pressure of his lips. Her body relaxed, and he tightened his grip on her, as if he were afraid she, too, would dissolve into nothingness. She remembered how it had been to kiss him, how it had seemed like nothing else in the world existed.

And then other memories started rushing in, crashing into her like rolling waves. The smell of a newborn baby, an olive-skinned toddler chasing seagulls around the harbor, a pink backpack bobbing behind a little girl on the first day of school. An argument over a man one wanted to know and the other wanted to forget. The midnight glow of pyramids in the Egyptian desert. A frightened child screaming for her mother on a pile of rocks in the Atlantic Ocean.

Gasping, Cedar pulled away from Finn and looked at him, her eyes burning.

"I remember her," she said. "I remember everything."

CHAPTER 17

It took Nuala a moment to realize her eyes were open. A dark mist swirled around her, thick and pungent with an unfamiliar smell. She peered ahead, trying to focus on her memories of Tír na nÓg. She pictured the fields of flowers that reached out to caress those who walked past, waterfalls of crystal nectar, trees that sang and danced and hung heavy with fruit, one bite of which would fill a person with energy for days. She strained her eyes and thought she could see vague outlines and forms in front of her. She moved a hand through the air and found that the dark mist clung to her skin. It was sticky, like cobwebs. She let go of Eden's hand to wipe it away, and Eden took a step forward.

"Wait," said Nuala. "Something isn't right. I don't know why it's not clear."

"I do."

The voice came from Eden, who turned around to face her. But it wasn't a small, frightened child who approached her now, moving through the fog as if it were the crystal air of a spring morning. She was taller, and her hair fell down her back in thick waves. She was wearing a dress of black gossamer lace that looked as if it had been woven from the same material as the mist that surrounded them. The gown clung to curves that did not belong to a six-year-old body. When Eden stopped in front of her, Nuala realized they were the same height now, staring eye to eye. The eyes that bored into hers were not wide with innocent wonder, but deep and old and fierce. Nuala looked away, and noticed for the first time that she herself was dressed in mottled gray rags.

"It is not clear because there are things you do not wish me to see," Eden said in a low, throaty voice. "But it does not matter. We are in my dream now."

"No," whispered Nuala, closing her eyes and trying to wrest control of the dream, focusing all her powers of concentration on one singular image, the glade where she had spent countless hours, no, years, listening to the water nymphs singing and bathing in the nearby stream. After several long moments she opened her eyes, fully expecting to see the sunlight dancing off the golden leaves, but instead she was looking into a pair of golden eyes that were now rimmed with mirth.

"While we're here," Eden said, "we might as well have a look around." She took Nuala by the hand and started pulling her along, fragments of the gossamer gown drifting off her body as she moved, only to be replaced by new wisps of the surrounding mist.

Nuala moved behind her, partly because she didn't want the girl-woman to get away, and partly because she had no choice—Eden's grasp was as strong as if someone had poured molten lead on their hands, sealing them together. As they moved through the darkness, Nuala heard a sound that made her skin crawl. She listened more closely. It was the sound of a small child crying. It echoed as if the child were alone in an empty, cavernous room. Nuala strained her eyes but could see nothing. They kept moving, and the child's crying faded, only to be replaced by a new sound. This, too, was of a child, who was calling out, "Mummy? Mummy!" The voice had the same echoing timbre as the one before it. She could hear footsteps, soft at first, then loud and fast, the sound of bare feet pounding against wood. The cries rose in pitch and volume until the child was screaming hysterically, "MUMMY! WHERE ARE YOU?"

Then it was quiet.

"Who—" Nuala began, but Eden turned and silenced her with glance.

"Listen," she said. Then the chanting began. It sounded like many voices; a dozen or a thousand, Nuala could not tell. They chanted in unison in the same dull, deadened tone. She could not see them, but she could sense that the chanters were rocking back and forth, back and forth, keeping rhythm with the words as they swayed through the air. "I hate you, I hate you, I hate you, I hate you…"

"Eden, stop," Nuala said, her voice swallowed up by the growing number of voices around her. "Stop!" she shouted. "Tell me what this is!"

Eden broke her viselike grip on Nuala's hand and spun to face her. They were only an inch apart, and Nuala gasped when Eden bared her teeth, pointed like a row of tiny daggers, and made a growling sound deep in the back of her throat.

"This is me," she hissed, raising her arms into the air in a sudden, swooping curve and thrusting her palms outward. As if a brisk wind had swept in, the mist blew away, rolling back like the morning fog off the ocean. Nuala looked around and gasped. They were standing in Tír na nÓg, just as she remembered it. Immediately, her body relaxed, and she could feel herself filling with the power freely given by the earth beneath her feet. The peal of a water nymph's laughter erased all memory of the ghostly children. A light breeze lifted her hair off her shoulders and caressed her body as if to welcome her home. Even so, she could tell this was Eden's dream, and not her own.

"How do you know?" she snapped. Eden's gossamer gown was now white, and she was idly weaving a chain of flowers the color of sunrise into her hair. "How do you know what this place is like?

Have you known all this time?" She stepped in front of Eden, fury pumping through her veins. If this was the girl's dream, and she knew Tír na nÓg so intimately, then she had been lying to her all along. Nuala felt suddenly and unexpectedly betrayed.

Eden looked up, as if she were surprised to see Nuala standing there. Then she looked around. "This place? Mmm, it *is* lovely, isn't it? But it's not what you are looking for."

"This is exactly what I'm looking for, you lying wench," Nuala snarled. "I know exactly where we are, and you must too, or else you wouldn't have been able to re-create this place. Tell me how!"

Eden appeared unfazed by Nuala's growing rancor and gazed around curiously.

"I don't believe I've been here before," she said. Her voice, which had been low and husky, was now light and airy. She reached up to a blooming tree and pulled down a bough heavily laden with purple blossoms, burying her nose in them and then laughing with delight.

Nuala stared at her.

"Oh, yes, I have seen this place before," Eden said, as if just remembering. "It came from you, from your memories."

Nuala's eyebrows shot up, and then relaxed. "Then the dream-sharing did work," she said. "Now we just need to wake up."

"Mmm, I don't think so," Eden said in singsong voice.

"What do you mean?" Nuala snapped.

"This is how you remember Tír na nÓg, not how it is."

"What are you talking about? This is exactly how Tír na nÓg is! This is my home!"

Eden released the tree bough and watched it bounce gently back into place. She moved slowly toward Nuala, shaking her head sadly.

"No," she said. "If this is how Tír na nÓg truly is, then dear Brighid's painting would have been enough for me to open the sidh." She spun around, waving her arms through the air. "This is Tír na nÓg as it was, and as it should be." Then she stopped and looked at the ground. "But now…well, I do not know what it looks like now, but it does not look like this anymore. The land has been poisoned. Some fear it is beyond repair. And you…you wish to help him who would utterly destroy it." Eden's shoulders slumped.

"I don't," Nuala protested. "I mean no harm to the land. I just want to go back to my home, where I belong."

Eden raised her chin and looked her captor in the eyes. "Don't deceive yourself, or insult me with your lies. You don't want to *go* home. You want to *rule* home. You hate Ériu because you have no power there, no influence, no admirers. That is what you crave, and you think if you return to Tír na nÓg, the status that was once yours will be returned to you tenfold. Only there may not be any Tír na nÓg left by the time he and you are done with it."

Eden glided toward Nuala until they were facing each other. She took a long finger and pressed it into the center of Nuala's chest.

"I have seen *your* heart, Fionnghuala. You see yourself on the throne of Tír na nÓg and of Ériu, putting those you think are beneath you in their rightful place. Your desires run deep, and dark." Then Eden's somber expression shifted, and she smiled brightly at Nuala, who blinked in surprise. "Shall we continue?" Eden asked.

"Continue where? We need to wake up. We need to find your father, remember?" Nuala ran to catch up to Eden, who was suddenly several paces ahead of her.

Eden threw her head back and let out a peal of laughter. "Yes, yes, my father! Waiting for me in Tír na nÓg!" Then she stopped without warning, and Nuala narrowly avoided running into her.

"Here are my friends," Eden said, waving her arm forward. "They wish to meet you."

Two rows of imposing figures stood in front of them, forming a corridor through which they were clearly expected to pass. The figures were dressed in fine robes that wrapped around them like closed butterfly wings. Circlets of gold and silver sat on their heads, and their skin shone like sunlight reflecting off a rippling stream. Eden's face broke into a grin, and she began to jog toward them.

"Wait!" Nuala called, and Eden turned around. "Who—" Nuala began, and then she looked closer at the figures and grew pale. "Are those…the Elders?"

"Yes!" Eden smiled. "And some of the others who have gone on."

"How do you know them?" Nuala asked. "How do you even know *of* them?"

Eden shrugged, causing the fine lace of her gown to ripple delicately. "I suppose a part of me has always known them. I only meet them here, however, in my dreams." She looked wistful. "But someday I shall see them face to face. At least, that's what they tell me." Without looking to see if Nuala was following, Eden bounced forward to greet her friends.

Nuala slowly followed. She watched as Eden hugged and kissed the first figures in the columns. They were laughing and smiling, too, as if nothing delighted them more than she did. But as Nuala approached, the smiles slid from their faces and were replaced by hostile frowns. She held her breath and tried to make herself as small as possible as she passed between their ranks. Some of the faces she had known before they had returned to the Four Cities. Others had fallen in battle before she was born, and she had only heard tales of their grandeur. The Dagda. Nuadu of the Silver Hand. Manannan mac Lir. Aengus Og. Lugh. Ogma. Dian Cecht. Bodb Derg. The columns stretched out before her and she rushed to catch up to Eden, but she could not outstrip the wave of anger and judgment that emanated from those who had made the Tuatha Dé Danann a race worthy of legend.

Finally, Nuala could see that Eden had stopped just ahead in a small clearing. She walked up to the girl, trying to control her trembling. She glanced over her shoulder and was relieved to see that the glaring Tuatha Dé Danann had disappeared and two rows of stately birch trees now stood on either side of where she had walked.

When she turned back around, a small cry escaped her lips. Across the clearing ran a river, and on the far bank stooped a woman dressed in nothing but her long, raven black hair. Crows perched on her shoulders and head as she squatted down to wash something in the running water. The clear water turned red and murky as it flowed past.

"The Morrigan," Nuala whispered. She had never met the Morrigan, and was glad for it, but she knew about her all the same. The Morrigan was the goddess of death. There was a time when every soldier in Ireland had lived in dread of stumbling upon a woman washing his clothes in the river, for it meant he would soon die in battle. Despite herself, Nuala moved closer, staring at the cloth in the woman's hands. Then the woman stood up and rung out the cloth, and Nuala screamed, for the very rags she was wearing on her violently shaking body were turning the river red with blood.

❦

Nuala flung her eyelids open like the door of an escape hatch. She saw nothing but blackness and reached out with the rest of her senses for something to hang on to. She tasted blood and heard a ghastly scream. She forcibly closed her mouth and the screaming came to a sudden stop. She tried to move and realized that one of her hands was tied to something, to another person. She jerked at it and heard a small moan from the body next to her. Then she heard a trembling voice from somewhere in the air above her.

"Nuala," the voice whispered. "Are you awake?"

Nuala looked in the direction of the voice, but still she could see nothing.

"Who are you?" she asked. "I can't see you."

"Open your eyes," the voice said.

Nuala started to say that her eyes *were* open, but then she realized that no, they were not. She did as the voice instructed and found herself looking into the lined face of Maeve McLeod.

"I'm awake," she said. She sat up, turning her head sharply to look at the other body in the large chair. Eden lay there, looking exceptionally small and frail, her hair fanned out on the arm of the chair and her cheeks flushed. Nuala breathed heavily through her nose as the humiliation of the dream returned to her.

She felt bile rising in her throat. She remembered the blood running from her clothes, staining the Morrigan's hands and dripping from her elbows. She remembered the glares of the Tuatha Dé Danann, the disgust in their faces as she passed between them. She could still hear the ghostly wails of the children echoing off the walls of her mind. It was just a dream, she told herself, Eden's dream, and none of it was real.

Eden opened her eyes, and Nuala watched her closely, relieved to see no trace of the older dream-Eden. She did not have to be afraid of this strange child. She was still in control.

"Eden?" Maeve said, leaning past Nuala to help her granddaughter sit up. "How do you feel?"

Eden looked over at Nuala, then back at Maeve, and then her face crumpled and she began to cry, her face pressed up against Maeve's chest. Maeve held her close and looked at Nuala in alarm.

"What happened?" she asked. "Did it work?"

"No, you useless hag, it didn't work. It was nothing but nonsense. You should be glad I don't kill you on the spot," Nuala said.

She snapped her fingers in front of Eden's face, causing the girl to look up. "Eden! Do you remember the dream? Do you remember what you saw?" For a moment, she thought she saw a flicker of the older Eden in the six-year-old's eyes, but then the girl shook her head, sniffling. "I don't know. I feel weird."

"What do you remember? Tell me!" Nuala snapped.

Eden cowered back into her grandmother's arms, which was difficult given the fact that her wrist was still bound to Nuala's. Maeve made soothing noises and stroked Eden's hair. "You had best answer her, dear. It's okay now; you're awake. Tell us what you remember from your dream."

"Flowers," the girl whimpered. "There were flowers."

Maeve looked up at Nuala. "You said the dream was nonsense, but she remembers something. Is it Tír na nÓg? Is it enough?"

Nuala stood up, dragging Eden with her toward the door. "Open it," she said. "Think about the flowers you saw in the dream." Eden opened the door, but they only saw the yard out front, and Maeve's blue car. Nuala slammed the door closed. She was not surprised that it hadn't worked. If what Eden had said in the dream was right, then even she herself did not know what Tír na nÓg looked like anymore. She sat back down in the armchair, frustration and fear and desperation building inside of her, wishing she could set something on fire or tear apart a boulder with her hands. She was running on borrowed time, but she would not give up. With Eden at her disposal, she could stay one step ahead of the rest of the Tuatha Dé Danann rebels. Soon they would wish they had just let her go, instead of pursuing her like a hound pursues a hare.

She whirled around and snapped, "What time is it, druid?"

"Six o'clock in the morning," Maeve said, "on Tuesday. You were asleep a long time."

"A long wasted time," Nuala snarled, her fear fueling the vitriol in her voice. How much closer were Rohan and the others to finding her now? Had the druid alerted them? She knew she had stayed in one place for too long. They needed to leave, and now—but there was still the matter of the druid. She closed her eyes and opened her mind, reaching out to Maeve. She delved deep into the druid's heart, and found what she had seen before. Maeve's desires were simple, strong, and glaringly obvious. All she wanted was for Eden to be safe. Nuala almost smiled. This would be easy.

Maeve, however, anticipated her. "You don't have to charm me," she said, her voice urgent. "I *want* to help you. Please. I will be more effective if I'm acting of my own free will."

"I doubt that," Nuala said, her voice dripping with scorn, "but I'll give you one more chance. Then we can try it my way."

"Let me go to Cedar," Maeve said. "She will tell me everything she knows. It may give us an idea."

Nuala stepped close to her and bent down so she was staring Maeve in the eyes. "And how do I know you will not betray me?" she asked softly.

Maeve did not quail under Nuala's glare. "Because I want to keep my granddaughter away from the Tuatha Dé Danann—*all* the Tuatha Dé Danann. If Rohan and his people find her, they will heed the prophecy and take her to battle against Lorcan. They will think nothing of her life, her safety. Frankly, I don't care about your world, or your war. I only want my grandchild to be safe, and to stay that way. I will take her far from here, and hide her, using everything at my disposal. And I won't fail this time," she added bitterly.

Nuala considered this, and then nodded. "Then go. Now."

Eden suddenly yanked hard on the ropes that bound her to Nuala and strained toward the door, knocking Nuala so off-balance that she almost fell. She gave Eden's arm a firm tug, twisting it sharply enough for the girl to howl in pain.

"Do that again and I'll rip your arm right off," Nuala hissed. Eden kept screaming and started flailing at Nuala with her free arm.

"Do you want your grandmother to live, you useless child?" Nuala snarled. "Shut up and do as I say, or I'll chop her into little bits, I swear it!" She stopped, breathing heavily, then spoke in a softer voice. "Do as I say and you can go home soon." She opened the door and walked out into the sunlight, dragging Eden with her. She turned around to see Maeve still standing inside the workshop, a tortured expression on her face. "Go! Hurry!" Nuala yelled, and stood watching as Maeve fastened the building's locks, cast several protection spells, and ran to her car. As Maeve drove away, Nuala dragged the hysterical child toward the empty house.

CHAPTER 18

For a moment, Cedar felt perfectly happy. She felt well rested for the first time in days, and she could feel the warmth of Finn's body against her back. The weight of his arm draped over her waist was like an anchor, tethering her firmly to this peaceful place. She could hear the birds singing outside her window, their sound carried on the same light breeze that was stirring the muslin curtains. Finn's breath on her neck was slow and steady, and she tried to keep from moving, wanting to fix this moment of perfection firmly in her memory. Then she thought of Eden.

"Oh," she said, the sound slipping from her lips like a child's dropped toy.

Instantly, Finn's eyes were open. He propped himself up on one elbow and leaned over to see her face. "What is it?" he asked.

She turned and burrowed into his chest, seeking the strength and safety it promised before she made herself vulnerable to reality, and whatever cruel plans it had for her today.

"It was just that for a moment I felt happy, like everything was okay. Then I remembered that nothing is okay. And it probably won't ever be okay again."

Finn wrapped her in his arms and cradled her like a small child, perhaps expecting her to cry or scream. She did neither, but shifted slightly to draw herself nearer to him. She closed her eyes and tried to fight off the wave of despair that threatened to crash over her.

"We're going to find her, Cedar," he said. There was no hint of uncertainty in his voice, and she drew strength from his confidence.

She allowed herself the luxury of a few more seconds in his arms, then wiggled her way out of them and sat up on the edge of the bed.

"I'm ready," she said.

"For what?"

"For whatever this day will bring. For whatever I have to do to find her." She allowed herself a hint of a wry smile. "After the last few days, nothing can surprise me."

"Glad to hear it," he said, tossing back the covers and swinging his long legs out of bed. "But first, breakfast."

"You make breakfast," she told him. "I'm going to shower." Once she was under the hot, steaming water, she was tempted to stay there all day, but she forced herself to keep moving. She had just pulled on a clean T-shirt and pair of jeans, and was towel-drying her hair when she heard a knock at the front door.

She hurried out of the bedroom and said, "I'll get it," to Finn, who was coming out of the kitchen.

"Wait," he said. "Let me get it."

She rolled her eyes, but stood back and watched as he opened the door.

"Mum!" she exclaimed. Maeve was standing in the hallway, being carefully watched by Brian, who was apparently still on guard duty.

Maeve started to enter, but stopped short when she saw Finn.

"Good morning, Mrs. McLeod," he said, nodding at her.

"Finn," she said, seeming stunned. Then she recovered herself. "Good morning," she said stiffly.

"Where on earth have you been?" Cedar asked. "Everyone has been looking for you. They went to your apartment and you weren't there, and we've been calling your cell. I was starting to get really worried."

"I'm sorry, dear," Maeve said. "I've been busy."

"Doing what? What is going on with you?" Cedar closed her eyes, trying to control her frustration.

Maeve glanced at Finn, who was watching them silently. "Could you give us a minute, Finn?" she asked.

Finn's expression was unreadable as he studied the older woman. "Yes," he said slowly. "I'm sure Cedar has many questions for you, questions I am unable to answer. Perhaps you could answer them. I would be most grateful if you would." He nodded at them both, then turned and walked out of the apartment.

"What was that?" Cedar asked as soon as Finn left.

"That was Finn's not-so-subtle way of saying I should tell you the truth. The whole truth," Maeve answered, sitting down on the sofa. "And it's about time you knew. Sit, dear, we have a lot to talk about."

Cedar sat. "The whole truth about what?" Her mother looked dreadful. Her gray hair, usually smooth, was frizzy and tangled, and her clothes looked like she had slept in them. The wrinkles in her face were deeper than usual, and the circles under her eyes were so dark they looked like bruises.

"Did they tell you what I am?" Maeve asked without looking at her.

Cedar frowned. "What you are? No. They didn't tell me anything about you."

"Is that so? I'm surprised. Well, best you hear it from me, anyway. I'm a druid."

"A what?"

"A druid. I am one of the very few humans schooled in a certain kind of ancient knowledge…and magic."

215

Cedar stared at her mother. While she had said she was ready for anything, she wasn't sure she had meant this. She swallowed. "Is that why you've been acting so weird? Because you didn't want me to find out? How is that even possible? How could I live my whole life with you and not notice that you were a...a druid?"

"Don't blame yourself for not noticing. I wanted you to grow up as normal as possible, and not as the daughter of what some would call a witch. I used my arts on the rarest of occasions, and even then only out of necessity. I have had to revive my skill over the past few days. I've been doing everything in my power to find Eden. It's why I had to stay away." There was a pause, and Maeve's voice softened. "I am sorry for not telling you about it. It's one of a lifetime's worth of regrets."

Cedar didn't know what to say to this. Was nothing in her life as it had seemed? "Why didn't you tell me, especially given everything that has happened?" she demanded.

"I should have told you," Maeve said, "but I didn't think you would believe me. And, I'll admit, I was angry that you chose to go with them. It's no excuse, I see that now."

"You didn't think I would believe you?" Cedar asked incredulously. "After seeing what Eden could do?" She exhaled loudly. "You're just like the rest of them. You didn't think I'd be able to handle the truth, so you hid it from me."

"I thought I was doing the right thing. I was trying to find Eden. I'm *still* trying to find Eden."

"How? How have you been trying to find her?"

"I've been using the art of divination to try to get some handle on where Nuala may have taken Eden. There are many methods of seeing beyond, and I've tried every way I know how."

"Did it work? Did you see them?" Cedar asked.

Maeve shook her head, her eyes sliding to the floor. "No, it didn't work." She looked up at Cedar, her eyes filled with a sudden eagerness. "There is more for us to talk about, but first, tell me what *you* have been doing. What is Rohan doing to find Eden? What is his plan?"

"I don't know what his plan is," Cedar admitted, wrenching her mind away from her mother's revelation and back to the events of the last few days. "I don't know if he has one. He doesn't exactly confide in me. He'd prefer it if I stayed out of the way, actually."

Cedar gave her mother an abbreviated version of what had happened since they had last talked, and took some satisfaction in Maeve's shocked reaction.

"I was right. You never should have gone with them," Maeve said, leaning back into the sofa's cushions. "You could have been killed." Cedar started to protest, but Maeve waved her hand. "Wait. I need to think," she said, and Cedar fell silent. She wished she could tell what her mother was thinking, and was about to ask when Maeve muttered, "That must be why it didn't work. Tír na nÓg has changed since the war."

Cedar looked at her sharply. "What do you mean? You think that's why Brighid's picture didn't work?"

"Perhaps," Maeve said, her eyes showing that she was still deep in thought. "I've never been to Tír na nÓg, but I know it is more than just a place. It's like a person, with a soul and a life of its own. Nothing changes a person's heart more than war or betrayal, and Tír na nÓg has seen too much of both. There's no doubt it has changed. It might be unrecognizable."

Cedar stared. Who *was* this woman beside her? Usually their talk consisted of Eden's schedule and not a whole lot more. She was starting to realize she had no idea who her mother really was.

Maeve took Cedar's hands. "I've been doing a lot of thinking over the past few days. It's time you knew the whole truth."

Cedar frowned. "I thought you just told me the truth. You're a druid."

"That's part of it, but it's not all. There is a lot more I haven't told you. I've told you who I am. Now it's time for you to know who *you* are."

Cedar's breath caught in her throat. Who *she* was?

Maeve continued. "You and I, we haven't always had the smoothest relationship. I'm sure you think I care more about Eden than I do about you. I do care for Eden. But I love you so much, Cedar. And it"—her voice broke, and she sniffed, squeezing Cedar's hands tightly—"it has been an honor to be your mother. I know you might despise me once you know the truth, and you'll be well within your rights to do so. I didn't ever want to face this moment. I thought I could put it off forever, but I suppose it's inevitable, things being what they are. And even if it wasn't, you would still deserve to know exactly who you are."

Cedar sat perfectly still, hardly daring to breath lest her mother change her mind. She didn't say a word, or ask any of the thousand questions burning on her tongue. She just sat, and eventually Maeve began speaking again.

"You are not my biological daughter," she said, speaking slowly, as if to gauge Cedar's reaction. Cedar's face was blank, but inside the truth was erupting like a volcano that had long lay dormant. It had never crossed her mind that she wasn't who she had always thought she was, but now it made perfect sense. She wondered why she hadn't seen it before.

Maeve continued. "When I was young—too young—I met and fell in love with one of the Tuatha Dé Danann. He was beautiful, and I was too, back then. He had a wife in Tír na nÓg, but I didn't know about her until later. He came and went as he pleased and I, fool that I was, just sat around waiting for him. It was he who arranged for me to become a druid. I thought it was so we could be closer to each other, but now I wonder if he was just grooming me to be his servant."

The pain in Maeve's voice was so strong that Cedar almost reached over and took her mother's hand. But she remained still, listening. "Then he left," she continued. "He said there was a war brewing in Tír na nÓg, and so there was. We had been together for years, and I didn't look seventeen anymore. I thought he was leaving me because I was too old or was outgrowing my usefulness to him. He didn't leave me with nothing, mind you. He gave me the house you grew up in, and a full bank account. But he left all the same, and why not? Why would he stay with me when he had a wife among the Tuatha Dé Danann, one who would always be as beautiful as he was?"

There was a pause, and Maeve bit her lip. Cedar remained still, transfixed as the story of her life unfolded before her.

"And she *was* beautiful," Maeve continued. She stared off into the distance, as though she had forgotten Cedar was there. "Her hair was as golden as mine was red, the color of the midday sun." She paused for a moment, and Cedar could tell she was somewhere very far away. "When Brogan left, he assured me I would never hear from him again."

The name Brogan sounded familiar to Cedar. She was sure she had heard it before in connection with the Tuatha Dé Danann, but she couldn't remember where, or why it was important.

"But I did hear from him again," Maeve said. "Almost a year later. He came to me in a dream, saying that terrible things were happening in Tír na nÓg and I was his only hope of saving"—she paused and tried to calm her voice, which had started to tremble—"of saving his wife and their unborn child." Maeve raised her chin so that her eyes, shining with unshed tears, met Cedar's, which were wide with growing comprehension.

"That child was you," Maeve said.

That child was me, Cedar repeated inside her head. *I'm one of them.* It didn't make any sense. "That's…that's impossible," she protested, once she had found her voice. "I'm human, like you are. I don't have special abilities or anything. The Tuatha Dé Danann have that sound they emit to each other, the Lýra. I don't have that; if I did, they would hear it."

Maeve looked absolutely wretched. "Let me finish, and you will understand." She sighed deeply. "I was never very good at denying Brogan anything. As angry as I was with him—well, I was heartbroken more than anything. I still loved him. I thought if I helped him, if I showed him I was willing to help even his wife, he might come back to me.

"He told me all the sidhe between Tír na nÓg and earth had been sealed, except for one, which no one knew about but the two of us—the one he had created in my cellar, which I couldn't go through. He wanted to send Kier, his wife, to me for safekeeping until the war was over and she could return. I agreed. I went down to the cellar and waited to receive this rival." She looked up at Cedar, and there was a flash of anger in her eyes, even three decades later. "I hated her," she said, "but I loved Brogan and would have done anything to help him, even then.

"When Kier came through the sidh, she was badly wounded. The Tuatha Dé Danann are strong, much stronger than humans. They heal quickly and do not succumb to old age or sickness, but if they are wounded gravely enough, they will die. She was covered in blood and screaming from the pain, not at all what I had expected. She was so far along, and clutching her swollen stomach as if to keep you inside. I made a tea that would help with the pain so I could see to her wounds. I'm not a healer, but all druids learn basic medicinal skills, and I thought if I could just stop the bleeding, her body would be able to heal itself. But she had already lost too much blood, and then she started screaming again…and that's when you came into the world."

Cedar stood up and started pacing the room. The shock of Maeve's revelation was wearing off, and she could feel the anger building within her. Her own life, her own identity had been nothing more than a lie.

"What happened to her?" she asked.

"She knew she was dying," Maeve said, a note of defensiveness in her voice. "She was barely strong enough to hold you. She knew who I was; she clutched my hand and begged me to take care of you, for the sake of the love I bore her husband. You were so helpless, and I could see him in you. How could I say no?"

Maeve took a deep breath. Cedar wondered what could possibly be coming next.

"And then she asked the most extraordinary thing. She asked me to help her make you human."

Cedar stopped pacing. "Why would she want me to be human?"

"She was terrified, for your sake. Your father was the High King. She knew Lorcan wouldn't stop until he had tracked down and snuffed out Brogan's line completely. But she knew she wouldn't be around to protect you. She wanted to hide you, to give you the best disguise she could so that he would never be able to find you. And she needed my help; her power was draining. To change the very nature of a being is a complex and dangerous branch of magic, one I had certainly never attempted before. It was far beyond my ability, but it was something she could not manage alone either, not in her weakened state, maybe not at all. This is why druids and the

221

Tuatha Dé Danann are meant to be together, because together we are capable of greater magic than we are alone.

"So I made the preparations as best I could. I created a potion, and she supplied the one missing ingredient—her own blood, given freely. I drank it, and then together we spoke the incantation. At first, it didn't seem to be working, but then, as we chanted, fresh wounds opened on my body, and she pressed herself against them, allowing the blood from her wounds to flow into mine. In so doing, she bound her life force to mine—giving me power equal to her own for a time. Together, it was enough to complete the spell, to make you human. She poured everything she had into you, through me. When it was over, she was gone. She had not even saved enough energy to keep herself alive. And I was holding a completely human child."

Cedar realized she had stopped breathing and struggled for a moment to fill her lungs with air. For several heartbeats, she just stood there, reeling. "And my father?" she asked. "I mean, the man you told me was my father, who died when I was a baby? Did he even exist?"

Maeve shook her head.

"Why?" Cedar wailed. "Why didn't you tell me this before?" Finally, she had answers, and yet she had never suspected this. All her life she had believed she was normal—a fatherless child, a struggling artist, a woman in love, then a woman abandoned, a single working mother. Now that foundation had cracked, and she could feel herself falling.

"She made me swear to never tell you, or anyone, who you were," Maeve said, looking at Cedar with desperate eyes.

"But the rest of the Tuatha Dé Danann know, don't they?" Cedar accused. "It explains everything—the half truths, the whispers. No wonder they look at me with pity and revulsion. I'm a freak in both worlds. I'm not really human, but I'm not like them either, not anymore. This is what Finn wanted you to explain, isn't it? How is it that everyone knows the truth, except for me?"

"I had no choice but to tell them!" Maeve protested. "Rohan called me as soon as you left their house the day you met them. He demanded that I explain how you could have birthed a Danann child. Riona came by, trying to see Eden in order to prove their suspicions, but I wouldn't let her in. But they insisted I meet with them, which I did—alone—after you returned home that day. As I said, I had no choice. He had the goblet of Manannan mac Lir; I couldn't lie to him. And then he made me swear not to tell you, not yet. It was Eden they wanted, not you. They thought if you knew too much, you would make things more difficult. You're the daughter of the High King…but a human. It's something that in their minds should not be. I swore an oath not to tell you who you were, but I'm breaking it now, for you. Don't you see? And Finn, he swore an oath too, but he wanted me to tell you."

"*Why has everyone sworn an oath to lie to me?*" Cedar raged, her face distorted. "My whole life has been nothing but lies! Am I so weak, so pathetically human you didn't think I could handle knowing who I was—or who I could have been?"

Maeve stood up and held out her hands in a calming gesture. "No, Cedar, it wasn't like that. I wanted to tell you—"

"Did you?" Cedar interrupted. "If you had really wanted to tell me, you would have. Your oath isn't stopping you now, is it? I bet you enjoyed keeping it a secret, knowing you had Brogan's child all to yourself, telling yourself you were keeping me safe while clinging to the memory of the man who rejected you!"

Maeve winced as if Cedar had struck her across the face, but Cedar didn't stop. It was too late now; this storm was going to run its course. "All of this is your fault! If I had known who I was, none of this would have happened! Now Eden is gone, and who knows what's going to happen to her!"

"She'd have been in the same amount of danger if I had told you the truth!" Maeve snapped back, her eyes blazing. "Everything I have done has been to protect you, and to protect that little girl. If I had told you who you are, and who she is, you would have delivered her straight to them. They give too much weight to that damn prophecy."

"What are you talking about? What prophecy?" Cedar asked, vaguely remembering Deardra and Rohan's argument on the beach.

"Eden is the dyad, don't you see?" Maeve said. "*The dyad that should not be will rise from the ashes and purge the land of the coming poison.* They've been clinging to that prophecy ever since Lorcan gained power. If they find her, they'll raise her to be a warrior and send her to fight Lorcan. That is why I didn't tell you about what she might become. I needed to keep you away from them! But you went to them anyway."

"Did you think I wouldn't find out?" Cedar asked, her cheeks still burning with rage. "That I wouldn't wonder when she started opening magic doors all over the place?"

"I honestly didn't think it would happen," Maeve said, her shoulders drooping. "I thought it was impossible."

"Why?"

"Only two members of the Tuatha Dé Danann can produce another, and I thought you were, well, you *are* human. That's why Eden fits the prophecy. She's the impossible result of mating between a Danann and a human. But maybe I was wrong, maybe there is some Danann left in you, or..." Maeve trailed off, looking at Cedar as though she'd never seen her before.

"What?" Cedar snapped.

"I just realized how…" she stared at Cedar for a few more seconds, her mouth slightly open. Then she closed it firmly and shook her head. "Nothing. It's nothing," she said.

At once, Cedar fired up again. "Have you heard anything I've said?" she shouted. "No. More. Secrets."

Maeve opened her mouth again to respond, but before she got a word out her eyes fell on something behind Cedar. All at once, the blood drained from her face as she stared in undisguised astonishment over Cedar's shoulder. Cedar turned to see what had caught Maeve's attention and noticed that the necklace Finn had given her in New York was lying on one of the bookshelves behind them.

Maeve's voice was barely a whisper. "Where did you get that?"

Cedar glanced at the necklace again and then back at Maeve, who was swaying slightly on the spot. "The necklace?" she asked. "Finn gave it to me. It's Riona's. He called it a starstone or something."

"I know what it is," Maeve said in the same ghostly whisper. "Yes, of course, that might work."

"What are you talking about?" Cedar asked, coming to stand right in front of Maeve. She waved a hand in front of Maeve's unblinking eyes, which were focused on something far away. "Are you okay?"

Maeve looked at her suddenly. "Yes," she said. "I'm fine. But I must go."

"Go? Go where?" Cedar demanded, hands on her hips. "I'm not letting you do this again. Tell me what's going on!"

Without a word, Maeve picked up her purse and headed for the door, almost colliding with Finn in the hallway. She pushed past him, her purse swinging wildly as she ran down the hall.

Cedar followed Maeve into the hallway and stared after her with an open mouth. Then Finn spoke in a soft voice.

225

"She told you?"

Cedar should have been angry with him for not telling her. She wanted to rage and scream and accuse him of horrible things, but the weight pressing down on her was so heavy she could barely breathe.

She nodded, her mouth in a tight line. "Why didn't you tell me?"

For such a powerful being, he looked incredibly fragile at that moment, like smoke drifting from a recently blown-out candle. When he spoke, it was ever so gently.

"I didn't know, not when we were together. I had no idea. Last week, when Rohan first told me, I wanted to rush to you, to tell you everything, but he made me swear not to say anything. He made me promise that if I told you, I would leave you again." He shook his head. "So I stayed silent, hoping you would find out another way, hoping that when the time came you would find it in your heart to forgive me…again."

Cedar stared at the spot where Maeve had disappeared around the corner. She didn't want to see his face right now. She didn't want be reminded of what she had lost. "Just go," she said. "Go back to your people. They're always going to come first with you."

"Cedar, please believe me," he pleaded. "I learned who your parents were when I was summoned back here, when they told me about Eden. It was only days ago. But it doesn't change how I've always felt about you. I didn't lie to you."

Cedar looked up at him, disbelief written across her face. "You don't think you lied to me? Pretending all this time not to know who I was? Letting me think Eden was special just because you're her father, and I had nothing to do with it?"

She shook her head, and her voice broke when she said, "I'm so stupid. How did I not see it? I was so convinced that I was completely normal. I *am* normal. Human," she corrected herself. "I thought Lorcan just wanted Eden so he could open the sidhe, but it's more than that, isn't it? She's the heir to the throne. Assuming I don't count, and I'm sure everyone agrees that I don't, she's the only heir of his greatest rival, which also makes her his greatest threat." Her throat seized up, and when she could speak again she whispered, "There's no chance he'll let her live."

"He will. He needs her alive, remember? Besides, it hasn't come to that yet," Finn said firmly.

"How could you possibly know that?" Cedar asked, her voice rising with frustration. She stalked back into the apartment. Finn followed and immediately picked up where he had left off.

"Don't start thinking that way. Don't give up. She is still here, still in this world, I'm sure of it. If the painting didn't work, there's no other way for her to get to Tír na nÓg. Nuala can't run forever. We will find her. We'll find Eden."

He tried to put his arms around her, but she jerked away and glared at him. "No," she said. "I don't want to be with you, Finn." She spoke every word clearly and firmly, even though she felt a little bit of herself dying with each syllable that left her mouth.

For a moment he looked stunned, and then, to her surprise, angry.

"This isn't just about you, you know," he said, with an edge to his voice. "Eden is my daughter too."

She looked at him coldly. "You impregnated me. Don't delude yourself into thinking you are her father in any way other than that. You've never even met her."

"And I will never get to meet her if you give up on her! Do you have any idea what it's like for anyone else? Yes, they lied to you, they didn't tell you who you were, and I'm not saying they were right to do that. But in Maeve's case, it was only to keep you safe.

She didn't have to raise you, but she did, as a single mother, and you know how hard that can be.

"I'm not blaming you," he said in a quieter voice. "I have no idea what you went through when I left or what it's been like to raise Eden on your own. I will never forgive myself. But you need to realize that other people have made sacrifices too. Maeve devoted her entire life to you. I spent seven years in exile to keep you safe from Nuala, knowing I would spend every day of the rest of my life aching for you. My parents, and the others like me, fled the land they loved out of the desperate hope that they might find Kier and her child here, only to be told by the druid that they were dead. Can you imagine how they felt, more than two decades later, when they realized Brogan's daughter was alive after all—the hope that must have inspired? But then to find you had been made human…all the hopes they had treasured for years shifted to Eden, who was clearly one of us. Then she was taken, from them as much as from you." Cedar started to speak, but Finn held up his hands and continued.

"I'm not saying she belongs to them, or that they have any claim on her. They don't. She's your daughter, and you're right, I haven't been a father to her. But I *want* to be. If you could only try to understand what she means to me, what she means to all of us. She is more than a way for us to get home. She's even more than our rightful queen. She is *hope*. She's a second chance, a sign that all is not lost, that maybe, just maybe, everything sad can be undone. And we're not ready to give up on her yet."

Cedar could feel his gaze, but she kept her eyes trained on the floor. She tried to imagine escaping a war zone and starting over in a strange land, with only a slim hope of ever returning home. She remembered being curled up on Maeve's lap as a girl, and wondered how it had felt for Maeve to raise a child born to the wife of the man she loved. She thought of her own daughter, and how hard it had been at times to look at her without seeing Finn, and how much more difficult it must have been for Maeve. And yet Cedar had never felt unloved as a child. She thought of Finn, and tried to imagine being forced to leave him in order to save his life. She would have done it in a second.

Tears pricked at her eyes, but not from anger this time. "I haven't given up on her," she said softly.

"And neither will I," said Finn, his face grim with determination. "Ever. Nor will I give up on you."

There was a pause, and then he asked, "Did Maeve have any new information? Did she tell you what she's been doing?"

"Just druid stuff. Divination and other things out at the old house. But she said it didn't work, and then she just took off."

He raised an eyebrow. "Really? Why?"

She told him about Maeve seeing the necklace and asking about it, and about how strangely she had reacted.

His face darkened as he considered this. He walked over and picked up the necklace, studying it.

"What do you think it means?" she asked.

"I'm not sure, but I don't think it's good. Why else would she leave so suddenly, without any explanation? If she has a lead on Eden, she should tell us."

"She doesn't trust you," Cedar said. "Any of you. She thinks you want Eden to lead you into battle against Lorcan, because of some prophecy. Do you?" She remembered what Rohan had said the morning after Eden had disappeared. *We will take full responsibility for her. She needs to be raised as part of this family—her true family.*

Finn exhaled slowly. "No, I don't. I don't set much store in prophecies. There are too many interpretations, too many ways they can be twisted to suit one's own ends. But not everyone feels that way. There *are* those who think she is the dyad, and that she will play a key role in restoring Tír na nÓg to peace." He paused for a moment, considering. "I suppose that helps explain why Maeve hates us so much, if she believes we only want to use Eden. Between that and what happened with Brogan, I can't say that I blame her. But I don't like this—her leaving like that. If she's acting against us…" he trailed off, his expression dark.

Cedar bit her lip. "I'll call her, find out where she's headed. But…you should go."

The expression on Finn's face almost made her change her mind.

"I'll call you later," she said. "I want to be alone right now. I need to wrap my head around all this—who I am, who my mother is, who my daughter is. I need to figure out whom I can trust. And honestly, I don't know if that's you anymore."

CHAPTER 19

Maeve urged her car to go faster as she sped toward the old house. It was almost over; she could feel it. She had found a way to free Eden and send Nuala back to Tír na nÓg. If it worked, it would be worth all the lies.

She had called Nuala as soon as she left Cedar's apartment. "I think I've found another way," she had whispered. Nuala had sounded annoyed—and very far away—but Maeve was certain she would show up, and she would have Eden with her. Sure enough, when she pulled into the driveway, she saw two figures outside the workshop. Eden was sitting slumped on the ground. She rushed toward her. "Eden!"

Eden looked up but did not stand. Instead, she gazed at Maeve with dull eyes filled with wariness. Maeve felt the eyes stab into her, and she winced. *It will all be over soon*, she thought, and someday Eden would understand that everything she had done was for her sake, to keep her safe.

"Are you okay, dear?" she asked the girl on the ground.

Eden shrugged.

"Well?" Nuala asked impatiently.

Maeve looked nervously back at Eden. Then she said to Nuala, "It's not something a child should see."

Nuala rolled her eyes. "If you think I'm letting her out of my sight for a moment, you're stupider than I thought. She's going to have to deal with it, whatever it is. Now hurry up. What did you discover? What is their plan?"

Maeve spoke quickly and hoped Eden was tuning them out, since she was staring off in the opposite direction.

"I was at Cedar's, trying to find out what they were up to," she began, "and I saw on her bookshelf one of the seeing amulets, a star-stone. It was set into a necklace; she told me it was Riona's. Apparently the elder Donnellys have given their set to Cedar and Finn."

"What of it?" Nuala snapped.

Glancing again at Eden, who was picking at a twig on the ground, Maeve said, "It reminded me of a similar necklace I have seen before. I had completely forgotten about it, I confess." She lowered her voice to a whisper. "Kier was wearing one when she came through the sidh and into my cellar. It's buried with her."

Nuala was staring at her, eyes shining. "And the other stone is still in Tír na nÓg," she breathed.

Maeve nodded. "One can only assume so. If we activate her half of the pair, we may be able to get a real-time picture of Tír na nÓg. Of course, there's no guarantee. The other half may be lost or buried," she said, thinking of Brogan's body lying beneath the earth.

"It's unlikely," Nuala said, her voice eager. "All the bodies were searched. There's no way the king's body would have been left unspoiled. Someone over there has that stone. But we need the song—do you know it?"

"I do. At least, I think I can remember it," Maeve said.

"Show me. Where is Kier's body?"

Maeve bit her lip. "Under the cedar tree," she said, pointing. "Please, Eden should not see this."

Nuala shook her head. "Then she can close her eyes." She smirked. "What, do you not want her to see her true grandmother? Or are you worried it might be too gruesome? You should have no fear of that. The bodies of the Tuatha Dé Danann remain quite unspoiled, even in death. Now uncover the grave, druid. If you are worthy of that name, it shouldn't be a problem."

Maeve walked over to the large tree and placed her forehead against it. Silently, she began to speak to the spirit of the tree. "We have been friends for many years," she said, "and you have done much for me. Please, I ask for only one more favor. Release your hidden treasure, which you have valiantly protected all these years. Let me see her again, and remove but one thing from her, which will only be used for good, to save her daughter's daughter." She waited, and felt the tree become perfectly still as it considered her request. Not a single needle moved, even though there was a strong breeze in the air. After a moment, her body began to shake as the tree's roots shifted beneath the ground. She held onto the trunk with both hands as the ground opened up, then fell still. She whispered her thanks and stepped away from the trunk, kneeling down near the edge of the newly opened grave.

It was not deep, only three or four feet. The grave was rimmed by thick roots, interwoven so that it looked like an intricate basket had been lowered into the earth. The sides of the hole were lined with more roots, which sheltered the treasure that lay at the bottom. Maeve's lips tightened as she gazed down at Kier, still so beautiful, so young. Her blonde hair was spread out around her, and her dress lay smoothly, as if she had been buried in a coffin of glass and gold instead of roots, dirt, and slugs. But there were no insects or other creatures of the earth around her. All signs of blood and violence were gone. Her pale skin was unmarked, and her long lashes lay peacefully against her cheeks. On her chest, the stillness of which was the only sign she would never awake from this sleep, lay a richly decorated gold necklace with a large stone the color of onyx set in the center.

A shadow fell over the body. Maeve glanced up to see Nuala standing behind her, with Eden at her side. Eden was looking into the grave with wide eyes.

"Who is she?" Eden asked. "Is she a princess?"

"She is queen of Tír na nÓg," Maeve answered.

"She *was* the queen," Nuala corrected. "I will be the new queen."

Maeve was surprised. "Is that what you think is going to happen, that you will unseat Lorcan from the throne?"

Nuala's face was impassive, as cold as a damp winter chill. "In case it has escaped your attention, people tend to do what I tell them. Look at you, groveling in the dirt, betraying your own daughter, and I'm not even trying. Lorcan wields many powers, but they will all bow to mine once I am in Tír na nÓg. Now bring me the amulet before I toss you into the grave with her."

Maeve cast a worried glance at Eden, who was still staring at Kier's body, her small brow furrowed, and then lowered herself into the grave. The roots shifted slightly to support her, giving her a small shelf on which to kneel. Up close, Kier's body gave off a light floral scent, and her skin was supple and smooth, although there was no color in her cheeks.

"I have done as you asked," Maeve whispered, reaching behind Kier's neck to find the clasp. She shivered as her fingers grazed the pale skin. "I kept your daughter safe, and hidden, for as long as I could." Then her face twisted. "And she hates me for it. That is the only legacy you left me."

"*Now*, druid," came Nuala's voice from above. Maeve stood and began to climb out, the tree roots obliging her by forming small steps in the side of the grave.

Wordlessly, she handed the jeweled necklace over to Nuala, who took it hungrily. Then she looked at Maeve suspiciously. "The song—you said you knew it."

Maeve nodded. "It's been a long time, of course, but I believe I can remember it." How could she forget? It had seared itself into her heart like a brand. She would always remember the sound of Kier singing the song through her moans of labor, clutching the stone around her neck as if it might save her, wanting desperately to see her husband one last time, to know he was safe.

He had never answered her call.

The stone had remained black and cold, and when Maeve had finally abandoned all attempts to revive Kier, turning her attention to the squalling infant, it had taunted her with its silence. She knew what it was, what the Danann woman had been trying to do, and the fact that Brogan was not answering his wife's desperate call meant that something was horribly, impossibly wrong. Maeve had wrapped the baby in a blanket and laid her against her mother's cooling chest. Then she had touched the necklace, cupping it in her hand. Softly, she had sung Kier's song and waited for a response. She had concentrated on Brogan's face, picturing it clearly in her mind and trying to weave a psychic message into the song. *Your wife is dead. I have your child. Come back for her. Come back for me.*

Silence.

She told herself it was war; he was fighting, or in hiding. He could not be dead. He would come back when he could, looking for his wife and child, and when he did, he would find his mistress and child instead. She would be there to comfort him, and the child would love her like a mother. He would stay, or would take them both back to Tír na nÓg.

Ten years later, a ragged group of survivors had appeared in her cellar and told her the horrible truth: Brogan was unequivocally, irrevocably dead. And by then she loved Cedar and wasn't willing to give her up to these strangers. So she told them the child had died along with her mother, and they believed her, too accustomed to death at this point to question her. Without the Lýra, there was no reason for them to suspect that the human child running around her house was the missing princess they so desperately sought.

No reason, that is, until Cedar showed up on Rohan's doorstep with stories of a child who could open portals with a touch of her hand.

Maeve reached out and took the necklace back from Nuala, and began to sing. The song was simple but haunting, and her aging voice did not do it justice. But the notes were the same, and her lips formed the words of the ancient language reserved for the most intricate of spells.

As she sang, the black stone began to swirl like angry clouds. Watching it, Maeve felt as if she were floating through the air. Nuala looked over her shoulder and gasped. Then she grabbed the stone.

"Come here, Eden," she said, yanking the girl over to her. She knelt so Eden could see the stone, which lightened to a uniform gray. They all peered into it. The color shifted again to a dull brown that was slightly textured. It looked like dead grass.

"Yesss," Nuala hissed, putting her hand on the back of Eden's neck and forcing her to look closer. "Someone has the other stone," she said. "Look, child, *this* is Tír na nÓg, your home and mine. Look closely."

Maeve stiffened at Nuala's words. "*This* is your home, Eden, don't ever forget that. Your home is with the people who love you."

Eden looked back and forth between the two women, then back at the stone. The picture in the stone swung about to reveal a barren landscape. The image was small, but perfectly clear. In the foreground was a dead tree, tall and ghostly white. In the background of the tiny picture was a dry gully where perhaps a river had once run. The image did not linger; soon it blurred as if moving, and they heard a voice, "King Lorcan! Your ring, it's glowing."

Instantly Nuala reached out and pushed Eden to the ground, ordering her to stay silent. She moved away from them, holding the amulet so only she could see what appeared in it next. Maeve noticed Nuala's hands were shaking. She helped Eden to her feet and pulled her close.

A voice came from the stone. It was as soft and oily as the selkie that swam in the Irish Sea. It was a voice accustomed to being obeyed.

"You are not Kier Mhic Airgetlam," the voice said. "Who are you, and how did you come by this stone?"

"My lord Lorcan," Nuala said with a bow of her head. "I am your servant Fionnghuala."

"A traitor, then," Lorcan said slowly, "and yet one who calls me lord and professes to be my servant. You answered only one of my questions."

"K-Kier is dead, my lord," Nuala said with a slight stammer. "I took the amulet from her body. I wish to beg forgiveness and to bring you a great gift."

There was a moment of silence, and Maeve was sure Lorcan himself could hear the pounding of her heart. *What gift?*

Then Lorcan spoke again, his voice so smooth and quiet that Maeve took a step closer to the stone to hear him. "Bring me? We have overturned every pebble and twig of Tír na nÓg looking for the sidh through which you cowards escaped. Are you telling me it is still open?"

Nuala licked her lips and glanced over at Eden. "I have found a way to reopen the sidhe, my lord. That is the gift I am bringing you."

The impact of Nuala's duplicity struck Maeve suddenly, almost knocking her to the ground. For a fleeting moment she allowed herself to feel like a fool for trusting this woman, for believing she would hold up her end of their bargain. But there would be time for guilt later. Now, she needed to act, and quickly. Low and soft, she began to sing Kier's song, just barely audible. She saw Nuala frown in concentration at the stone in her hand.

"My lord? Can you still hear me? My—" Nuala looked up and saw Maeve's lips moving, then she turned back at the stone, which had gone completely black.

"Stop singing!" Nuala roared as she advanced on Maeve.

Maeve stood her ground, moving Eden behind her. "No. I will not fall prey to you," she said through clenched teeth.

"You will do as I say," Nuala said, staring at Maeve intently.

Maeve laughed, an unhinged sort of laugh that made Nuala's eyes widen. "Look inside me, if you will. Do you think there is anything in there you can use? Do you think there is anything I want in this world other than to keep this child safe? Your power won't work on one whose only desire is the opposite of yours."

Nuala said nothing, but continued to stare intently at Maeve. Again, the older woman laughed. "Find anything yet? I didn't think so. I'll tell you about the only things I've ever wanted in my life. I wanted Brogan to love me, but he's dead, so you can't use that. I wanted his wife to be dead, and she is. The only desires I have left are for my daughter's love and my granddaughter's safety, and I see now you are trying to take both from me. You have no power over me."

Nuala looked down at the girl cowering behind her grandmother's blowing skirt. "Eden! Did you see it? Did you see Tír na nÓg through the stone? Do you remember what it looked like?"

"I…I don't know…" Eden stammered.

"DID YOU SEE IT?" Nuala bellowed, her spittle landing on Maeve's cheek.

"Y-y-yes," Eden whimpered.

"Run, Eden," Maeve said, keeping her eyes on Nuala's contorted face. "Run to the house. Use the door and go to your home—your mother and father are there."

"You will stay here!" Nuala screamed at Eden. Then she turned back to Maeve. "Do you really think she can outrun me, or even that she would? Do you even *know* your so-called granddaughter? She *wants* to go to Tír na nÓg. It is her destiny."

Maeve glanced behind her to see Eden frozen in place, her eyes wide with fear and confusion.

"My father is at home?" she asked Maeve. Then she looked at Nuala, "You said he was in Fairyland."

"Is that what she told you?" Maeve exclaimed. "Eden, my dear, no. Your father has been looking for you, just as I have. He is at your house right now, waiting for you, with your mother."

"She lies!" screamed Nuala, and Eden's head swiveled up sharply. "She does not want you to go, Eden, she does not want you to be a princess. Remember everything we talked about—a magical kingdom of your very own, servants, the most beautiful dresses, as many ponies and horses as you can ride. And your father is there, he wants to see you so badly."

For a moment Maeve saw a shadow flicker behind Eden's eyes. Then it passed.

"No," Eden said. "I don't want to go there anymore. I want to stay here."

Nuala's voice was low and deadly when she spoke. "You will open that sidh, and you will come with me."

"NO!" Eden yelled, then turned and sprinted toward the house. Nuala darted past Maeve and stood in front of Eden, blocking her path.

"Do you think I survived the war by being slow or weak?" Nuala called to Maeve, who was running toward them and breathing heavily. "I may not be able to control you, but I can still hurt you. Now, child, open that door to Tír na nÓg, or I will hurt your grandmother very much."

"No, Eden!" Maeve gasped as she tried to catch her breath. "No matter what happens, do not open that door for her. She is taking you to a very bad man. He will kill all of us."

"Fool!" Nuala screamed, then reached out and struck Maeve across the face. The blow sent her flying across the yard. She landed on the gravel driveway and felt a sharp spasm of pain in her hip. Breathing hard, she pressed her palm into the rocks beside her, whispered some ancient words, and then lifted her hand into the air. Stones rose from the ground and swirled like a whirlpool in the air. Maeve flung her arm in Nuala's direction and the stones spun out of the whirlpool and headed straight for her, assailing her with enough force to make her scream in pain and cover her face. Maeve struggled to get to her feet as Nuala tried to ward off the stones. As she straightened herself, she heard Eden cry out. Nuala had grabbed the child and was using her as a shield. With a few hurried phrases from Maeve, the stones landed softly in the grass at their feet.

"Leave her alone," Maeve snarled. "This is between us now."

"*You* are the only thing standing in our way," Nuala said. "Let us go peacefully, and I will let you live. Continue fighting, and I will kill you. Then I will force the child to open the sidh. This is a fight you cannot win, druid."

Maeve stared at Eden, who seemed paralyzed with fear. Nuala had a firm hold on one of Eden's arms, and Maeve could tell she was in pain.

"You're hurting her," she said. "Let her go, and we will end this. Or are you afraid to face me without a child to protect you?"

"Eden," Nuala said as she backed away toward the house, still keeping the child between her and Maeve. "We are going now. Say good-bye to your grandmother."

At this, Eden snapped out of her paralyzed state. She struggled and kicked and tried to pull away from Nuala, screaming, "Let go! Let go! You're hurting me!"

"Good girl," Maeve said under her breath. Eden was no match for Nuala's strength, but at least she was distracted, which gave Maeve a slight advantage. She whispered a few more words and watched as the ground behind Nuala rippled and formed a small ridge. Nuala, who had been expecting flat ground and was concentrating on keeping a firm grip on the squirming child, tripped and fell. Her hand flew off Eden's arm, and Eden made another dash for the house, now only steps away. As soon as Eden was out of range and before Nuala could get to her feet, Maeve flung out her arms, and the ground beneath Nuala fell away.

Maeve shouted once again to Eden, who was standing on the front porch, watching the dust rise into the air where Nuala had been standing only seconds before.

"Go, Eden! Go home! I'll follow you there!"

Eden turned toward the front door and reached out her hand. Before Maeve could see if she made it through the sidh, she felt a searing pain in her side. It was only in retrospect that she heard the bang. She felt herself fall to the ground and looked in astonishment at the blood spreading in a large blotch on her blouse. When she looked up again, Nuala was standing a yard away and pointing a dull black gun in her face.

"I know you're still here, Eden," Nuala said without taking her eyes off Maeve. "And that's good. That shows that you want your grandmother to live."

Maeve looked at Nuala in astonishment. She had expected a battle of power between them, Nuala's incredible strength and speed pitted against her own brand of magic. She had never imagined Nuala would stoop to such a crude human weapon. But there it was, pointed directly between her eyes, and Maeve knew that the moment she started to utter a spell, she would be dead.

"That's right," Nuala said. "I didn't think I'd have to use this, but you're a stubborn, selfish bitch, you know that? You could have let her go, with your blessing, even, to become what she is meant to be. Now her last memory of you is going to be of you lying in the dirt in a pool of your own blood because you tried to keep her from her destiny."

Maeve tried to block out the pain in her side, tried to think of nothing but Eden. She opened her mouth to speak, but all that came out was a weak, whimpering, "Go, Eden. Go."

She tore her eyes from the gun and looked over at the porch. The child looked so frail, standing there alone with one hand on the doorknob, the other hanging limp at her side. Her golden eyes were dripping with tears that left tracks down her dirt-smudged cheeks. She looked at Maeve for an agonizingly long second, and again Maeve saw that strange shadow pass behind the girl's eyes. "It's going to be all right, Gran," she said. Then she looked at Nuala, who was still pointing the gun at Maeve's forehead. "I'm ready." She gave the door a hearty tug. The last thing Maeve saw was an expanse of brown, dead grass and a tall white tree through the open door. Then everything went black.

❦

Cedar listened to the phone ringing, silently willing Maeve—she couldn't bring herself to call her "Mum" anymore—to pick up. The phone rang and rang, and Cedar waited for it to click over to voice mail. But then she heard the ringing stop, and a thin voice at the other end whispered, "Cedar?"

"Mum?" Cedar asked automatically, and then corrected herself. "Maeve? Where are you?"

"Cedar, you must come, you must hurry," Maeve said in a voice so quiet she could barely make out the words.

"Come where? Where are you? Are you okay?"

"No, no, I'm not. I'm at the old house. Hurry, dear."

The line went dead, and Cedar stared down at the phone in her hand. She grabbed her bag from the counter and headed to her car. Brian, the sentry Rohan had placed in the hallway, yelled after her, but she gave him a few choice words about minding his own business and how she could go anywhere she damn well pleased.

She drove as fast as she dared through the city and onto the highway. She saw an eagle circling in the sky above her, as if it were eyeing its prey, and her heartbeat quickened. Had one of Maeve's druid spells backfired? Had she found Eden? No, she would have said so on the phone. Cedar wondered if she should call one of the Tuatha Dé Danann, maybe Felix or Riona, but it might have nothing to do with them. Perhaps Maeve had just fallen down some stairs and twisted her ankle. She would wait until she found out what was going on. Besides, the Danann didn't care about Maeve, or Cedar herself, for that matter. All that mattered to them was Eden.

She finally sped onto the road leading to her childhood home. She turned into the driveway and pulled up in front of the house.

"Mum? Mum?" she called, throwing open the car door and running out into the yard. Then she saw her.

Maeve was lying just feet from the small set of steps leading up to the veranda. For a second Cedar was relieved. She must have just fallen down the stairs; it couldn't be too bad. Then she saw the blood. She rushed over and knelt beside her.

"Mum, can you hear me?" she asked, and then gasped as she saw the gash on the side of Maeve's face, as if someone had struck her hard.

Maeve's eyes flickered open. "Cedar," she whispered. "Thank the gods you're here. She has taken her; they have gone to Tír na nÓg."

Cedar stared at her in shock. "How do you know this?"

"I tried to stop her; it's my fault. She swore she would leave Eden behind if I helped her. I believed her. I thought I could get Eden away from them all, from all the Danann." Tears ran through the blood that was still sticky on her face.

"What do you mean, you helped her?" Cedar whispered.

"The starstones…Kier's and Brogan's. Oh, Cedar, I'm so sorry."

Cedar said nothing. She felt empty and light-headed. Eden was gone, really gone, beyond her reach. She tried to speak, but no sound came out.

She whirled her head around at the sound of approaching footsteps. Finn stood behind them, his face ashen.

"What are you doing here?" she asked.

"Brian called me, and I followed you, as an eagle," he said simply and then knelt beside Maeve and started examining her wounds.

"Eden's gone," Cedar said.

"I heard," Finn answered, not looking at her. "I'm still not giving up. If she could create a sidh to Tír na nÓg, she can create one *from* there as well. She can come back."

Cedar nodded woodenly, wanting to believe his words, to take comfort in them, because to believe otherwise would surely kill her.

Finn stood up, pulled his phone out of his pocket, and then pulled Cedar a few paces away. "She's in bad shape. I'm calling Felix. He needs to get here right away. I'd take her back to the city, but I'm worried about moving her too much."

Cedar went back to Maeve's side while Finn called the healer. Maeve's hand reached out for Cedar, and Cedar took it in both of hers and held it tightly. "Finn is calling Felix," she said. "You're going to be okay." All the anger she had felt an hour earlier had melted away. It would come back later, perhaps, or maybe not. Right now, there was only pain.

"Listen to me," Maeve said, and Cedar bent closer to hear her. "I'm not going to make it. I can feel the other side calling for me. I'm ready to go. I tried...I tried to be a good mother to you. And I'm sorry. I hated them so much. I couldn't forgive him for leaving me."

Cedar squeezed Maeve's hand back. So this is how it would happen; she would become motherless and childless in one fell swoop. "You were a very good mother to me," she said, "and an amazing grandmother to Eden." Her voice broke on the last word.

Maeve tried to shake her head, but winced. "It's not too late, Cedar. You can still save her, I know it. And you must, or else he will kill her. What the Tuatha Dé Danann believe about Lorcan is not true. Brogan did not die by Lorcan's hand. He can and will kill Eden to take her ability. But *you* can save her. You must save her!"

"How?" Cedar asked. Hot tears were running down her cheeks. She barely registered what Maeve had said about Lorcan and Brogan. "How can I save her? She's gone where I can't go. Nuala and Lorcan are so powerful. I'm just human."

"No," Maeve said. "*No.* You are the daughter of the great High King. I was wrong, Cedar. You are *not* human—you are one of the Tuatha Dé Danann. What your mother and I did, I didn't understand at the time, not fully. We did not change who you are, we only masked it. We weren't taking away your gift; we were *giving* you one. Don't you see? Few, if any, of the Danann would recognize it as such, but a gift it is. We gave you the gift of humanity. It's a strength, not a weakness." Her eyes opened wide, and she stared at Cedar intently. "Oh, why didn't I see this before? *You* are the answer they have been seeking. Not Eden. *You* are the dyad—both human and Danann. *You* are the one who can end this. Use your humanity."

"*How?* How can I end this?" Cedar asked again, but Maeve did not answer. She had closed her eyes, and her breathing was barely detectable. "Mum?" Cedar asked. She put her ear to Maeve's chest, and heard nothing.

"Mum!" she wailed. This couldn't be happening; it was impossible that she could lose them both. The pain ripped through her and she cried out unintelligibly, her hands in her hair, pulling at it as if the physical pain could lessen the torture she felt within. She was shaking, and when Finn knelt down and wrapped his arms around her, she tried to fight him off. He tightened his hold and kept her from falling apart as she sobbed uncontrollably into his chest.

Then she heard his voice in her ear, and there was an urgency to it that made her glance up. "Cedar, look," he said. She looked where he was pointing. On the other side of the driveway, near the old workshop, grew a tall cedar tree, and Finn was staring at it.

"What?" she said, not understanding, not caring.

"Can you see it? The tree, it's shimmering," he said.

Cedar looked back at the tree and squinted her eyes, still blurry with tears. It looked the same as it always had, thick with blue-green needles, tall and foreboding. She had always been a little bit afraid of that tree as a child.

"Look again, look harder," he urged.

He helped her to her feet and she walked closer to the tree, staring at it intently, trying to see the tree as he did. Maeve's voice came back to her. *You are the dyad—both human and Danann.* Slowly, she began to detect a slight glimmer on the outer branches. Then it spread, needle by needle, as though a curtain were being drawn to let the sun through.

"Watch out," Finn said, and grabbed her arm. She had been looking at the tree and not the ground beneath her, and had almost stepped into a deep pit. She tore her eyes from the shimmering branches to look down, and jumped back with small cry.

"Who—" she began, unable to finish the sentence.

Finn knelt at the edge of the grave. "This is Kier, your mother."

She knelt down beside him and gazed at the peaceful face nestled among the roots. "One of my mothers," she corrected him, the tears still running down her cheeks.

"Maeve did well to bury her here," Finn said. "The land will keep her in peace." He got to his feet, his eyes searching the ground near the tree. He saw what he was looking for and walked over, scooping Kier's necklace from the ground. "Perhaps you would like to keep this," he said, handing it to Cedar.

She took it from him wordlessly and gazed at it. "Thank you," she said, closing her hand tightly around it. Then she looked back up at the shimmering tree.

"What does it mean?" she asked him.

"It's a sidh," he said.

She looked at him unbelievingly. "How?"

He shook his head. "I don't know for certain, but I think it must be Eden."

Cedar grew pale. "Or Lorcan." Haltingly, she told Finn what Maeve had told her about Brogan and Lorcan. His face darkened.

"Even if that's the case, I don't think he did this," he said. "It's not his style. This is subtle, beautiful magic."

"But this isn't a door. Eden needs a door."

"Maybe not. Eden is the only sidh-opener I've ever heard of who used a door, and who was able to make one appear in the other place. The others before her, they could turn any object into a sidh, as long as there was a corresponding object on the other side. A hillside to a hillside. A waterfall to a waterfall. A tree to a tree. Maybe in Tír na nÓg she can use her power in ways she couldn't here." He took another step toward the tree-sidh, and then stopped. He looked back at her and held out his hand. "There's only one way to know for sure."

Again, Cedar heard Maeve's voice in her head. *You can still save her.* She didn't know how, but she knew that if Eden had created this sidh, she was summoning her. Hope flooded her veins. All was not yet lost. She looked at the glimmering tree and thought of the world beyond it, a land of war, where a ruthless warrior was bent on the destruction of everyone she loved. She thought of Riona's strength and kindness, and Felix's easy smile. She even thought of Rohan, of how he tried to lead and protect his people despite impossible odds. She thought of her father, a great king of the Tuatha Dé Danann who had loved a frail human, and of Kier, lying in the grave at her feet, who had given all her energy to bestow Cedar with a gift that would conceal her true identity and ensure her safety. Kier could never have known that Cedar would meet and love another of the Tuatha Dé Danann, or that she would feel more alive, more at home with him than with any other man. She could never have known they would bring a Danann child into this human world, a world some wanted to protect and others wanted to destroy.

Cedar took Finn's hand, and together they walked through the open sidh.

CHAPTER 20

To her surprise, Nuala did not have to force Eden through the open sidh—the child went willingly. But once they had walked through the shimmering air in the doorway of Maeve's house, Eden didn't even seem to notice that they had crossed into a fabled land, the Otherworld, the land of Faerie, the land of Tír na nÓg. Instead, she stood with her hand still on the doorknob, looking back at her grandmother, who was lying unconscious on the ground.

"She'll be fine," Nuala said, not unkindly. "Now close the sidh." When Eden showed no sign of obeying, she said, with an edge to her voice, "Or would you rather leave it open so the bad guys can go through and find her?" Eden swung the door closed, and it disappeared. She continued to stand there silently, and quite still.

Nuala looked around. She could feel it as soon as they had walked through the sidh. There was no question in her mind they were in Tír na nÓg. And yet the Eden she had met in the dreamscape had been right; it was not the Tír na nÓg she remembered. When she had fled with the other so-called rebels, the land had been showing signs of strain—fruit withering and falling from the trees, the streams not as full as they should have been, the days more cloudy than sunny. But this was nothing like the land she had left. Everything around them was a variation on gray. Even the brown, dead grass beneath their feet was tinged with a sickly gray pallor.

The sky, the trees, the bushes that had once been brilliant with color all looked ashen, like a corpse that had been many days dead.

But the war is over, she thought, looking around in astonishment. *The land should have recovered.* She continued to stare, letting the shock of what she was seeing sink in, and then she saw him.

She had seen him before, of course, years ago. He was handsome, as were all the Tuatha Dé Danann. He looked every bit the warrior-king, tall and strong, with chiseled features and steely blue eyes. As she watched Lorcan advance on them, she hesitated slightly. What if the druid had been right, and he would kill the child the moment he knew who she was? But there was no turning back now, so she raised her chin and waited for him to approach, focusing her power and readying herself to take control. This was the moment she had been waiting for.

A Danann warrior walked on each side of the king. When they drew close, the soldiers stopped and stared at her openly. She smiled slightly. She knew they, at least, were feeling the effects of her charm, even though it was not directed at them.

Lorcan's eyes, however, did not glaze over. They stared at each other for a moment, as if sizing one another up, and then she gave a slight bow. "My lord," she said, "I have brought you a great gift, as promised."

He looked behind her, not yet paying attention to Eden. "Did you create that sidh?" he asked, staring intently at the spot where it had been.

"No, my lord," Nuala said. "I did not make it, but I brought you the one who did. The child you sought, many years ago." She indicated Eden, who had walked over and sat down at the base of the tall dead tree they had seen through Kier's necklace. Her eyes were closed and she was leaning against the trunk.

Lorcan breathed out in a long, slow hiss as he looked at the girl. "That was many years ago, and yet she is still a child. How is that possible?"

"She is Brogan's grandchild," Nuala answered. "His own child, this girl's mother, has been made human through a druid's craft. But *this* child has the gift you seek. I found her, and have gone through much danger to bring her to you. I remember your words, your promises to the one who could bring you the child with the king's gift."

Lorcan tore his eyes from Eden and narrowed them at Nuala. "*I* am the king," he said slowly.

"Of course," Nuala faltered, confused. Her power did not seem to be having any effect on him, and she could not understand why. A chill ran through her, though the air was hot and dry. "I only meant that I brought her here as a sign of my loyalty. I was deceived when I left Tír na nÓg, and have been searching for a way to return to your side ever since. I hope to claim the mercy and reward you promised."

He sneered at her. "I am known for many things. Mercy is not one of them. However, you have done well, very well, to bring the child to me. For that, I shall spare your life, provided you agree to use your considerable talents in my service, of course. That should be reward enough, don't you think, Fionnghuala?" Then he leaned over so that his lips were touching her ear. "How are your charms working so far?" he whispered, and then pulled back, mockery written across his face.

Nuala took a step back. The chill deepened, and she felt goose bumps rise on the smooth skin of her arms. How could her power have no effect on him? He was not a closer like Rohan or Finn. He had very real, very obvious desires. She did not even need to look inside his heart to see the hunger for power that consumed him. It should have been easy to control him, to convince him that he needed her.

"You don't think I walk around unprotected, do you?" he said. "Not all my loyal subjects are as willing to serve me as you are." His handsome features twisted into a smirk. "I shouldn't take all the credit. This shield of protection used to belong to someone else, someone who is now dead, of course. No, don't bother trying to see it. You can't. But it's there, protecting me from you, and everyone else who would wish to kill me." He paused. "But I don't think that was your plan, was it?"

"Of—of course not, my lord," Nuala said. "I would never dream of such a thing. I only wish…" she hesitated, unsure how to proceed knowing he was not under her spell. "I only wish to assist you. I believe in your cause, and I have done what I can to help by bringing you the sidh-opener. However, I can be of much more service. With your many powers, and my ability to persuade, we could make a formidable team, my lord."

Lorcan raised a blond eyebrow into a perfectly pointed arch. "Team? Ah, I see it now. You think this favor you have done for me merits a reward greater than the mere gift of your life. You think I should make you queen." He reached out and ran a smooth finger along her cheek and down her neck. He trailed it along her collarbone and traced the neckline of her shirt to where it dipped between her breasts. She held still, barely daring to breathe, and tried to soften her features as she gazed at him seductively.

"You do have a certain charm, even though I am shielded from your power," he said. "Your ability will no doubt be useful to me." He paused, slowly running his tongue across his lips as he ran his hands over her body. "I could kill you and take it for myself, of course, and I may, in time. However, I'm sure I can think of some use for you until then." He looked at his guards. They were still gazing at Nuala with undisguised lust through their glassy, slightly dazed eyes. "Or maybe they can," he said with a short laugh.

Nuala looked at him in horror, simultaneously shutting down all vestiges of the seductive threads she had been sending his way.

The other men shook their heads, as if trying to get water out of their ears.

"Come!" Lorcan commanded with a sweeping turn. "This is a momentous occasion, and there is still much to be discussed." One of the men took Nuala by the arm and shepherded her in Lorcan's wake. The other man was pushing Eden along in front of him. Nuala shook with fear and anger and hissed, "Let go of me at once."

The guard immediately dropped her arm and stood to the side, letting her pass. Lorcan stopped and turned around, a look of mock disappointment on his face.

"You're not going to be difficult, now, are you? Look at how easily the child obeys," he said, indicating Eden, who was standing still beside her guard. "You may have noticed that Tír na nÓg has changed since you left. You're in *my* Tír na nÓg now, Fionnghuala. Believe me when I say I can make things very difficult for you. There is no place to run." He turned to her guard. "Let her walk freely," he said, then continued apace in front of them.

Nuala stood her ground for a second, and then fell into step beside Eden, who was following Lorcan. She glanced over at the child.

"Are you okay, Eden?" she asked. Eden just shrugged and kept walking. Nuala let out a frustrated breath. What did she care if the child was okay? Her entire plan was in ruins. This wasn't the Tír na nÓg she had longed for. This was a wasteland. Even Ériu, as much as she despised the place, held more attraction for her than this vast expanse of gray, every tree and rock a dismal reminder of the glory she had left behind. Were the Tuatha Dé Danann who remained here also only shadows of their former selves? Would she find the same race of dignified, powerful beings she had once adored and been proud to be part of, or would they have withered under a cruel king's reign, until they cowered and simpered like humans?

She forced herself not to dwell on such despairing thoughts. She just needed a new strategy, one that would put her in a position of power. She would neither simper nor cower—but she could be patient.

Nuala remembered Lorcan's hands on her body, and shivered at the thought of playing whore for him. But if she could get him alone, if eventually she could get him to let down his shield of protection, it would only take a few carefully chosen words to shift the balance of power in her favor.

∞

As soon as Cedar crossed through the tree-sidh, she started looking around frantically. "Eden!" she called out. She felt Finn's hand clamp over her mouth.

"Quiet!" he whispered, pulling her down behind a dry patch of brambles. Beside them was the tree that had served as the connecting sidh on this side. It was a tall, dead thing, gleaming ghostly white. Together they stared at it. Cedar could detect a faint glow, but she wasn't sure if that was because it was a sidh or because the whiteness of the tree's bark contrasted so much with the dingy grays and browns around them.

Finn whispered, "I think we can leave it open. I barely recognize it as a sidh, and I'm looking for it. I don't think it will be easily noticed, and it will be good for us to have a way back in case…in case we need it."

"What about the others?" Cedar asked. "You called Felix. Will they follow us through?"

Finn shook his head. "I don't think so. I was on the phone with him when I first noticed the sidh. I told him I would go through, and asked him to be ready in case someone from Tír na nÓg tries to get to Ériu. My father can close it if it comes to that. If not, they'll wait, at least for a while. The more of us there are over here, the more likely it is that we'll be discovered."

Cedar looked at Finn and felt a rush of warmth that bolstered her against the terror playing at the edges of her mind. She was glad he was with her, and not just because he kept her from feeling completely and utterly helpless. She had thought she might feel different here—bolder, more confident. This was, supposedly, her ancestral home. Still, she felt small and ordinary and exhausted, and filled with the same desperation to find her daughter before it was too late.

"So *this* is Tír na nÓg?" she asked, taking in the barren landscape.

He nodded, his face grim. "It is, or it was, I should say. This isn't Tír na nÓg as I knew it, but we're in the right place, if that's what you mean."

"Where do you think she is?"

He shook his head. "She could be anywhere, but if Lorcan has her she'll be at the Hall, the seat of the High King."

"Which way?" she asked, looking around.

"Hold on," he said. "We need a plan." He was quiet for a moment, still crouched in the brush.

"We need to get going! We can't just sit here!"

"We'll be of no help to her if we get ourselves killed before we even find her," Finn said, laying a hand on her shoulder to keep her from standing. "Cedar, I know you're not going to like this, but…I think you should go back."

Her eyebrows raised and her jaw dropped. "Are you insane? We're so close to her! We don't have time to argue, so you might as well save your breath and drop it."

He gave her a look that said he would drop it, but wasn't happy about it. Then he said in a hushed and hurried voice, "Fine, but

I'll reach her quicker if I go alone. I can shift into something small and fast. The fact that we're still alive right now means it probably wasn't a trap. Eden must have created this sidh, which means she doesn't need a door anymore. She can create a sidh from anything. Maybe she's already escaped! If not, she's probably being restrained somehow. I just need to free her, and she can use whatever is around us to make a sidh and escape to Ériu, back to Maeve's. She can close the sidh behind us, and we'll both be safe."

Cedar listened to his plan with an uneasy feeling in her stomach. His reasoning made sense. She was slow and loud and weak, all things that would imperil their rescue mission. And yet Maeve had told her *she* could save Eden. *We gave you the gift of humanity,* she had said. *It's a strength, not a weakness.*

Cedar's forehead wrinkled as she tried to concentrate on what Finn was saying. She couldn't help but feel that she was missing something, that they were all missing something. Surely, it was not as straightforward as merely finding Eden and spiriting her away. If Lorcan was so easily tricked, how had he stayed in power for so long, and brought an entire race of superbeings to its knees?

Use your humanity.

Cedar gasped as the answer came to her. She nearly laughed from the sheer simplicity of it. She put her hand on the trunk of the tree to steady herself. She was sure of it now. She *was* the dyad, the two-in-one, and the answer to the prophecy, just like Maeve had told her. She saw now how she could rescue Eden and prevent Lorcan from ever coming after her again. At the same time, she would be fulfilling the prophecy by purging the land of the poison that was Lorcan, saving not only Eden, but also Tír na nÓg…and earth.

She turned to Finn, who was looking at her with concern. "I need to go with you," she said quietly but firmly.

"Cedar, I just finished listing all the reasons why that would be a bad idea."

"Listen, you have no idea what you're facing, right? There are a thousand things that could go wrong, and if you're captured or killed, Eden is as good as dead. I can be Plan B."

"What could you possibly do?"

She hesitated, and for the first time knew how Finn must have felt when he had hidden the truth from her to protect her. She took one of his hands in hers and said, "I have a plan, but I can't tell you what it is, not yet. You're going to have to trust me."

He brushed a stray strand of hair out of her face. His eyes, slightly wounded, were intent on hers. "I do trust you, and I love you. You don't have to tell me your plan. But plan or no plan, this is too risky. Please, just stay here and wait for me to come back. If I'm not here by sunset, go through the sidh and see if Eden got back to Ériu alone." He stood up and pulled her to her feet, then brought her in close against his chest.

"I spent years thinking I'd never see you again," he said. "You don't know how much it means to me to have you back. It's as if I've been given back my life. I can't risk losing you again."

"This isn't about us," she said, her voice muffled against his chest. "It's about Eden. She needs me. I know I can save her." Cedar felt moisture on her cheeks and wiped it away with the palm of her hand. "Please understand," she pleaded. "I have to do this. I have to do whatever it takes to keep her safe."

"You could be killed," he said, his voice trembling.

"I'm not as helpless as you think I am," she said, trying to fill her voice with conviction. "I'll be careful. I'll stay out of the way, hidden, just close enough to help if I can. But I need to be there. We have the starstones. Find out where Eden is, and let me know. Maybe it will be easy, like you say. If nothing goes wrong, we won't have anything to worry about. I'll head straight for the white tree and meet you on the other side. But I'm not going to stay here, not without knowing whether you and Eden are alive or dead or being tortured somewhere. I'm going with you."

CHAPTER 21

Finn flew above her in his eagle form, occasionally swooping down to tell her to wait or hide or change course based on something he had seen from high above. Without the sun, it was difficult to gauge how long they had been in Tír na nÓg, but finally Cedar saw in the distance a grand building that had to be the Hall. It was like no place she had ever seen on earth. Its towering walls of pure white would have been blinding in the sun. The Hall's many spires twisted and danced through the air above the walls, and many-colored banners hung limp from them. She tried to imagine what it would have looked like on a sunny day, or with a slight breeze to send the banners soaring into the air.

To the west of the Hall stretched a large lake, or what Cedar assumed had once been a lake. She could see water in the distance, but it had obviously been steadily receding, leaving a vast swath of dry, parched earth in its wake. Beyond this once-lake rose a gray mountain range. Cedar squinted at one of the mountains, which seemed oddly misshapen, as if a giant had ripped it in two. She wondered if they would encounter any giants in Tír na nÓg.

She continued through the brush, avoiding the dusty road that led to the Hall, until at last she followed Finn into a small copse of trees, where he resumed his normal form.

"You should be safe if you stay here," he said. "There are guards at the front entrance, but other than that there is little activity in the outer grounds. This place used to be alive and filled with people, but now…" He gave Cedar a long, searching look, then shook his head. "This is a mistake. I should have come alone. If something goes wrong…" He trailed off, his eyes full of a sudden panic.

Cedar wrapped her arms around his neck. "They think it's impossible that either one of us could be here," she said, trying to reassure him. "Even if you're caught, they'll think you acted alone. They won't be looking for me. Do you have the starstone?"

He pulled out the pocket watch and quietly began to sing the song that made both stones glow with a soft light. She closed her eyes and listened to the sound of his voice, trying to fix it in her mind, hoping she could take that memory with her where she was about to go.

When she opened her eyes, he had stopped singing, and his face was only inches away. Then his lips were crushing hers, and she responded in kind, kissing him as hard and fierce as she could, as if she hoped to make a permanent imprint of herself on his body. When he reluctantly started to pull away, she held onto him.

"Finn," she said urgently. "If I don't…if something goes wrong, make sure you think of Eden, not of me. She has to come first, do you understand? No matter what happens. Get her home and take care of her. I know you'll be a great father. And I forgive you for everything, for leaving, and for not telling me the truth. I know you were just trying to protect me. And now you have to protect her. I'm trusting you with her life. Just…tell her how much I love her, how much I've always loved her. Tell her she's the most important thing in the world to me. You'll be fine. You'll both be fine."

She kissed him again, but softly this time, trying to communicate everything she wanted to say but dared not.

"We're not saying good-bye," he said. "We're *all* going to be fine. I'm going to save Eden, and we're all going home together.

We'll get to know each other again. You'll paint, and we'll have more children, and we won't have to worry about any of this."

She tried to smile at him and control the shaking in her voice. "I know," she said. "I'm sorry, I don't mean to be so melodramatic, I'm just nervous. And…I love you. I want to make sure you know that."

He kissed her forehead and whispered, "I know. I'll see you soon." Then he was gone. She couldn't tell exactly what he had transformed into; all she could see was a small brown shape moving quickly through the dry grass.

As soon as he was out of sight, Cedar crept toward the edge of the trees and peered out. She thought about waiting to see if he did, in fact, succeed. Then she thought of him facing Lorcan, whose power apparently had no limit, and shuddered. No, she had to go through with her plan before both Finn and Eden were killed. She took several steps out into the open, and then stopped. Still she could see no one, so she started jogging in the direction of the Hall. Soon she saw a couple of guards standing by a small side entrance. They saw her coming and tensed, waiting. She saw them exchange a confused glance as they realized she had no Lýra.

She stopped several feet in front of them and then raised her voice and said, "I am the daughter of the true High King, of Brogan and Kier. Take me to Lorcan at once."

"Fionnghuala."

Nuala opened her eyes to see Lorcan standing before her. She had fallen asleep, and it took her a moment to remember where she was. Then it came back to her, and she fought back a shudder. She would not show weakness to this bastard, not if she were still determined to conquer him.

"My lord?" she asked. She was lying on a bed in a round, windowless room. She struggled to sit up, a feat made difficult by the chains fastening her wrists to the wall behind her. Lorcan waved his hand, and the chains fell off.

"Crude, I know," he said, "but you have not yet proven yourself."

Beside her on the bed lay Eden, fast asleep or drugged or unconscious. Nuala couldn't tell. The girl was chained, too, both hands and feet, with enough freedom to lie down, sit up, and use the chamber pot under the bed, but not enough to reach the room's only door. There were no guards outside the door, no one within earshot of Nuala's voice, but she knew that these rudimentary chains weren't the only things restraining them. Had she been so restrained on Ériu, she would have been able to break free easily. But this was Tír na nÓg, where everything was stronger—people, chains, enchantments.

She had been allowed to live, despite her role in the rebellion against Lorcan. He had plans for her, or so he had said while he was extracting all the information she had about Eden and the Tuatha Dé Danann on Ériu. He did not have her power of persuasion, not yet, but his own power had not been exaggerated, and she'd had no choice but to tell him everything he wanted to know. She had planned to tell him, anyway. It wasn't as if she cared what happened to Ériu or the people there, whether they were human or Danann.

"According to my guards, the child's mother is here," Lorcan said. "You told me she was human. Explain how this is possible." His face was unreadable.

"What?" Nuala said, shocked. "That *isn't* possible. Eden closed the sidhe from Ériu, I saw her do it. I *made* her do it. There is no one else with that ability, and you've kept her unconscious and in chains. I told you, she needs an actual door to open the sidhe."

"And yet, the mother is here. Fascinating, is it not?"

Nuala felt her skin go clammy. If he thought she had somehow tricked him…

"I suppose I shall just have to ask her myself," he said, "before I kill her." He paused for a moment to relish that concept, and then said, "Wake the girl. It is time to make an example of her and claim what should be mine."

Nuala gaped at him in horror. "But you need her alive. If you kill her, her gift dies with her!" She remembered what Maeve had said, how the woman had begged her not to take Eden to Tír na nÓg. She looked at Eden lying there on the bed, so innocent and weak. The girl had come willingly, to save her grandmother's life. Nuala felt a strange, unfamiliar feeling sweep over her—a sense of loss…and guilt.

Lorcan tossed back his golden head and laughed, rubbing his hands together. "Is that what you thought? Looks like Brogan's lies have backfired, doesn't it? No, my dear, no one is immune to my power. If I kill her, her gift becomes mine. The only reason she is still alive is so I can make an example of her. I will show my people what happens when they sympathize with humans."

"She's just a child," Nuala said, looking again at the small girl lying beside her, the way her hair stuck to her forehead, her mouth slightly open, as if she was peacefully asleep.

"She's an abomination, and will not be permitted to exist," Lorcan rasped.

∽

Cedar was led through a dizzying series of corridors, past marble fountains and towering statues and across grand open spaces where gardens had once flourished. Her mind registered them all, but as if from a distance. She was not bound, and the guards walked an arm's length away. They did not look at her, but she sensed that they were walking slower than normal, as if they were unsure what to do with her.

She picked up the pace, forcing her guards to keep up, although she did not know the way. It was too late for regrets or second thoughts. All that mattered now was that she arrived in time.

Finally, the guards stopped and held out their hands for her to do the same. She stood perfectly still. They had reached an entrance to a large courtyard—one of many entrances, for the walls of the courtyard consisted of a series of large white stone arches. Between the arches stood tall white birch trees, leafless but still imposing in their height. Their faint white glow reminded Cedar of the sidh she and Finn had passed through, and her heart sped up. Standing in every archway was a warrior of the Tuatha Dé Danann. Was Eden in there? Had Finn managed to slip past the guards? Had he succeeded in finding her?

For a moment, she allowed herself to hope, but then she reminded herself again what was at stake. Rescuing Eden this one time was not enough, not if Lorcan still lived. He would always want her gift, he would always hunt her, and Cedar was the only one who could truly defeat him.

One of her guards was speaking with the warrior at the archway. The tall, bearded man turned and stared openly at her. She defiantly met his gaze. She was determined not to be intimidated by these so-called deities. If she had learned anything about the Tuatha Dé Danann over the past few days, it was that they were as flawed as she was. Stepping forward, she spoke to the bearded warrior.

"I am Cedar, daughter of Brogan and Kier," she said again. "Take me to Lorcan."

"Wait here," the warrior said quietly, then turned and walked into the courtyard and out of sight. Cedar could see other men and women entering the courtyard through the other arches, milling about. Some of them stopped and gaped at her, and Cedar knew it wasn't only her lack of a Lýra that told them she didn't belong. Her dirty, bloodstained clothes stood in stark contrast to the delicate robes and gowns that sheathed the Tuatha Dé Danann as naturally and beautifully as petals on a flower.

She tried to see inside the doorway, but her two silent guards stood in front of her, blocking her view. After a few minutes, the warrior returned. He looked at her gravely, and then said, "Come."

She followed him through the archway. The crowds of Danann lords and ladies parted to let them through, and the air felt heavy with their silence. At the far end of the courtyard loomed a dais that was several feet high. Behind it stood a row of white birch trees like the ones between the archways surrounding the crowd.

A man was seated in the center of the dais, on a beautifully crafted throne of woven branches that seemed to be growing up through the marble platform. Cedar knew at once who he must be, but her eyes merely skimmed over Lorcan as she sought the one she had come here to save. Eden was there, standing behind his right shoulder—still wonderfully, gloriously alive. Cedar's body nearly gave out, so great was her relief.

"Eden," she whispered as she was led to the foot of the dais. "I'm here."

Eden watched her approach but betrayed no sign of movement, except that her eyes filled with tears that spilled down her cheeks and onto her grubby, stained clothes. She stayed still and expressionless, as if she were frozen, although Cedar could see no restraints. Still, she was alive and would soon be free. So intent was Cedar on her daughter, it barely registered that Nuala, too, stood on the dais, slightly behind Eden. Looking at her now, Cedar could see she wore a Danann robe in a mossy green color that set off her creamy skin and red hair. Despite the fine clothes, she looked miserable and ill, and her whole body trembled.

"Well, well," Lorcan said, inclining his head at Cedar. "I do believe this is a first." He looked out at the faces filling the courtyard. "Ladies and gentlemen, we have a human in the court."

A murmur spread throughout the crowd, low and anxious. Lorcan raised his hand, and silence fell at once.

"I know all about you, of course," he said, addressing Cedar. "Your friend Fionnghuala has been very cooperative. What she has been unable to tell me is how you, a human, made the journey from Ériu to Tír na nÓg. Don't tell me you share your whelp's ability. Power like ours cannot reside in such a weak vessel. And yet I have rendered the girl immobile since her arrival, so this cannot be her doing. Tell me at once. How did you come here, human?"

Cedar hesitated. She had no doubt Nuala had told Lorcan everything, but if Nuala didn't know about Eden's tree-sidh, she wanted to keep it that way. "My father was Brogan, your High King. I have his gift. I made the sidh," she lied in a loud, clear voice. She had expected more murmurs, but the air stayed silent, as if all those who heard her had suddenly stopped breathing.

"Yes, your father," Lorcan said in almost a purr, but loudly enough to be heard by everyone in the courtyard. "Your father, the coward. Your father, who preferred human whores to his own queen. Your father, who was so afraid of my power that he dared not face me himself. Your father, whose blood was so weak he produced a human child. Do not insult our company with your lies. You have no power. The power, you see, is all mine." He glanced over his shoulder at Eden. "Or very soon will be."

For a moment, Cedar said nothing. She was not here to defend her father's honor, and yet she needed to keep Lorcan's attention on her and away from Eden. She needed him to see her as the bigger threat.

"My father was a greater king than you could ever hope to be!" she said, raising her voice and trying to project a confidence she did not feel. "He was loved, not feared. I know all about you too. You are nothing without the power you take from others! You're nothing but a leech!"

"Silence!" Lorcan roared, and she felt all the breath rush out of her as if she had been struck hard in the chest. She collapsed to the ground, wheezing, and he leered at her. "Your time here will be short enough, do not hasten your death with idle insults. *I am the king.*" He lifted his face to the crowd behind her. "I AM THE KING!" he bellowed. In one voice, the people in the court chanted back, "You are the king," but to Cedar's ears it sounded rote, and far from enthusiastic.

"My subjects!" Lorcan said, standing and spreading out his arms. "May I introduce to you the human spawn of your former king, who would have had you bow down to humans rather than defend yourselves against them. She has been hiding among her kind in Ériu, and has now come back as a spy to finish her father's work, to bring the armies of Ériu against the Tuatha Dé Danann once more, seeking to eradicate us once and for all. She and what is left of her family of traitors will be dealt with severely, so you will see I have no patience for those who would stand against our cause." Lorcan's voice rose as he spoke, and he raised his arms in the air. The birch trees shook, and above his arms came an answering rumble from the sky. Cedar, who had managed to regain her breath and was making her way shakily to her feet, watched in awe as he seemed to grow to twice his normal size. His voice boomed out over them, drowning out the thunder that still rumbled in the sky above.

"It is time for us to reclaim Ériu for our own!" His eyes glowed brightly as he strutted in front of the throne. "We will take the humans by surprise. We will destroy their armies. We will exact our revenge on those who once tried to destroy us, and would do so again!" There was another rumble from the sky, a burst of applause in the otherwise silent air.

He put his hand under Eden's chin and forced it up so she was looking at him. His voice quieted. "This child, abomination though she is, has brought us a parting gift. Once she is dead, we will be able to open the floodgates of the Tuatha Dé Danann until humanity is utterly destroyed."

Cedar heard her own voice scream, "No!" and she flung herself forward. Her guards, caught by surprise, came up behind her and grabbed her by the arms. She strained against them, feeling her muscles tear as she fought to reach Eden. "It's me you want!" she screamed. "I am Brogan's daughter! I have his gift! Kill me, not her!"

Lorcan slowly removed his hand from under Eden's chin and turned around. "Let her go," he said to the guards. As soon as they had released her, Cedar felt herself lifted through the air as if by invisible strings. She floated, unable to move, several feet above the marble dais. Looking out over the crowd, she spotted the one face she did not want to see at this moment. Finn was standing in front of one of the arches, his face a portrait of agony and fear. As her eyes met his, the invisible strings holding her in the air were suddenly cut. Her body met the marble floor and she felt her arm break as her breath was forced from her lungs once again. The pain was blinding, and she would have screamed if she'd had the breath for it. Instead, she lay crumpled at Lorcan's feet, unable to move.

Just do it, she thought, wishing Eden didn't have to watch.

CHAPTER 22

Enough!" roared a voice from what seemed to be very far away. She struggled to her knees and looked around. She heard it again, and this time there was no doubt in her mind who was speaking. *Finn, no,* she thought frantically, lifting her unbroken arm to touch the amulet still around her neck, as if it could enable him to hear her thoughts. *If he kills you, who will look after Eden?*

Finn's voice rang out, filled with passion. "What has become of our people, that you would believe such lies, that you would stand here and watch while this usurper to the throne murders an innocent child?"

Lorcan moved away from Cedar and stood on the edge of the dais. He seemed entirely self-possessed, as if this new interruption were almost expected.

"Is that you, Fionnbharr son of Ruadhan?" he said with a sneer. "Have all the traitors returned? Excellent. Now I can kill you all at once and save myself the trouble of hunting you down. Show yourself, coward!"

Cedar looked out again over the sea of faces. Every head was craned, searching for the subject of Lorcan's demand. Where could Finn hide? He had to be in his true form in order to speak. She couldn't see him anywhere, so she started to crawl awkwardly toward Eden, who was still standing immobilized.

"Listen, friends!" Finn was saying. "Your fear has betrayed you! You have believed his lies, because the alternative was certain death." There was the sound of an explosion and falling marble, and then Cedar heard Finn's voice coming from another direction.

"But where has this brought you? Tír na nÓg was a land of peace and beauty. Humans are not to blame for its destruction. This is something we have brought upon ourselves through war and violence."

Cedar reached Eden, ignoring Nuala, who was now standing at the back of the dais and watching everything with wide, frightened eyes. She wrapped her good arm around the girl, and then flinched in shock. Eden's body was as cold and hard as the marble they were standing on. But her eyes moved and locked with Cedar's.

"It's going to be okay, my heart," Cedar whispered to her. "I love you so much, and I'm going to save you. You're going to be all right." She kissed the cold, hard cheek.

She turned her attention back to the cat-and-mouse game between Finn and Lorcan. She could feel a wall of heat radiating from Lorcan. Out of the corner of her eye, she saw a huge ball of fire shoot from his hands and into the assembly. He roared with rage and screamed, "Bring him to me!" Cedar realized that Finn must be taking his true form for only long enough to speak. She heard the movement of those gathered below, but no one brought Finn forward. Then she saw him briefly, landing as a tiny bird on the uppermost limb of one of the white birch trees encircling the courtyard. He flew down to a lower branch and transformed back into himself. "None of us are blameless, and yet you allow Lorcan, who has shed the blood of countless of our race, to rule you. You know he is not worthy of that task!"

Cedar could not see what shape he took next, but he disappeared just in time to avoid Lorcan's sword, which sliced through the tree as if it were made of silk and then returned at once to its enraged owner.

She heard Finn's voice again, and saw heads in the crowd swivel to search for him. "This child holds the gift of the sidhe, and if you allow Lorcan to kill her, his power will be so great it will destroy us all! Now rise up with me!"

Then she could not help but see him, for he was once again the horrifying creature that had terrified her on the Irish beach. He rose from behind the farthest of the marble arches and started advancing toward the throne, a mass of tentacles and fangs and talons. The Danann all backed away from him, and Cedar heard several of them cry out in alarm. Lorcan had dropped his sword and was standing with his feet spread apart and his hands in the air. It was an odd posture, as if he meant to embrace the creature once it drew near. Cedar did not know what it meant, but it filled her with dread, and she knew she had lingered too long.

Finn came at Lorcan, intent on annihilation, and it seemed as though the usurper was going to do nothing to defend himself. The Finn-monster struck him, or seemed to strike him, but from Cedar's vantage point she could tell that he had only struck the air in front of his target. Then the huge scaled and winged body seemed to puncture and deflate, and Finn lay in his Danann form on the dais.

Cedar screamed. She stared at Finn, who was lying motionless on the ground, his skin mottled with dark purple bruises. She struggled to her feet. *Now.* She had to act now.

Lorcan was ignoring her and had turned his attention back to his subjects. They had started to swell forward in Finn's wake, but now they stood still, shocked and silent.

"Oh, yes," Lorcan said. "I *am* invulnerable. I wield the true shield of protection, which cannot be penetrated by those with ill intentions. No one in Tír na nÓg or in Ériu can stand against me. Try, if you must. Use all your powers and arts against me, but the price you will pay is your life. If this traitor had been in his true form, the impact would have killed him at once. As it is, I shall finish him off now." He held out his hand and his sword flew into it.

Cedar cast one last glance back at Eden, but met Nuala's eyes instead. Nuala had come up beside Eden and was covering the child's eyes with her hand. Then Cedar turned and ran straight toward Lorcan, focusing all her hatred and fear and anger on him.

The last thing she felt was a burst of pure, white-hot pain. Then, nothing.

∽

Nuala stood as still as the immobilized girl beside her, frozen with shock as she watched the events unfold around her. When Cedar hit Lorcan's shield, she immediately fell to the ground, unmistakably dead. Her body was red and raw, as though she had been flayed, and her eyes were open and unseeing. Nuala tightened her grip over Eden's eyes.

Then several things happened at once.

Lorcan lowered his sword, picked up Cedar's body, and lifted it like a trophy into the air.

"Who will defy me next?" he roared, throwing her body back onto the floor in front of his feet like a rag doll. He turned back to Finn, who had managed to get as far as his knees and was grop- ing for Lorcan's dropped sword. Lorcan kicked the sword away and reached for Finn as if he were going to rip him apart with his bare hands.

And then the mist rose.

It was barely noticeable at first, but Nuala knew what it was. She had seen this scene repeated far too many times over the course of the war. Several people in the crowd cried out, and Lorcan twisted around to see the mist drifting toward him. He looked at Cedar's body in surprise, and then started backing away from it. But it was too late. The mist surrounded him, disappearing into him like a sponge soaking up water.

He must have been able to feel the change, must have known what was taking place, for even as his body started to wither and shrink, he let out a roar of protest and anger. But his strong voice was now feeble, and before the eyes of those who had feared him above all else, he transformed from an ancient, all-powerful ruler of the Tuatha Dé Danann to a very old human.

Nuala heard the murmurs as the crowd began to understand what had happened. Of course, the great High King Brogan and his noble wife, Kier, could not have bred a human child. This woman who had so valiantly defended her own child against the ruler who had terrified them all, she was Tuatha Dé Danann. Her gift, her ability—it was humanity.

And now it was Lorcan's.

The shrunken, aged body stood for a moment on legs so pale and thin they shook with the effort. Then Lorcan's white head was neatly separated from his shoulders by his own sword in Finn's hands.

Chaos erupted. Nuala felt Eden warm and soften in her arms, and she released her grip on the child, only to wrap her arms around her again and whisper, "I'm sorry, Eden. But your father is here, he really is. He'll look after you now." Nuala saw Finn looking around for them. She gave Eden one last embrace, and then ran. When she was beyond the marble arches she turned to see Finn crouching over Cedar, shaking her, picking her up and half carrying, half dragging her over to where Eden was running to meet him, screaming for her mother. She saw Finn grab at the girl, say something to her, beg her, and then together, Finn still carrying Cedar's body, they staggered to one of the marble arches and, after only a second's hesitation, disappeared. Others tried to follow, only to find themselves on the other side of the arch. Nuala started running and didn't look back.

CHAPTER 23

It was overcast on the day they buried her. The sky mingled with the fog, as if the clouds had descended to walk among them, to share in their grief.

They buried her under the great cedar tree at the country home. The tree still shimmered slightly. Around it, the Tuatha Dé Danann stood in a ring, surrounding the two graves, their faces somber.

Finn and Eden stood closest to where they had laid Maeve in the ground. Her body was in a simple wooden coffin, still open. Riona had dressed her in a long green gown that billowed around her, and had placed a bouquet of wildflowers in her arms. It looked as though she were lying in a field of grass at springtime. Seeing her there, one could almost picture her as the young woman who had captured the heart of the High King of the Tuatha Dé Danann.

Eden, clutching Baby Bunny in both hands, started to shake with sobs. Finn bent down and wrapped his arms around her, gathering her into his chest. He nodded at Riona, who stepped forward and looked into the grave at Maeve's closed eyes, her peaceful face. Then Riona spoke.

"Maeve McLeod, druid and friend to the Tuatha Dé Danann, rest well in this place. You were one of the last of your kind, a woman of wisdom and skill, of fire and spirit. You were proof that humans still play a part in the destiny of our people." Riona paused for a moment, her face full of sorrow. Then she continued.

"You had little love for us, and I understand why. Our race was not kind to you, and for that, I am so very sorry. Thank you for raising Cedar as you did, for taking her in and loving her as your own. You spent your life protecting her, and you gave your life protecting Eden. You will forever have the gratitude and respect of all the Tuatha Dé Danann. May your spirit find the love and peace you so deeply deserve."

Riona stepped back from the grave, and Sam and Dermot moved to close the lid of the coffin. Suddenly, Eden broke away from Finn's embrace. "Wait!" she cried, and the men stepped back. She walked to the edge of the grave and looked down at her grandmother. Then she gave Baby Bunny one last cuddle and dropped him into the coffin. "I don't want Gran to be alone," she said, before running back into Finn's arms. Tears streamed down his face and into her hair as he held her close. The only sounds in the air were the uneven sobs of a little girl and the soft thud of dirt hitting the wooden coffin.

At first, she didn't know where she was. The lights were off in the room, except for a lamp beside the bed. She glanced at it without raising her head off the pillow. It was the same Beatrix Potter lamp she'd had as a child. She sat up slowly and looked around. She was in her old bedroom at the country house. She held her breath and listened, but it was perfectly quiet. She was alone. *Is this the afterlife?* She swung her feet out from under the covers and stood up, feeling the grain of the hardwood under her bare feet and the fibers of the thin cotton nightgown brushing against her skin. *I shouldn't be able to feel anything*, she thought. She walked over to the window and pulled the curtains aside, wincing as the diffuse light from the overcast sky stabbed at her eyes. She could see people standing in small groups in the yard, some gazing at two fresh mounds of dirt on either side of the cedar tree. She squinted through the window at the figures below. She recognized Riona and Molly and several of the others, but she didn't see Finn…or Eden. *How is this possible? Did I fail? Am I alive instead of them?* Suddenly panicked, she moved to the door of the room and flung it open. "Hello?" she called. "Hello? Is anyone there?"

She heard a clatter like a tray being dropped, and then footsteps thundered up the stairs. She took a couple of steps back from the doorway just as Felix burst into the room. He let out a howl and clapped his hands together, his face breaking into a wide toothy grin.

"Well, I'll be damned! You're alive!" he said, grabbing her in a sudden hug. He let her go and stood there beaming, and then suddenly his face went stern. "Get yerself back in that bed right this instant and let me check you over. Need to make sure nothin's amiss." He strode over to the window, yanked it open, and bellowed, "Get in here, she's awake!"

"Felix," Cedar began, sitting back down on the side of the bed. "What happened? How did I get back here? Eden and Finn, are they…?"

"Hush now, they're both all right, thanks to you," he said, as he began to examine her. "That was a mighty fine thing you did, make no mistake, although I reckon Finn'll be havin' words with you over the matter. But don't fret. He's bound to be too overjoyed you've got air in yer lungs and blood in yer veins to give you too much trouble."

They're all right, she repeated to herself. *They're alive.* She felt her body sag with relief and sat farther back on the bed, leaning against the pillows.

"But how? Lorcan should have killed me," she said. "Did it work? Is he human?" She remembered rushing at Lorcan as he poised his sword over Finn's prone body. She had assumed that would be the end. She would be dead, but so would Lorcan, and Eden would be safe.

Felix grinned and looked like he was about to answer her questions when Riona burst into the room.

"Cedar!" she cried, and then she completely startled Cedar by falling on her, weeping. "You're okay," Riona said when she had sufficiently recovered herself.

"I am," Cedar said. "Where's Eden? And Finn? Are they here? Are they all right?" she asked again. A crowd was gathering at the door, but Felix growled at them to stay out while he examined his patient.

"Yes, dear, they're fine, they're fine," Riona said, patting Cedar's hand. "Anya's gone to fetch them. Finn took Eden back to your apartment after…well, we buried Maeve this morning. I'm sorry we didn't wait for you; we just didn't know how long it would be. Finn has hardly left your side, and Eden won't leave his, so we thought it would be good for them both to have a change of scenery, and for Eden to be in her own home for a while. They'll be back soon, don't worry."

Cedar's face fell and her heart clenched at the thought of Maeve, but she still had so many questions. "Felix, did you do this?" she asked. "Make me alive?"

Felix threw back his head and let out a booming laugh. "Me? Nay, I've not the ability to bring back the dead."

"Then how—?" Cedar began.

"We hoped it might happen," Riona interrupted, her cheeks flushed. "I mean, we had no idea you were going to do what you did. It hadn't even crossed our minds that Kier and Maeve had given you a new gift. We thought you *were* human. And, well, there will be time for apologies later, I suppose, but we certainly didn't treat you right, Cedar, and I'm sorry. When Finn brought you and Eden back from Tír na nÓg, he thought you were dead. You *were* dead."

A shadow passed over her face and she shook her head. "I'm glad you didn't have to see him then. Rohan and Murdoch wasted no time in going over to Tír na nÓg once Finn had told them what had happened. They're there now, trying to sort things out. It's a mess. The sidh is still open, the one Eden created in the tree. The poor girl seemed nearly as dead as you were. She's fine now," she added hastily at the look on Cedar's face, "physically, at any rate, now that Felix has seen to her. The rest, well, that will take time, but it will be much easier now that you're back with us."

"Yes, but how?" Cedar interrupted, sitting up straighter.

"Yer plan worked all right, if that's what yer wonderin'," Felix growled through a grin that seemed permanently etched on his face. "Lorcan shriveled up like a prune, and yer boy Finn lopped off his head with his own sword."

Cedar sank back into her pillows with relief. Lorcan was dead, truly dead. Of course, that still didn't explain how she was alive. Her face must have betrayed the question because Felix continued.

"No one ever really understood how Lorcan did what he did, how his ability worked. It's quite rare, you see. Turns out he's like a storage unit for a person's whole essence, not just their particular gift. And when he died," Felix shrugged expansively, "well, all those essences were freed. While they were trapped in his body they were unable to pass on, and for some reason instead of passing on once they were released, they went back to find their bodies." He shook his head. "It's quite remarkable. People comin' back to life all over Tír na nÓg. When we heard this had started happenin', well, we scarce wanted to believe it in case it wouldn't work in yer particular situation. Finn wanted to move you back to Tír na nÓg so yer essence could have an easier time finding you, but almost every bone in yer body was broken, and I didn't want you comin' back to life just to die from yer injuries. It's only been two days, but

I think I've got you healed up pretty good. The sidh was open, and we figured that if it was really yer essence he had taken, it would know how to find its way back to yer body."

"Mummy?" the tiny voice at the door caused them all to look around. Eden and Finn were standing in the doorway, holding hands. Finn's face was taut. He looked as though he were barely holding himself together. Cedar drank them both in with her eyes.

"She's okay, Eden," Riona said in a gentle voice. "Your mother is fine."

"Eden," Cedar whispered, then the tears started coming. Eden let go of Finn's hand and rushed to her, jumping onto the bed and into Cedar's waiting arms. "You're safe now," Cedar told her, clinging tightly to her daughter. "I'm so sorry for what happened to you, my heart. You're safe now. We're going to get through this together."

They lay entwined and crying for what seemed like hours. Eventually, Eden's sobs subsided and she snuggled close, her head against her mother's chest. Cedar kissed the top of her head and tried to rein in her own tears, which were still flowing. She closed her eyes and listened as Eden's breath became slow and steady. Then she opened them and looked up.

He was still there, standing in the doorway. Felix and Riona had gone. Finn's eyes were rimmed with red, and his face was blotchy with spent emotion. "Cedar," he breathed. "I'm so…how could you…I thought…"

"Shh," she said, reaching out her hand and pulling him gently onto the bed. He eased himself down beside her, careful not to disturb their sleeping child. "Don't be angry with me, not right now. We'll have time to fight about it later." She smiled at him softly, and ran her fingers along the stubble of his jaw and over his lips.

"Okay," he said, covering her hand with his own. "Later."

❧

The fight never did happen, though Finn rarely let either Eden or Cedar out of his sight, even for a moment. Cedar oscillated between euphoria and exhaustion, as she came to grips with the death of the woman she had believed was her mother, while at the same time reveling in the joy of Eden's safe return and her reunion with Finn. Eden was quiet and withdrawn, and would rarely talk to them about what had happened with Nuala, but seemed to take comfort in just being together with them. Cedar didn't push it, not yet. Instead, the three of them spent hours getting to know one another all over again, reading books, and sharing their memories of Maeve. Finn told Eden stories of the Tuatha Dé Danann, and she listened with rapt attention. Cedar listened closely too, and there was no hint of the skepticism she had felt when Finn had tried to tell her these stories years ago. She knew now that they were true, and that they were stories about her own people.

About a week after the events in the Great Hall at Tír na nÓg, Finn asked Cedar the inevitable question. They were lying in bed together, back in Cedar's apartment, early in the morning. Finn rolled over and faced Cedar, propping himself up and gazing at her intently.

"So what happens now?" he asked.

She didn't have to ask what he was referring to. She had been thinking long and hard about what they should do next, now that Eden was back and she had received Felix's bill of clean health. She returned his gaze steadily.

"I think we should go back," she said. "We should go to Tír na nÓg." She saw the relief in his eyes and smiled. She knew he wanted to return to the land of his childhood, though he hadn't said so. She knew he would want to be part of the restoration, to help rebuild

Tír na nÓg into the great land it had once been. And she had come to realize that she wanted that too. She wanted to be part of something bigger than herself. She wanted to embrace who she was, and discover more about her biological parents and their home. And above all, she wanted a safe place for Eden, where she wouldn't have to worry about her accidentally opening a sidh in front of her friends or teachers and ending up in a government lab or military institution. School was starting soon, and Cedar thought it would be best if they were gone by then. She told Finn all this, and he leaned back into the pillows and looked up at the ceiling.

"I agree, but it won't be easy," he said. "From what Rohan tells me, things are a real mess over there. It's hard to tell the people who actually agreed with Lorcan from the ones who were just supporting him out of fear. The Council has taken over for the time being. They're well respected, and they used to advise the High Kings before Lorcan disbanded them. But who knows if they can sort through the chaos and set things right again."

"All the more reason we should be there," Cedar said. "Maybe we can help. Has there been any word on Nuala?"

"Nothing," Finn said, frowning. "No one has seen her—or at least no one is letting on that they have."

Cedar's stomach squirmed uncomfortably. She didn't like the idea of Nuala on the loose. She was sure that the redhead would not give up her delusions of power so easily. But Eden, at least, was safe. There was no one besides Lorcan who could gain her power through her death, and Eden's gift would be treasured by all the Tuatha Dé Danann. Yes, she thought, it would be safer for Eden there, among her own people. Yes, they would go, and face Nuala again if they had to. But this time, they would be together.

THE END

ACKNOWLEDGMENTS

There are not enough words to express my deep gratitude to my friend and mentor Chris Hansen, who selflessly shared his vast knowledge of story and painstakingly walked me through the creation of this one. Chris, you changed my life. I cannot thank you enough.

There are many other people to whom I am grateful. Here are but a few: Justin Sherwin; Mark and Kari Petzold; Jason and Christie Goode; Janelle deJager; Kelley Stuart, Andrea Penner, and their books clubs; Carla Sbrocchi; and my parents, Judi and Allan McIsaac, for their unwavering support and invaluable editorial assistance.

I am so grateful for the hardworking, überprofessional, and very fun team at 47North, including David Pomerico, Katy Ball, Patrick Magee, Kelly Borgeson, and Angela Polidoro. You have all made my first foray into the publishing world an incredibly positive experience.

Of course, I'm very grateful to my husband, Mike, who allowed this book to invade our lives, helped me find time and space for this passion of mine, and cheerfully served as a perpetual sounding board; and also to my children, Lauren and Willow, who never seemed to grow tired of the refrain "Mummy's writing" and had their own helpful suggestions for what to include in Mummy's story (cue Baby Bunny).

To everyone else who believed in me: thank you.

ABOUT THE AUTHOR

 Jodi McIsaac grew up in New Brunswick, Canada. After stints as a short-track speed skater, a speech-writer, and a fundraising and marketing executive in the nonprofit sector, she started a boutique copywriting agency and began writing novels in the wee hours of the morning. She currently lives with her husband and children in Calgary. This is her first novel.